# The Christmas Catch

## by Clare Lydon

custard
books

**First Edition October 2022**
**Published by Custard Books**
**Copyright © 2022 Clare Lydon**
**ISBN: 978-1-912019-06-9**

Cover Design: Kevin Pruitt
Editor: Kelli Collins
Typesetting: Adrian McLaughlin

Find out more at: www.clarelydon.co.uk
Follow me on Instagram: @clarefic
Follow me on Twitter: @clarelydon

## Also by Clare Lydon

### Other Novels
A Taste Of Love
Before You Say I Do
Change Of Heart
Christmas In Mistletoe
It Started With A Kiss
Nothing To Lose: A Lesbian Romance
Once Upon A Princess
One Golden Summer
The Long Weekend
Twice In A Lifetime
You're My Kind

### London Romance Series
London Calling (Book One)
This London Love (Book Two)
A Girl Called London (Book Three)
The London Of Us (Book Four)
London, Actually (Book Five)
Made In London (Book Six)
Hot London Nights (Book Seven)
Big London Dreams (Book Eight)

### All I Want Series
Two novels and four novellas chart the course
of one relationship over two years.

### Boxsets
Available for both the London Romance series and
the All I Want series for ultimate value. Check out
my website for more: www.clarelydon.co.uk

# Acknowledgements

I love Christmas. The movies, the music, the lights, the food. But most of all, I love the lead-up to the big day, with all the anticipation that involves. I love that everyone is in the mood to celebrate. I love that for a few days, everything stops, and you get to take time off. I don't wish it could be Christmas every day as that would take the magic away. But I'm thrilled we get to anticipate Christmas and be in the mood for three months every year. Consider this book the start of your festive celebrations.

I hope you enjoyed reading The Christmas Catch as much as I enjoyed writing it. This story is one of the all-out funniest I've written in a while, and puts my two leads, Morgan and Ali, into a myriad of tight spots. I loved making them suffer, but I also loved the journey they went on and how they came out the other side. This story is about finding love where you least expect it, and overcoming adversity. Your worst days might turn out to be your best. That's what Morgan and Ali discover.

Thanks to Angela, Sophie, Kathy, Miira and Hilary for their first read and encouraging comments. Also, to my fantastic advanced reading team for their eagle eyes that picked up all the last-minute issues. I couldn't do this without you, so you get all the plaudits!

Heaps of praise to my wonderful team of talented professionals who make sure my books look and read the best they possibly can. Kevin Pruitt for the Christmas-tastic (with bells on) cover. Kelli Collins for her ace editing. Adrian McLaughlin for his typesetting prowess and general loveliness. Also, to my wife for supporting me at every turn, and for indulging my Christmas obsession with good grace and humour. You're the best, darling.

Finally, thanks to you for buying this book and supporting me on my writing journey. I appreciate it more than you could ever know. You buying this book means I can stay a full-time writer and keep producing books for you to enjoy. Thank you, from the bottom of my heart, and merry Christmas!

If you fancy getting in touch, you can do so using one of the methods below:

Website: www.clarelydon.co.uk
Email: mail@clarelydon.co.uk
Instagram: @clarefic
Facebook: www.facebook.co.uk/clarelydon
Twitter: @clarelydon

*Merry Christmas. I hope this year is your best one yet!*

# Chapter One

"What is it you want this project to do for the company, Cinnamon?" Every time Morgan said the woman's name, she craved a cinnamon bun. Like, seriously. However, she was in the middle of a work meeting. It wasn't the done thing.

She glanced at Cinnamon, her face folded in thought. With her blonde hair, white skirt and white jacket, she looked like you could pick her up and put her on top of your Christmas tree. All she needed was a pair of wings. However, in this meeting, she'd displayed admirable fighting qualities. There was no way Cinnamon would allow herself to be a tree-topper. She preferred to be on ground level, in the thick of it.

"I want it to get our name out there. To truly make this the brand on everyone's lips." Just like the taste of those rich, sweet buns were on Morgan's.

Cinnamon raised her left eyebrow, asking if that was the right answer.

Morgan adopted her best poker face. She wasn't here to give answers. She was here to facilitate. At least, she was for the next seven minutes and 54 seconds.

"And you, Antonio. What is it you want?"

Antonio shot Cinnamon a withering look, then turned on his charming smile for Morgan. "I also want what's best for the company, just like my colleague." He kept his eyes firmly on Morgan. "But if we do it my way, we'll get quicker, more agile results."

Morgan had to hand it to him. Antonio knew the right buzzwords to use. But it wasn't going to win any points in this room.

"Agile results?" Contempt laced Cinnamon's words. "This is what I'm talking about. Stop speaking in riddles, Antonio."

Morgan raised a hand, looking from one to the other. "We've only got a few minutes left, and I think you've had time to air your points of view. You've both got valid concerns, but let's leave it there. You can each write the three things you've taken away, and the three things you want to keep discussing. Then we'll move forward and see if we can conclude when we get back in January."

Cinnamon drew in a long breath and shook her head. "I'd rather get this sorted before the Christmas break so it's not bugging me all holiday long."

Morgan folded her arms across her chest. "You can, if you both do the homework and get in a room without me. In fact, there's nothing I'd like more."

"We tried that before you stepped in to mediate. There's a reason you're here." Antonio gave Cinnamon a pointed look.

"Maybe you've come further than you think in the past three days we've been talking," Morgan countered. "Maybe you could work it out just the two of you now."

Cinnamon sighed. "You're asking for a Christmas miracle."

The timer on Morgan's phone buzzed, and she stabbed it with her index finger to silence the beeping. "Okay, that's time. Great work today. If you two could find it in yourselves to work out a compromise, it would make everyone in this office believe in Christmas magic. Including me. I'd love to stay around and help," (she was lying), "but I have Christmas plans, and I have to get all the way home to Devon to do them." She picked up her grey leather backpack and began packing up her laptop, wires and notepads. "If you manage it, you're doing me out of work, but it's money I'm prepared to lose." She paused. "Why don't you go for a mulled wine together and hash out the details?"

A strangled sound emerged from Cinnamon's mouth. "Is that an approved tactic from the mediation handbook?" She didn't look convinced.

Morgan gave her a sweet smile. "Nope, it's a life tactic. A glass of wine makes most things better." She shrugged on her navy-blue peacoat and pulled back her shoulders. "Merry Christmas, you two. I hope to not see you in the New Year."

\* \* \*

Morgan strode down Argyle Street, then pulled her scarf closer around her neck. The wind had teeth today. Would it be any better back home? It had to be. Four hundred and eighty-two miles, plus a few curled vowels and strident consonants separated Glasgow and her home town of Dartmouth in Devon, but it might as well be another galaxy. Yes, she'd grown up there, but Morgan hadn't lived in Devon since university. But she was going home for Christmas, just like always.

Ahead, an illuminated reindeer towered over last-gasp shoppers determined to find that perfect gift. Morgan could feel their panic as the days to buy diminished. Conversely, all her shopping was done. What had her school report said all those years ago? 'Morgan is always prepared, always ready'. Not much had changed in the two decades since. Was that a sad state of affairs? The jury was still out.

Morgan breathed in the smell of roasted chestnuts from a cart across the street. She stared up at the liquorice sky, the surrounding air crispy. The forecast was for light snowfall. She screwed up her face as her stomach twisted tight. Light snowfall she could deal with. Heavy snowfall that would ground her plane? Not so much. It happened often enough in Scotland for it to be a concern. But she wasn't going to focus on that. The power of positive thinking was what she preached in her job. That would get her home, too.

She shifted her bag on her shoulder and felt in her coat pocket. Her phone was still there. She'd lost it twice this year, having never misplaced it before in her life. She had no idea what she'd done to offend the phone gods, but the upshot was she constantly checked her pockets now. She wasn't going to lose another one. If nothing else, it was a mighty expensive habit to foster. She took her hand away, and her phone vibrated. She retrieved it. Her sister's name flashed up on-screen.

"Hey sis." Morgan walked left to avoid an oncoming loved-up couple who weren't going to unlink their hands for anyone. What was it on pavements with couples and their territorial rights? It always irked her.

"Hey yourself," Annabel replied. Morgan could picture her younger sister at their parents' large marble kitchen island, her dark hair tied up in a messy bun. She also knew her sister's belly would be touching the counter first, too. "Just calling to check everything's still okay for tomorrow? Mum is beside me, making pastry for mince pies and fretting. She wants to check you haven't agreed to fix the problems of any more companies as you normally do?"

Morgan smiled. Her job was relentless and there were always more relationships to be fixed and training to be given, but she'd carved out this Christmas holiday and made it clear to everyone that she wasn't available from today. She was having a proper festive break. What's more, she was going to spend the first week solely with her family. She couldn't wait.

"Nope, no last-minute Christmas emergencies. Only that I still haven't got a present for Josh. What would he like?" Her sister's husband was a cycling freak, but Morgan had exhausted most cycling paraphernalia on previous birthdays and Christmases. A bike-wheel clock. Personalised bike tool kit. Leather, monogrammed bike coffee holder. Plus, there were only so many cycling-related socks, mugs and T-shirts a man needed.

Annabel sighed. "Nothing. He knocked me up and now my ankles are like puff pastry tarts, so he deserves nothing. Gruel. A vasectomy. You choose."

Morgan smiled. Her sister was never one to mince words. "As a relationships specialist, I have to tell you that's not a great starting point for a happy home."

"Bite me."

"Okay, a bottle of whisky it is." Morgan knew that would make Josh smile.

"And he still gets to drink," Annabel huffed. "Pregnancy is a special form of torture, you know that? Whoever thought it up had just been dumped in the worst way by the worst woman ever. And it was definitely a man."

"But in the end, you get a cute little bundle of wonder. Did I mention I've bought lots of presents for Bump?"

"Aww," her sister replied. "I would say you shouldn't have, but I'd be lying. Buy Bump another gift and forget Josh. That's my vote. Or buy him whisky and I'll drink it once I've birthed said bundle of wonder. I'll hide it under the bed. The whisky, not the baby. You are in the right place to bring me the best, after all."

"You see? I knew you'd find the silver lining." Morgan looked left, then right. Both sets of lights were on red, and the main road was clear. She made a dash for the cab rank on the other side.

Just as she moved, she saw something dark moving towards her out of the corner of her eye.

She stopped, then focused fully right.

By that time, the cyclist was almost on top of her. No lights on, and the rider wearing no hi-vis clothing.

Morgan jerked backwards as the cyclist swerved around her. She just about avoided the collision, but in the melee, her phone leapt from her hand. To her left, a car slowed as Morgan let out a squeal. She rushed to the other side of the road where her phone lay in the gutter, spinning.

Fucking cyclists.

Josh was getting whisky, no argument.

Her heart thudded in her chest as she bent to pick up her phone. Sweat broke out on the back of her neck. Damn it all to hell. The screen was smashed. Frustration boiled in her as she stepped onto the pavement before another bike mowed her down. She held it up to her ear just in case her family were still on the other end.

"Hello?" Nothing. Now they were sure to think she'd expired on the mean streets of Glasgow. Her family didn't understand her motives for living so far away. If she carked it here too, they'd never forgive Scotland.

She dropped her phone into her bag and stood in the queue for the cabs. On December 21st, with everybody laden with shopping bags, it wasn't a short line. She should get the bus. But it was too cold, and this week had been too long. Plus, she'd just nearly died. She deserved a cab. Her friend Crystal would tell her to walk. Then again, Crystal was born and bred here, and still didn't own a coat. It was the Scottish way. Morgan was always the soft southerner.

Fifteen minutes later, she was in the back of a cab, the driver asking which football team she supported. She didn't think Plymouth Argyle was going to raise his interest. Morgan's mind wound forward to tomorrow. To her plane ticket being digital, and so on her phone. Could smashing her screen have happened at a more inconvenient time?

She made a quick mental to-do list in preparation for her midday flight.

1. Get to the phone shop and get her screen repaired.

2. Email Ryan and tell him to have a stern word with Cinnamon and Antonio.

3. Borrow her neighbour Harry's phone to call her family and tell them she wasn't dead.

# Chapter Two

Ali Bradford waved her arm to get served. The guy behind the bar looked through her every time, only serving the women with long hair. Blondes especially, she'd noted. The world wasn't a fair place, particularly for a thirsty short-haired lesbian surrounded by office Christmas parties. Ali hadn't gone to her own. This was her makeshift party with her friends before she headed home. At least, it would be if she ever got served.

Behind the bar, the pretty bar staff were still resolutely ignoring her like it was some sort of sport. She was just about to turn and tell her friend Sasha to try instead—she had long hair, after all—when the man beside her pointed the nearest bartender in her direction.

Ali blinked. "Thank you." Apparently, chivalry was not dead yet. She ordered a Peroni for her, a Coors Lite for Sasha, and a Soave for Tobias ("criminally underrated" according to him). She flashed her card at the terminal, picked up the drinks, and walked back to their booth.

When she got there, Sasha frowned at Tobias. "It's got to be Christmas trees, right?"

Tobias shook his head, his dark fringe flopping in his eyes. "Nope." He put his right cheek in the palm of his right hand and tilted his head to their friend. "Guess again."

Sasha pursed her lips, then snapped her fingers. "Advent calendars."

"Wrong!" Tobias loved guessing games, while Sasha hated them. He took his wine from Ali's hand, "Thanks hon!", then trained his gaze back on Sasha.

"What are you two talking about?" Ali slid into their booth. She pushed their pile of coats against the wall, giving herself more room on the red leather seat.

A cheer erupted from the booth behind.

She hadn't drunk enough for this bar.

"What festive tradition we got from the Dutch," Tobias told her. He drained his previous glass and gave Sasha a smug grin.

"And obviously, I'm hating every minute," Sasha told her.

"Obviously," Ali replied.

The music in the bar changed to Wham's 'Last Christmas', and an accompanying cheer went up all around. She tried to ignore the table behind, but it wasn't easy. Ali put a hand on her beer. Every time they slammed their table, her beer vibrated.

Both Tobias and Sasha temporarily paused their chat as their eyes widened at whatever was happening behind Ali. When she twisted to look, their booth neighbours stood on their seats, belting out the words to the Christmas classic as if they *were* George Michael. Ali didn't want to be the bearer of bad tidings—you only brought good tidings at Christmas, right?—but they were more on the level of Andrew Ridgeley than George.

"Is the tradition we inherited getting pissed up at Christmas parties and murdering the classics?" Ali turned back to face her friends.

9

Tobias snorted. "No, but good try. I think we made that tradition up all by ourselves."

Sasha shrugged, then sipped her beer. Last year, she wouldn't have been seen dead drinking it, but the low-calorie version had made it acceptable now. "I give up. And I hate you. Tell us."

"The tradition we got from the Dutch is leaving out milk and cookies for Santa." Tobias grinned like it was obvious all along.

"We'd never have guessed that!" Ali slid her fingers under the table to check her bags were still there. They were. All her last-minute Christmas shopping done today, before the long trek home started tomorrow. It was at this time of year she envied her Scottish friends. Their families lived in the same city. Her family lived almost as far away as you could get in the UK, without falling into the sea.

The song ended, and a cheer went up.

Ali turned to see one of their neighbours now in a heap on the floor. One too many festive sherries. She had it all to look forward to back at the family pub, too.

"Ready for your long trip home tomorrow? Final Christmas before your big move?" Tobias's question snagged her attention back to the here and now.

"No." She wasn't even packed yet. "I still have to wrap my presents, so I can't stay long."

Sasha rolled her eyes, then tapped a finger on Ali's wrist. Sasha's fingernail was painted matte white. "Wrapping presents tipsy is part of Christmas. Stay for another drink, live a little. We won't see you much next year after you head to New York, will we?"

Ali glanced out the window, where the promised light snow flurries had begun. She gritted her teeth and hoped the airport did the same to the runway.

"You'll see me plenty. I don't go until mid-January."

But first, she had to get home. This Christmas was going to be strange, but she was determined to make it as near to normal as possible. Even if it was impossibly different already.

"What time's your flight?" Tobias asked.

"Midday."

He held up his beer. "A toast, then. To us all having a merry Christmas. But especially me, living it up in Ali's flat. Me, Snowy, and *The Holiday* on repeat."

Tobias was cat-sitting for the next week while Ali was away. If he survived and didn't kill her cat or burn her flat down, he was moving in permanently next year.

She clinked his beer, but held him in place with her stare. "It's a very serious business looking after Snowy. She's a delicate creature, like her owner." Ali paused. "And I hate to reiterate this, but I fear it needs saying. No having sex in my bed while I'm away."

Tobias gave her a butter-wouldn't't-melt look. "Only with myself, I promise."

\* \* \*

Ali wrinkled her nose and filled Snowy's bowl full of Whiskas, ignoring the grim smell. Then she got Snowy's biscuits and rattled the metal tin. Sure enough, her cat appeared in the kitchen in seconds.

"You're always here for your biscuits, aren't you, girl?" Ali bent to stroke Snowy's pure white fur as her cat purred at her feet. Then she put her food on her mat, and Snowy's attention was fully consumed as she got stuck in. She wasn't to know this was the last day she'd get to have breakfast with her owner for a week.

Ali walked across her black-and-white chequered kitchen and stared out through her patio doors at the snow-covered grass beyond. It was perfectly festive. She'd love to spend a Christmas here one day. She had a cat, she had a home, but she'd like a girlfriend to share them with. Also, an excuse to stay here. Not that she didn't love going back to Devon. But she'd like just once to not have to rush around for the holidays. To stay where she was and enjoy the home she'd made. Maybe next year. Or perhaps then, she'd still be in New York City. Her future was wide open.

Snowy's warm body pressed against her left calf.

Ali crouched down and stroked her. It was an uncharacteristic display of love. Maybe she could sense she was about to be abandoned.

"You going to be a good girl for your Uncle Tobias while I'm away? But not too good. Wake him up with a dead mouse in the bed one morning. Get it over with when I'm not here."

Ali picked Snowy up and kissed her neck.

Unimpressed, Snowy wriggled out of her arms and went back to her food.

Ali glanced up at her kitchen clock: 7:30am and she still hadn't packed. She swept up her pile of clean clothes from the kitchen table and took them into her bedroom, where her suitcase was already open. She put the clothes into one side, then pulled open the underwear drawer of her solid teak 1950s dresser she'd picked up in a second-hand shop around the corner. Finneston, Glasgow's hipster district, was full of such treasures. When she turned back with five pairs of knickers in one hand and socks in the other, Snowy sat in the other side of her case. Ali laughed. What was it with cats and suitcases?

"You're not coming with me. We already had this conversation, remember?"

Her phone beeped, and she saw a message from Tobias.

*It's tomorrow you're leaving, right?*

Fucking idiot.

*Today, and you know that.*

*That's right. Today's the day I get the key to my Christmas Shag Palace. I've already had a word with Snowy. She says so long as I bring her a parade of pretty ladies to rub herself against, she's all for it.*

Ali rolled her eyes.

*Are you even out of bed yet?*

Tobias lived two floors above with two other flatmates. Which made him living here easy, as he didn't have to worry about forgetting anything.

*I'll be there in 20 mins. Put the kettle on.*

Ali threw her phone on the bed, then picked up a distinctly unimpressed Snowy. She'd had the vague hope her clothes wouldn't be covered in white fur when she went home, but that dream had already sailed. "It's a good job you're cute, isn't it?"

She walked around her bedroom, going through the list of things she needed. Jumpers. Jewellery. Perfume. Foundation to cover up the bags under her eyes. Her new reindeer-print shirt to impress her mum on Christmas Day.

Her phone rang, and she furrowed her brow.

She picked it up without looking at the screen. At this hour, it could only be Tobias again.

"I'm still leaving today. And no, you still can't have sex in my bed."

There was a pause on the other end of the line. "I'm not sure who that was directed at. Definitely not your mother."

Heat warmed Ali's cheeks. "Shit," she spluttered.

"Still not very eloquent, I hate to tell you."

"Sorry, I thought you were Tobias."

"Tell him your mum says he's not to have sex in your bed, either."

Ali laughed. "I will. Why are you calling? I'm going to see you in a few hours."

"I was just watching that lovely BBC weatherman—he's gay you know, I can tell—and he was talking about snow in Scotland. I just wanted to check your flight was still okay?"

Ali walked over to her window and moved a space between the blinds with her thumb and index finger. A light snow covering, but it was far from a winter wonderland. "It stopped snowing last night, so it should be fine. If anything changes, I'll let you know."

"Great," her mum replied. "Nicole's coming over later with Harrison. We're all excited to see you."

Ali's stomach plunged. It wasn't a dig, that wasn't her mum's style.

It didn't matter.

Guilt still nibbled every inch of her.

"Stuart will pick you up from the airport."

Ali gulped. That was different. But this year was different, wasn't it? She'd stayed away for too long, she knew that. But it was Christmas. All the more reason to get back. "That's great. Listen, I better dash. Tobias is turning up any minute, and I've gotta get Snowy out of my case."

"Okay. See you soon. Can't wait!"

Ali smiled as she hung up. She wasn't sure how she'd cope back home, but she was going.

It was long overdue.

# Chapter Three

Morgan could hardly believe it. She'd asked the cab driver to drop her at a phone shop near the airport. He'd done just that, and she'd handed in her phone, pleading with the staff for a quick turnaround. Now, a woman with a sharp buzz cut and a smile the width of the Clyde walked towards her. She presented Morgan with her phone. Maybe the season *did* contain magic.

"You're in luck. Our repair guy was able to resurrect your screen. It's as good as new."

Morgan plucked the phone from the woman's hands and held it at arm's length, with a reverence usually reserved for a newborn. Which it sorta was. If it wasn't frowned upon, she'd have leapt across the counter and placed a kiss on the woman's lips. Thirty-five minutes ago, she'd arrived flustered and desperate. Now, with her link to the rest of the world back in her hands, she was leaving as a woman restored.

"Thank you. You don't know what this means." Morgan glanced at her watch. She really had to go. She had a plane to catch, family to hug. She paid her Christmas miracle worker, gave her an extra tenner along with a "Merry Christmas!", then ran out of the store, the wheels of her sleek suitcase rumbling on the cracked pavement beneath her. She hailed another passing black cab, and heaved her suitcase into the back, breathing a sigh of relief as the driver sped off.

Ten minutes later, they skidded to a halt outside Departures at Glasgow Airport, the driver braking suddenly to avoid an incoming cab ploughing straight into them.

Morgan threw out her arm to stop herself from crashing to the floor. She succeeded, but also cracked her elbow on the side of the cab. She slammed back into her seat as silent swear words formed in cartoon bubbles above her head. She sucked in a long breath and held her elbow, waiting for the searing pain to stop.

Up front, her driver yanked open his door and strode towards the other cab, shouting something in Glaswegian that Morgan couldn't quite make out. From his frantic gestures, she guessed he wasn't wishing the other driver season's greetings.

Once she could move her elbow without wincing, Morgan opened the door and got out of the cab, grateful to be alive. Her solid black Samsonite case landed on the pavement with a thump. She pushed it closer to the main building, but then realised she still needed to pay.

A woman got out of the cab that had caused all the trouble in the first place, her feet encased in black boots that weren't tied all the way up. She wore a green duffel coat and a mustard scarf, and her hair—undercut, longer on top, perfectly styled—held huge queer energy. Morgan studied her for a hot moment, then raised an eyebrow as the woman hauled the same black Samsonite suitcase out of her cab and placed it beside Morgan's.

They stared at each other for a few seconds.

"Black Friday sale?"

Morgan scrunched her face.

The woman pointed at her case. "The Samsonite. I got mine on Amazon in the Black Friday sale."

Morgan laughed. "Snap." There was something about this woman that looked familiar. She was sure she hadn't slept with her—there hadn't been enough for Morgan to forget one—but perhaps one of her friends had? But that wasn't about to be her opening gambit. Did Morgan detect a slight accent? Her mind hummed trying to work it out.

"See you for drinks on Friday then," Morgan's cab driver shouted, then walked back to his open door.

Morgan blinked. That wasn't how she expected the altercation between the two drivers to end. "You want to pay by card?" he asked her, before he slid back into his seat and shut the door.

Morgan nodded, then got out her Mastercard.

The other passenger (who Morgan still couldn't place) held up her card, then walked over to her taxi, leaning in the window to pay.

Morgan's cab had a fixed pay station, which was in the back. She went to hop in, but unfortunately tripped on the step up and fell straight onto her elbow.

Pain shot up her arm as if something had just sliced through her. She rolled onto her side and clutched her elbow again. Goddammit, why was she such a walking disaster these past 24 hours? At least it wasn't snowing. She had to look on the bright side. In a few hours, she'd be home, eating one of her mum's delicious mince pies. All she had to do was get up and get on the plane.

The cabby turned his face near to the Perspex screen. "You picking a fight with yourself there, missy?"

Morgan chuckled. It looked very much like she was. She struggled to her feet, paid the man, then jumped out, slamming the cab door.

She hoped the mystery woman hadn't noticed any of that. If she had, Morgan would never know, as the pavement only held her case, and nothing else.

The other woman had paid and left.

Disappointment scratched in Morgan's chest.

\* \* \*

Morgan was one of the first on the plane, having bought speedy boarding with her ticket. She hated queueing, and anything that nixed it got her vote. The flight wasn't long, but she was all for making travelling as comfortable as possible. It came from a childhood spent camping in the rain in Devon and Cornwall. Travel and holidays to Morgan meant getting as far away from that image as she could. She edged her way along the narrow aisle, smiling at an older gentleman just taking off his flat cap two rows ahead. He was the type of man who'd play the granddad in an ITV Sunday night drama.

"Going home for Christmas?" he asked as he unwound his grey scarf.

"I am. You?" She bet this entire plane would say the same, so it was a pretty safe guess.

"Going to see my daughter and her family," the man replied in a broad Glaswegian accent. "They've moved to Devon. Couldn't get farther away from me if they tried. I'm trying not to take it personally."

Morgan smiled. Her mum and sister said the same when she told them she was staying put after university.

She settled into her seat, flicking through the inflight magazine and food options. She'd already had breakfast at home, but something about planes always made her want to order more. At least a coffee and something to go with it. A bacon roll with ketchup? Four-finger KitKat? They both sounded good.

"We meet again," a low voice said nearby.

Morgan looked up from her magazine, then blinked. The mystery woman was back, standing over her. Her face was like an art exhibit, all sharp angles and shadows, with devastating brown eyes. They crinkled as she smiled in Morgan's direction.

A frisson of intrigue ran through Morgan. Who was this woman? Her face rang so many bells.

Maybe she *had* slept with her.

"What are the chances of your taxi nearly crashing into mine, and then us getting on the same flight to Exeter?" If she was a betting woman, probably less than one per cent.

Which is why she wasn't a betting woman.

"Slim to none." The woman gave her a warm smile, then slid into the seat across the aisle. She unwound her mustard scarf. It looked homemade. Had her gran knitted it for her? Her mum? Her girlfriend?

Morgan tried not to stare. She was just about to ask if they knew each other, when a family with toddlers walked through the aisle between them. When they'd gone, Morgan turned her attention back to the food menu. They didn't know each other. She was being stupid. The woman just had one of those faces.

"You don't recognise me, do you?"

Okay, so it wasn't just her. Morgan turned and put down her menu, then stared across the aisle. Salon-ready hair, questioning smile, smooth skin and vibe. The woman looked like a TV presenter. Maybe for E4 or women's football.

"You look very familiar, but I can't quite place you." Morgan winced. "I'm afraid you're going to have to put me out of my misery, sorry."

The woman smiled, then put a hand to her chest. "Ali Bradford. Nicole's sister. We went to school together at Hawthornes Academy?" She treated Morgan to her dazzling smile. "And I'm guessing you're going home for Christmas?"

Ali Bradford? The last time she'd seen Ali Bradford, she hadn't looked like this. Not even a teeny, tiny bit. She'd had longer hair, she'd been in braces, and she certainly hadn't exuded such queer energy. Now though, Ali's queer energy might turn the whole plane gay.

"I am. You are, too?" It was the best sentence Morgan could string together in the circumstances.

Ali Bradford. Her sister, Nicole, had been Morgan's best mate throughout their school years. Ali had been the little sister, always trailing in their wake. But now, Ali Bradford was all grown up.

"I am. Back to the homestead and all that entails." Ali gave her a forced smile.

Morgan had been home almost every year, but hadn't called in at Ali's family pub, The Rising Sun, nearly as often. She'd caught up with Nicole, but she hadn't seen Ali in maybe a decade. Morgan had always known Ali was gay, but she'd never looked like *this*. Like she could fill you in on the stats for the England women's football team, then take you out to the best sushi place and give you a night you'd never forget.

"How long's it been since we saw each other? Ten years? Maybe more? You look so different."

"Was I that bad before?"

Had Morgan offended her? *Shit*. She shook her head. "Course not, just…" She couldn't quite find the words.

"More hair?" Ali raised an eyebrow. "Less queer?"

Morgan laughed. Yes, the last time she'd seen Ali, she'd had chestnut locks halfway down her back. Not that you couldn't be queer with long hair, of course. But Morgan totally approved of this new look. "You looked fabulous before, but you look doubly fabulous now."

Ali gave her a broad smile. "Smooth. I'll take that from you, Morgan Scott."

Morgan beamed. She liked the way Ali said her name. Like she was someone famous. "I feel like I should have changed a little more now." She smoothed down her blonde hair. Still the same medium length as when Ali had seen her last.

"You're fine as you are." Ali held her gaze, then dropped it abruptly. She grabbed the food card from her seat pocket and studied it.

"Have you been home much lately?"

Ali shook her head, not looking at Morgan. "Not since summer."

"I've only been back once this year. Work's been crazy."

They stopped talking for a few minutes as the plane got busier with passengers boarding. Morgan's brain churned with all the information that had just been dumped in her lap. Her friendship with Nicole had a once-a-year catch-up vibe, and that suited them both. She'd mentioned Ali had gone to Edinburgh uni, but nothing more.

Morgan waited for the captain to tell her staff boarding was complete before she restarted the conversation.

"How come you're in Glasgow?"

Ali put her menu back in the seat pocket. "I live here."

She did? This was news. "Me, too. How did you end up here?"

"I went to university in Edinburgh, but fell in love with Glasgow. I mean, there could be more sun, but you can't have it all, can you?"

"Especially not sun." Morgan got up to let a person in her row into his seat. The man didn't say thank you. "What do you do in Glasgow?"

"I work for a software company that makes apps for hospitality. I saw a gap in the market and wanted to make my parents' lives easier. Then I got hired to create it."

Morgan hadn't expected that. "Anything I'd have heard of?"

Ali shook her head. "Industry things. Solving problems in business."

"Sounds clever and worthwhile, like you're making a difference."

Ali gave her an embarrassed smile. "What about you? You and my sister used to be as thick as thieves when I was growing up. I always thought you'd become a DJ or a film star."

Morgan snorted. "Really?" She had no idea why Ali thought that.

Ali nodded. "You used to host the school radio, didn't you?" Her cheeks turned pink. "Plus, you were always hosting

23

school assemblies. Nobody could shut you up, so I assumed you'd get a job that involved a lot of talking."

"I did, in a roundabout way. I work with companies and people sorting out their relationships and business issues. A communications specialist."

"I wasn't far off."

"I guess you weren't."

The plane taxied down the runway, and Morgan settled back in her seat, giving Ali a 'we don't have to talk the whole way if you don't want to' smile. She rummaged in her backpack for her headphones—there was a podcast she'd been meaning to listen to about relationships, and she'd downloaded it especially for the flight. Would it be rude to plug in now she and Ali had reconnected?

She couldn't feel her headphones, so she lifted her bag into her lap and peered in. The flight was almost an hour and a half. Even though it was nice to see Ali, they might have used up their conversation starters already. They both lived and worked in Glasgow. She wasn't sure where else to go.

Although, she really couldn't find her headphones. At this rate, she'd be forced to engage in chat for the entire flight.

"Ladies and gentlemen. This is your captain speaking. We've got a slight technical hitch with the plane, so we're going to be grounded here for a little while until it can be fixed. It shouldn't take too long."

Damn. She really needed her headphones now.

"I thought it would be snow that might ground us. I hadn't predicted a technical hitch." Ali gave her a tight smile.

"The captain said it wouldn't take long to fix. Hopefully, she was telling the truth."

Morgan pulled out her phone, her wallet, a packet of tissues and three pens, one without a lid. She felt around inside her bag with her fingertips, then studied them. No ink. At least the pen hadn't leaked. She wasn't putting it back, though. Instead, she slotted the pen in the netting in front of her. Morgan pictured her headphones on her bedside table. Probably where they still were. She sighed, put her backpack on the floor, then waved to a nearby crew member.

"Excuse me." She fluttered her eyelids. "I was just wondering if you had any spare headphones? I seem to have forgotten mine."

The air steward flashed her straight white teeth at Morgan and shook her head. Her fringe looked like it was made of Lego. "I'm sorry, we don't carry them for short flights." She had a Spanish accent that made Morgan smile. She once had a fling with a Spanish woman. She only had fond memories.

Morgan nodded, then spotted the woman's name badge. "No problem." She got a box of Cadbury's Heroes from her backpack and gave them to the steward. "These are for you, by the way. To share with your crew. Merry Christmas, Arianna."

From being polite but reserved, Arianna visibly brightened. "That's so kind, thank you."

"You're welcome." Countless work trips had taught Morgan that a box of chocolates often made a flight that much more comfortable.

Sure enough, minutes later, Arianna returned with a packet of headphones. She leaned down, putting her mouth by Morgan's ear. "I found these, but they're the only pair, so keep it on the down-low."

Morgan grinned up at her. "What a star. Thank you."

Arianna left, and Morgan plugged the headphones into the phone.

"Wow, impressive. Does that always work?"

Morgan glanced over at Ali. "Not always, but who doesn't love chocolates? If nothing else, I spread a little cheer. And sometimes, I get cheer back." She raised her headphones.

"I can see why you're a communications specialist."

Morgan grinned. "Years of experience."

# Chapter Four

Morgan. Fucking. Scott.

Okay, Ali really needed to keep her cool here. Not show how much a young Ali used to worship the ground Morgan walked on. It had irritated her sister beyond belief that Ali followed them around everywhere. Her parents thought it was sibling worship. And yes, there was an element of that. But there'd been more of an element of Morgan Scott worship.

Back then, Ali never put a label on it. She just knew that when she grew up, she wanted to be as funny as Morgan Scott. Plus, she'd always wanted to have a name as cool as hers, too. Alison Bradford was pedestrian in the face of Morgan Scott. The former sounded like a primary school teacher. The latter sounded like a film star with a row of blockbusters to her name.

And now, here she was, on the same plane.

Ali was doing everything she could to be calm, but it wasn't easy.

Of course, she wasn't 12 anymore. And Morgan Scott was not a film star or a DJ.

But seeing her threw Ali right back to that girl who'd always been in awe of Morgan.

It was only in later years Ali realised the *real* reason she'd followed her around like a lost puppy. Morgan Scott had been Ali's first bona fide crush. Three years older, she'd lived in a world far more glamorous than Ali could ever hope to inhabit. Morgan had cool friends (apart from Nicole), she ran the school radio, and people looked up to her. They listened when she spoke. Ali listened to everything she said, right up until Morgan left school, aged 18, and went to university. Fifteen-year-old Ali had known it was coming, but it still left her bereft.

But now, Morgan was chatting to Ali like it was an everyday occurrence. It wasn't. Ali might now be 35, but beside Morgan Scott, she'd forever be a stuttering, blushing 12-year-old.

Still, Morgan had plugged in her newly acquired headphones now, so the chat portion of their flight was over. That suited Ali fine. She needed time to regroup. Were her cheeks as red as she thought they were? She was glad she didn't have a mirror to check.

She looked up to the front of the plane, where the crew were in deep conversation. There was also a lot of head shaking. Was this technical fault going to delay them for longer than the captain had said?

She glanced at Morgan, who'd somehow got her brand-new headphones in a twist and was trying to untangle them.

Ali leaned over. "Can I help? You might be good at solving relationship issues, but I'm very good at solving stuff like that." She pointed at Morgan's headphones.

Morgan hesitated, unplugged them and handed them over. "That would be great, thank you. I'm not sure how I tangled them so soon. It's a special talent."

Ali said nothing as Morgan passed them over.

When their fingers touched, her breath caught.

Twelve-year-old Ali stood on a chair and punched the air. "I'm touching Morgan Scott!" she screamed.

Thirty-five-year-old Ali pursed her lips, ignored the wave of heat that rumbled through her, then carefully and quickly untangled Morgan's headphones and handed them back.

"Thank you." Morgan's gaze flicked up and down.

What did she see? Ali had no idea. She curled her toes in her shoes and prayed she wasn't the colour purple. Fifty-fifty chance. She was so glad this plane ride was short. She couldn't be in Morgan's space too long without saying or doing something really stupid, she was pretty sure.

The tannoy crackled, then a voice filled the plane. The captain.

"Ladies and gentlemen, I'm afraid I have bad news. The aircraft isn't fit to fly, and I'd rather know that when we're on the ground than when we're in the air, as I'm sure you'd agree. The upshot is, we're going to have to deplane you, and see what we can sort out in the meantime for getting you to your destination. I know this isn't the news you wanted, but let's look on the bright side. At least it's December 22nd, still three days before the big day, so hopefully that means you can all make it back to where you're going in time for turkey. Again, huge apologies, but this is out of our control. Please follow the crew instructions on what to do next. Thank you!"

Ali glanced at Morgan again, her forehead furrowed. "Not the best news."

Morgan sighed, unplugged her headphones and put them back in their plastic pouch. "No, but like the captain says, we have time to get home."

Ali nodded. "Plenty. How busy can Christmas travel be?"

29

\* \* \*

They got off the plane and rode the bus back to the terminal. Ali texted her family, letting them know what was happening. Then she slotted her phone back into her green duffel coat. Tobias said it made her look like a plant-based Paddington Bear. She had no issue with that. She liked Paddington. She liked marmalade sandwiches, too.

When she glanced out of the window, the snow, which was forecast, was now coming down in full force. Terrific. Would the rest of the flights even get off the ground if it kept up? She didn't want to think about that.

By the time they hurried through the airport doors for a second time that day, it seemed ten times busier, with flashing screens and harried customers. Beside the door, a bedraggled family of five wore frowns and crowns of fresh snow. Ali turned her head back to the scene outside, to the sudden blizzard that seemed to have come out of nowhere. She had a gnawing feeling this wasn't going to end well.

She joined the queue for the enquiries desk, but it wasn't moving. When she craned her neck to check what was happening, a man at the head of the queue gesticulated wildly, and the staff shook their heads slowly. She chewed on the inside of her cheek as the snow swirled against the floor-to-ceiling windows that lead to the airport tarmac. Should she try another route home?

Where was Morgan? Her charm might come in handy right now. However, when Ali stepped out to look to the front of the queue again, it was Morgan who was remonstrating with the staff at the desk. In seconds, she turned around and walked towards Ali, her face thunderous. Maybe blondes didn't always get their own way. She brushed past, not seeing her at all.

Ali put out a hand to stop her.

Morgan turned and shook her off. When she saw who it was, she blinked.

"Sorry, Ali." She rearranged her face from irritated to friendly. It almost worked. She sighed. "Getting home today was sort of important. My sister's pregnant, and due any day. I wanted to have some time with my family before that happened. We were going to make a gingerbread house tonight and decorate it."

Those were not the words Ali expected to drop from Morgan's mouth.

"It's a family tradition, so don't judge." Morgan pouted. "I've been looking forward to it all week."

Ali gave her a tiny smile. Morgan Scott wasn't a superstar, and she wasn't invincible. She might yet prove to be a normal person like everyone else.

"Your family bake gingerbread houses?" She should *never* offer to make her a cake.

Morgan blushed. "They do. We're good at it, too." She shrugged. "We like to bake. It makes us happy."

Okay, she was normalish. "*Eating* cake and biscuits make me happy, so we have something in common." Ali paused. "I take it you didn't have any luck with the woman at the desk? You should have saved your chocolates for her. Or baked her a cake."

A glimmer of a smile. "I definitely should have." She shook her head. "Especially with this blizzard. I asked about luggage, but she said they're not sure where it is. And now…" She pointed up towards the departures board, which currently was awash with one word: delayed. "If all the flights are delayed or cancelled, who knows when we'll get our luggage if they have to get the bags off *all* the planes. That's what the woman at the desk just told me, and that's when I might have lost it a little." She sighed. "Even communications specialists have off days." She put her palms together in front of her chest, then brought her eyes level with Ali. "But now I'm back on it. Back to problem-solving and getting people on my side. On *our* side."

"Our side?" There was an 'our'? Ali wasn't sure she was ready for that.

"You're going back to Devon, and so am I. Maybe we should travel together? I have a hatred of Christmas trains after being stuck on broken and overcrowded ones too many times. There are always too many people, too many presents."

"Hence you were flying."

"Indeed. But that might be up the spout now." Morgan tilted her head to the ceiling just as the old man from the plane walked by. Her blonde hair sparkled under the airport strip lights.

"Any luck getting your luggage?" he asked.

"Not much luck with anything right now," Morgan replied.

"Hope you get home eventually."

"You, too!"

He gave her a smile and walked on.

Morgan turned back to Ali. "I might have to bite the bullet and get a train. Although, I remember checking and they were all nearly fully booked months ago."

"They are. I checked last week. And then just now while I was waiting in line."

"Right." Morgan looked over Ali's shoulder.

Ali turned and followed her line of vision to the signs pointing towards the various modes of transport. Train. Bus. Taxi. Car hire.

"The buses will probably be rammed, too." Ali paused. Car hire. She really didn't want to be trapped in a car with Morgan the entire way home. It would be far too much for her 12-year-old self to take. But she might have to get over that. Or else, spend Christmas back at her flat. Not such a bad thought, but her mum would kill her.

So would Tobias.

"We could try car hire."

Morgan's gaze drilled into her.

Twelve-year-old Ali's stomach flipped. She rolled her eyes at herself internally.

"I can't drive."

Ali blinked. "You can't?" She didn't know anyone who didn't drive.

Morgan shook her head. "No. I mean, I can, but I haven't for ages. I don't have my licence on me."

"But I do, and I can." She glanced back at the sign. "So shall we try?"

Relief swept across Morgan's face. "Yes please."

Ali nodded in the direction of the hire companies. "Let's go."

# Chapter Five

No cars available. That was the sign on every single car hire desk when they ran through from the departures hall, dodging large swathes of confused passengers. They weren't the only ones in this predicament, which made it even more essential they made it out of the airport and the city before all routes out shut down. Yes, Morgan was thinking like she was in a disaster movie, but that was her jam today.

"Okay, let's think." Ali sucked on her top lip. Panicked queer energy had replaced her former cool queer energy. But she was still cute, if a little freaked.

But no, Morgan couldn't think about that.

There were more pressing matters at hand.

Like finding their luggage and a route south.

She held up a hand. She was trained to problem-solve. She needed to put her skills into action.

"We need to split up. You see if you can get our luggage before we leave." Because they were leaving, however it might happen. "I'll come up with a plan of action after I check buses and trains. Two-pronged approach for the win?"

Ali took in her plan, then gave a nod.

"Meet back by the cash machine in 30 minutes?"

"Should we exchange numbers in case we get stuck or lost?"

"Good plan." Morgan recited her number.

Ali's fingers shook as she entered Morgan's number. She'd either had too much coffee today, or she needed food. Probably both.

Morgan walked over to a spare metal seat in the airport foyer, deciding that whoever invented metal seating was clearly a sadist. The seat was next to a sad-looking Christmas tree with a severe lack of baubles. Ho bloody ho. She stroked the new screen on her phone, then flicked to the National Rail app to see if they could get on a train. However, the trains had something in common with the planes: most were cancelled. Maybe they'd have to get a bus all the way to Devon. They might just about make it by Christmas Eve, if they were lucky.

What had she done to deserve this? She'd worked her arse off this quarter, and satisfied all her clients. All she wanted was a festive break with her family.

A sob from nearby pulled her from her thoughts.

Morgan turned to find Mrs Claus crying on the end of the metal seating. Had Santa had an affair? Was Rudolph bed-bound with shingles?

Morgan fished in her bag and brought out a tissue. Maybe her problems weren't so bad.

She moved up the seating and sat next to the lady in red. "Excuse me," she said. "Would this help?"

Mrs Claus—who couldn't be over 25—brought her gaze up to meet Morgan's. She spotted the tissue, took it, then burst into tears.

"Thank you," she whispered, blowing her nose.

"It's been a rough day all round."

Mrs Claus nodded, then let out a hiccup. "You have no idea."

"Try me." Morgan had just about exhausted all transport avenues. She was very much up for some distraction. Mrs Claus was just that.

"My arsehole girlfriend stood me up, and then broke up with me by text."

Ouch. That had to hurt. "I'm sorry to hear that."

"We were meant to do a festive flash mob at the airport for a project we're doing at university. Hence the costume. Me, her and ten others. Only, the rest of them couldn't get here because of the snow, and then she messaged me saying she was having second thoughts and that we should break up. She's already got on a bus to go back to Manchester. I just can't believe it." She leaned forward, then put her head in her hands.

Mrs Claus was a lesbian. Or at least, a woman who liked women. That put a smile on Morgan's face. This was something she could help with. She was good at relationships. She was a queer communications professional.

"Mrs Claus," Morgan started.

"Call me Imogen," Mrs Claus mumbled into her hands. Then she unfurled herself and sat up with a sigh.

"Imogen Claus, I like it."

A smile ghosted across Imogen's face.

"Are you at university in Manchester?" It seemed an awfully long way to come if so.

"No. We go to Glasgow. I'm from here, but she was going

home to Manchester for Christmas later today. She moved her bus time."

"How come you're here if all your friends couldn't make it because of the snow?"

"I've got a car, and they haven't. Plus, I'm more reliable. I turn up for shit, you know? That was one of my girlfriend's gripes about me. She said I was too rigid. Not spontaneous. But I think being organised and reliable are good qualities."

Morgan sat up. Damn it, this girl sounded like a young her. She wanted to help.

Plus, Imogen had a car.

"Being reliable is an exceptional quality, and one your ex will see in time is something to celebrate." She waved a hand up and down Imogen's outfit. "I bet this didn't happen last minute, did it?"

Imogen shook her head. "No!" she wailed.

Morgan rubbed her back. "It's okay, better out than in." A plan formed in her mind. "Listen, Imogen. How long have you and your girlfriend—what's her name?"

"Sam," she said.

"Sam. How long have you been together?"

"Six months."

"Long enough," Morgan said. "And do you want to fight for her?"

Imogen turned her head. She'd gone all out for Mrs Claus on the make-up front, too. With her exaggerated red lipstick, blush and eye shadow, she could be a contestant on *RuPaul's Drag Race*. Morgan was certain they never got deliveries of Imogen's OTT stick-on lashes at the North Pole, either.

"I think so?"

She needed some persuasion. Morgan was the person to give it. "I'm a trained relationship specialist, so if you want some advice, I'm here for you." She leaned in. "I'm also a lesbian, so I understand where you're coming from."

Imogen's face crumpled. "That women are the worst?"

"The absolute worst," Morgan nodded. It had been a while, but they definitely were. "But if you think she's worth it, why don't you drive to Manchester and let her know? Do you know her address there?"

Imogen nodded. "I met her family a couple of months ago when we went for a weekend."

"There you are. If you want her, maybe you should go after her."

Imogen stared at Morgan, then twisted to look outside. "But the snow."

"The motorway will be clear," Morgan added. "Plus, I need to go that way, so how about I come with you? My plane's cancelled. I could coach you on what to say on our journey. It'll be like a road trip. Thelma and Louise!"

Imogen scrunched her brow. "That movie didn't end well."

She had a point. Poor example. But Morgan wasn't to be defeated. "But the whole gist of it was about female friendship and empowerment." Morgan paused, letting her words sink in. "If you go today, act on your gut. Maybe Sam just got cold feet over something. But if you confront her, you'll know. If you don't, you'll be stewing all Christmas until you're back at university. When is that?"

Imogen frowned, then took a moment before she replied. "Nearly a month."

"You don't want to wait that long. You need answers." She was really laying it on thick. But this was Morgan's ticket out.

Was Imogen going to bite?

"I promise, if we do this, we don't have to drive off a cliff at the end."

"There aren't many cliffs in Manchester."

"Exactly!"

The silence hung over them as Imogen processed. Then she jumped up and held out her hand to Morgan. "Okay, you're on. Road trip to Manchester. Sam will not believe I'd drive all the way there to confront her."

"You might end the day back on, and with all the answers you need. Wouldn't that be nice?"

Hope roared through Morgan. They could at least move south getting a lift with Imogen. Plus, she was Mrs Claus, so the best driver possible. She probably rode shotgun with Santa every year and took over the driving when he was tired or got stuck up a chimney.

Now she just had to locate Ali, and they could go.

Today was already turning into way more of an adventure than she'd planned.

* * *

They found Ali filling in forms at the luggage desk, along with hundreds of other passengers. It impressed Morgan she'd even got the forms.

When Morgan drew up beside her, Ali gave her a grin. "Just the woman. You need to fill in your email address. The whole luggage system has buggered up, and nobody is picking up the bags at the moment because of the snow. They're promising we can get our luggage eventually, but they can't say when. It could be today, but then again…"

"Holy shit."

"Holy shit is exactly what I said," Ali replied. "We're filling in these forms, and they'll text to let us know when the bags are ready. They might even fly them to Exeter so we can pick them up from there. I ticked that option."

At least they wouldn't have to come back to Glasgow for them. "Makes sense," Morgan replied.

"Now we just have to work out how to get there." As she spoke, Ali peered over Morgan's shoulder at Imogen.

Morgan straightened up. She needed to explain Mrs Claus to Ali. They were yet to be introduced.

"I might have come up with a plan for that." Morgan stepped back. "Ali, meet Imogen, aka Mrs Claus. Her girlfriend unceremoniously dumped her today, but Imogen's going to drive to Manchester to get her back in the manner of every rom-com movie you've ever seen, and we're going to hitch a ride that far with her. It's going to be an epic road trip and I've promised her we'll work out a solid plan of action to fix her love life in the car."

Ali's features didn't flicker.

"I've told her we're both seasoned lesbians, so we have ample experience."

Now Ali's eyebrow crept up her face. "Are you calling me a slut?"

Morgan's eyes widened. "No! I'm just saying, we have years on Imogen. We *know* women. We can be wise owls to her fledgling chicklet."

Ali didn't look convinced, but she shook Imogen's hand anyway. When she did, the tiny bells strapped around Imogen's wrist tingled. Other passengers glanced their way.

"Good to meet you, Imogen."

Ali thrust the pen and form into Morgan's hand. "Fill this in, and we can get going."

Fifteen minutes later, they climbed into Imogen's white Range Rover. If Morgan could have chosen a car to battle the current conditions, it would have been this one. She just wasn't sure what a university student was doing driving one. Range Rovers were normally the province of yummy mummies or posh boys, not spurned fancy-dress lovers.

"Great car for the snow." Morgan clicked her seat belt into place.

In the rear-view mirror, she watched Ali do the same. Now she reminded her of a famous footballer who played in the Women's Super League. Same stylish hair, same cool brown eyes. Did she have the same muscular calves under her trousers, too? Morgan cleared her throat. Those thoughts weren't helpful in getting them back home. They definitely wouldn't be helpful if Morgan ran into Nicole, either.

However, Ali wasn't an annoying 12-year-old anymore, was she? She'd even proved a useful teammate by sorting out the luggage. Morgan gave her corporate clients this sort of dilemma all the time to foster team-building. Now here she was, taking part in a real-life example, with Mrs Claus in the driving seat. Nobody would ever believe this story if she made it up.

"It's my dad's car." Imogen took off her red-and-white felt hat, hit the indicator, then the horn.

Morgan jumped.

"Sorry, it's pretty new, and this is the first time I've driven it. I only got put on the insurance at the weekend. My dad took some persuading. I borrowed it this morning when I needed to get to the airport. He's going to kill me going all the way to Manchester in it." Imogen located the windscreen wipers and set them going to clear the snow.

Oh fuck. Was this the car they were going to die in? Morgan had always had a slight fear of flying, but never of car journeys. Maybe that was about to change.

"You okay if I put the heat on?" If they were going to die, at least they could do it comfortably.

"Of course," Imogen replied.

Morgan turned the heat to full and cupped her hands around the air vent as if it were a fire.

Then Imogen reversed out of the space, narrowly missing an elderly woman pushing a trolley of suitcases taller than her. Imogen swerved at the final second, then let out a hiccup, followed by a giggle.

"Oops! My dad always tells me to watch out for people. But they're smaller than cars, aren't they? Trickier to see."

Morgan swallowed down her heartbeat and closed her eyes.

It was all going to be okay.

Probably.

"Can you key in Manchester on the sat nav?" Imogen pointed at the dashboard navigation system.

Morgan nodded. "Do you know the address?"

"Just put in the big Primark. If we head for that, that gets me on the right road and I know where to turn off beforehand."

Morgan glanced at Ali, her face ashen. She gave Morgan a tight grin and raised both eyebrows.

Five minutes later, they were out of the airport and on the road. They hadn't crashed. Yet. Morgan allowed her muscles to relax by ten per cent.

Imogen fiddled with the radio dial, keeping one eye on the road. She settled on a station playing Mariah's 'All I Want For Christmas' and tapped the steering wheel as she navigated onto the motorway.

"How long have you two been a couple?"

Morgan frowned at Imogen, then shook her head. "Oh no, we're not—"

"—a couple," Ali said decisively from the back.

Imogen glanced Morgan's way. "I just thought… you said you're both lesbians and you're travelling at Christmas together."

"I'm a lesbian." Morgan pressed her index finger to her chest. "I can't speak for Ali."

"I'm queer," Ali confirmed. "Sometimes I'm a lesbian. It depends on my mood." She gave Morgan a wink as she turned to her.

Now they'd met again, Morgan wanted to know more. Had they seen each other at queer venues in Glasgow? Had they slept with the same woman? That thought made Morgan suck on her teeth. It was possible, because the lesbian community in Glasgow was hardly huge. But now wasn't the time to ask that question.

In fact, she wasn't sure there would *ever* be an appropriate time for that one.

"Okay," Imogen replied. "How do you know each other?"

Her knuckles turned a little whiter as she gripped the wheel. "You do know each other, right? I'm not being kidnapped, am I?"

Morgan shook her head so there was no room for confusion. "Relax. We know each other from school. No kidnapping is taking place."

She could still picture baby Ali walking home behind her and Nicole. She was always told to keep a respectable distance. Far enough away for their school rep to remain untarnished, but not too far that it looked like they didn't care. Morgan's cheeks coloured at the memory. Being a younger sister must have been hard. "I really am a communications expert, and I can't vouch for exactly what Ali does, but I know her parents and they're lovely." Morgan glanced in the mirror again and met Ali's gaze.

As soon as she did, Ali dropped it.

"It's true. She knows where my family lives." Ali sat forward and put a hand on the side of each front seat. "In fact, we first met when Morgan came to my sister's eighth birthday party. We might have met before that, but that's the time I remember. Morgan won pass-the-parcel that day and walked away with a toy trumpet. I really wanted that trumpet. I was *so* jealous."

Morgan turned in her seat. "I remember that trumpet. I played it to death and drove my parents bananas."

"You've known each other forever." Imogen switched to the fast lane. She was no laid-back driver.

Ali held Morgan's gaze. "For as long as I can remember, Morgan has been in my life. Well, my sister's, which made it mine too. Because that's how families work, isn't it?"

What Ali said was true. She had been a part of her life forever. Just not when they were adults. Morgan turned to face front.

"It is," Imogen replied. "I've got 14-year-old twin brothers and they annoy the crap out of me."

"Give it time. You might like them when they're older."

"I doubt it."

"But you never quite grow out of the roles you had when you were younger. No matter how old Ali or I get, she'll always be my mate's little sister. One that I better get home safe or Nicole will kill me."

"I can get home myself just fine."

Morgan caught Ali's peeved tone, but she ignored it. "Anyway, enough about us. What about you? Tell us about you and Sam."

Now it was Imogen's turn to sigh. She flicked the wipers onto fast speed as the snow came at them in waves. The flashing lights on the overhead signs told her to lower her speed to 30mph. Imogen obliged.

"What do you want to know? We met eight months ago on our ecology course. Sam's very chatty, kinda brilliant. We began studying together, and then one night we went for a chai latte at a cafe in the West End, and Sam invited me back to hers. I didn't leave for six days." A wide grin spread across Imogen's features as she recounted the story.

"Look at your face! You can't give that up." Morgan remembered young love. Sort of. "Six days is an impressive shagfest. Did you eat anything at all or just survive on lust alone?"

A snort arrived from the backseat.

Morgan turned again. "What?"

"*Did you eat anything?*" Ali said. "You sound about 60, not 38. Who cares if she ate anything? She didn't need to. Lust is very filling, I hear."

Morgan tensed. Where had that come from? "I was just making conversation."

"We ate a lot of Battenberg cake. Good for energy. It still makes me smile when I see it." Imogen sighed again. "Or at least, it did."

Morgan reached over and patted her thigh. "It will again. You don't stay in bed with someone for six days if there's not a great connection. I'm sure it wasn't just sex and cake. There was some conversation, too?"

Imogen tipped her head as the traffic ground to a halt. As quick as the blizzard had arrived, it had now slowed, but so had the traffic. Imogen wasn't focused on that. She was too busy reliving the early days of her and Sam.

"So much of it. That's what I love about Sam. She's interesting and smart. Also, great tits."

Ali let out a hoot of laughter in the backseat. "You can't let her go, then. Tits are important."

Imogen slapped the wheel, and the car filled with the sound of jingle bells. "I'm glad you're a breast girl, too." She grinned at Ali via the mirror.

"Was she your first love?"

Imogen nodded. "First one where I've been away from home. I mean, I had girlfriends at school, and I really thought my first one was going to be the one I stayed with, but it didn't work out." She shrugged. "But Sam's different. Or at least, I thought she was different."

Morgan tapped her fingers on the dashboard. "In that case, if she's the one, you need to know why she's ending it."

"I wouldn't drive to Manchester for just anyone," Imogen replied.

"Although we've only driven 15 miles so far," Ali added, phone in front of her face when Morgan glanced her way.

It seemed like they'd been on the road for hours. But at least they were heading in the right direction.

"What about you, Morgan? Who was your first crush?" Ali leaned forward. "And if you say my sister, full disclosure, I will tell her when I see her."

Morgan laughed. "It was not your sister. It was actually a girl in the upper sixth. Her name was Sarah Kelly, and she wore her skirt just that bit shorter than anyone else, but in a 'fuck you!' kinda way." Morgan still recalled stopping in the corridor whenever Sarah walked past. The way her breath had caught in her chest. "I wonder where she is now?"

"I don't remember her." Ali's voice was quieter. "Did she move away?"

"Her family did, so she had no reason to come back. Probably for the best, because if she turned up in the pub, I might turn into my 15-year-old self and die on the spot."

"She might be married with four kids by now," Imogen told her.

Morgan shook her head. "It wouldn't matter. You don't forget your first and the effect they have on you, do you?"

At that, Imogen shook her head slowly from side to side. "No, you don't." She paused. "Are you both single now?"

Morgan glanced back as Ali nodded. "Yep. For the past three years. Happy to be so."

Imogen eyed Morgan. "And you?"

Morgan nodded. "Yes. This year has been too crazy to accommodate a girlfriend."

"Let me get this straight. You two are giving me relationship advice, when neither of you are in one, or have been for the past year?"

Morgan shifted in her seat.

She made a good point.

# Chapter Six

A li couldn't wait to get out of the car. This was possibly the worst road trip she'd ever had the misfortune to fall into. She'd done one with her ex when she was in her late 20s, and that had been a disaster as soon as they hit France and her ex began kissing boys on the sly. Or should that be, on the not-so-sly, because Ali kept seeing her do it. However, she still wasn't sure which was worse. Being cooped up with the woman she'd been in love with her entire teenage years. Or spending her days driving with her cheating, conniving ex.

Maybe she'd call it a draw.

"It's just intense, though, isn't it? First crushes and first loves?"

But apparently, it was all Imogen wanted to talk about.

Thankfully, Morgan had shut up in the front. Maybe she didn't want to think back on hers, for whatever reason.

Ali desperately wanted to look up Sarah Kelly, but she'd probably changed her name by now. Most women she knew had.

They passed a sign for a services where Burger King was the star attraction. Everyone knew an M&S Food outlet always trumped that, but they didn't get a choice. After half an hour, the snow had almost stopped, but the traffic was still slow.

"I need the loo, so I'm getting off here," Imogen said.

"Maybe we can get a coffee to warm us up for the rest of the trip, too?"

Morgan rubbed her hands together and blew on them. "Good plan. My treat for driving us. Might even get some gingerbread biscuits, too. Something festive and sweet." She turned around. "Fancy a coffee and a gingerbread, Ali?"

Morgan was oblivious to the effect she had on her, wasn't she?

"Sounds good. I need the loo, too."

Imogen flicked on her indicator, then pressed the accelerator to get past two cars on her inside. The obvious thing to do, rather than slowing down.

Ali clamped her eyes shut, so she didn't witness their certain death. However, when she reopened them, their car sped up the slip road and squealed around the bend too fast. She'd be glad to get out of this car alive. The bad news was she had to get back in.

Imogen parked up, and the three of them rugged up and walked cautiously across the car park to the main doors. A sign to the right of the entrance announced 'Christmas Trees For Sale: Free Local Delivery!', with an arrow pointing to a path beyond. As soon as they walked through the main door, Christmas music filled their ears again. This time, it was East 17 and their festive tune, 'Stay Another Day'.

Next to her, Morgan threw up her hands. "This is not a Christmas song, by the way. It's just a song that got released at Christmas and they added jingly bells. Why don't people realise that?"

Ali gave her a weird look. "But it's always played at Christmas."

"It's one of my mum's favourites." Imogen jingled for added effect.

Morgan rolled her eyes. "It's a deception. Even their lead singer, Tony Mortimer, admitted it."

"Okaaaay," Ali replied. Morgan flipping out about a song was not optimal right now.

Morgan sighed. "We've got bigger things to worry about, I know. It just winds me up every year."

Ali was getting that.

"Anyway, I'll get the coffees," Morgan said, taking charge. She did that a lot.

"Maybe we can drink them inside while I use the Wi-Fi to see if I can book a hire car for tomorrow? My reception has been patchy so far." She'd been trying ever since they began.

Morgan nodded. "Grab a table and I'll find you."

"I'm going to the loo before I do anything else." Imogen jingled as she walked away.

Ali found a spare table and sat down. She unwound her thick mustard scarf, specially knitted by Tobias's fair hands, then got out her phone and texted him. She had to talk to someone.

*Plane grounded. Now hitching a lift to Manchester. With Morgan Scott. Don't ask.*

Although, obviously, if *she* got that text, that was the first thing she'd do.

Within seconds, Tobias responded. She knew he would. His phone was surgically attached.

*OMG, I thought you'd be home by now! Are you okay? And who the fuck is Morgan Scott? Wait, was she in that Netflix thing you liked?*

She sounded like a film star! It wasn't just Ali.

*Remember when we sat up drinking wine at mine recently and we discussed our first crushes? Morgan Scott was mine.*

She waited for it to land, then his response.

First off, he sent a row of shocked-face emojis. Quickly followed by some aubergines.

*Wait. You're hitching a lift with your first love?* More shocked emojis.

*Looks like it. She's going home too, and we met at the airport. Our parents still live in the same village.*

Parent.

It was still new enough to shock her.

*I better go. She's just paying for the coffee.*

*Where are you now?*

*A service station somewhere south of Glasgow.*

*No shagging in the loos.*

Ali rolled her eyes. *No shagging in my bed.*

Tobias sent more aubergines, followed by a raised eyebrow.

She walked into that, didn't she?

\* \* \*

Twenty minutes later, Ali sat up straight. Elbows on the table, head turned left. Her gingerbread was gone, her coffee half-drunk.

Opposite, Morgan mirrored her pose.

Outside, Imogen walked up and down, phone stuck to her ear. Every now and again, she stopped, frowned, then started walking again. She was still dressed as Mrs Claus, so onlookers were probably worried Christmas plans weren't going well in the North Pole.

"You think it's her dad wanting the car back?"

Ali turned, and their faces were so close, she could almost reach out and touch Morgan. That face that was so familiar, and yet, so much a stranger. She sat back, putting some distance between them. "I hope not, otherwise we're screwed."

"I have a bad feeling," Morgan replied. "Although if it is her dad demanding she comes home, at least we won't die with Imogen at the wheel."

Ali snorted. "She is by far the worst driver with the nicest car I've ever had the misfortune to hitch a ride with." She paused. "If it cheers you up, I just booked us a car in Manchester for the morning. If we can get there, we just need to find a hotel, and we can drive home tomorrow."

Morgan's smile almost cracked her face. "Fucking hell, I could kiss you."

Ali went rigid, and her heart danced in her chest. Goddammit, she just wanted to get home and get away from Morgan. It was all too confusing. This was bringing back too much of her past, and Ali was all about existing in the future and beyond. She didn't want to be dragged backwards.

Imogen pulled the phone from her face, waved, then said something through the glass Ali couldn't understand.

Moments later, she sat next to Ali with a thump.

"I have good news and bad news. Which do you want first?"

"Good," said Morgan.

"Bad," replied Ali.

Imogen looked from one to the other. "Okay, I'll do it the way I want to. The good news is, that was Sam. She says she made a huge mistake. She read an article online last night about first loves and how I could be the one, and she freaked out."

Imogen shrugged, then ran a hand through her blonde hair. "The details aren't important. The key point is, she got off her bus at the first service station, and now she's back in Glasgow and waiting at my flat. She let herself in. She has a key.

"The bad news is that I'm going back to Glasgow. This is where our journey ends. Unless you want to come back with me and try again from there? Or you could try to hitch a ride from here? There are normally people on the way out of services, aren't there? Plus, you're both hot, so you should have no end of takers."

Ali blinked. She hadn't expected that from Imogen's mouth. But where did it leave them? Buggered.

"This trip is all about you getting back together with Sam, and it looks like that's going to happen. I'm thrilled for you!" Morgan gave Imogen an encouraging smile.

"Thanks for understanding. Sorry to leave you stranded." She stood up, jingled, then grimaced. "Give me your numbers, then if you're still stuck this evening and nobody's picked you up, we'll come and get you. Sam and I. You'll love her. She's gorgeous. Also, great tits."

Ali laughed, but keyed her number in just in case. "Thanks for getting us this far. Now, go have your happy ending." Ali got up and gave Imogen a hug.

"I'm so pleased I met you. Let's keep in touch!"

"See ya, Thelma." Morgan gave her a hug too, then checked she had her bag, wallet and phone.

Ali did the same.

"Go get your girl," Morgan added.

Imogen gave them both a wave, then disappeared out the door of the services.

"Well, now we're fucked," Ali said.

"Royally."

\* \* \*

After they got bored with freaking out, they hatched a plan. They were going to hitch a ride home.

They stocked up on chocolate, then bought a large pad of paper and a black marker. Morgan wrote the word 'Devon' in large block capitals on one sheet, after an argument about exactly what they should write. Ali had wanted to focus on a particular town, and write 'Exeter' or 'Torquay', both agreeing Dartmouth was too small. However, Morgan won out, saying people would more likely have a vague idea of the direction of Devon. Ali guessed they'd wait and see. If they hit the jackpot and scored a lift, they'd cancel their hire car.

They'd stood at the side of the road for around 20 minutes when a battered red Golf pulled up. Ali banged her hands together and leaned in, only to be confronted by two mean-looking dogs in the backseat. When Ali reached out a hand, one dog snapped its jaw.

Ali jumped back. She was cold, but she didn't want to be a dog's dinner.

"You're welcome as long as you don't mind sharing with Rod and Emu," the woman with a mass of frizz for hair told her.

Morgan gave Ali a definite shake of the head.

"Thanks, but my friend's not a dog lover," Ali replied.

"Shame, the forecast says snow again soon. Good luck, ladies!" With that, she drove off.

Ali breathed out, fogging the air in front of her. She

adjusted her new furry, wrap-behind ear muffs. She didn't like hats or normal ear muffs as they messed up her hair. "She has a point. I don't fancy standing here in a blizzard."

"If a blizzard whips up, we'll go back to the services, okay? I'd prefer that to getting in the back with those two dogs."

Ali hugged herself against the cold, but nodded. "Agreed."

They waited 15 minutes longer, the wind slicing Ali's face. She glanced at Morgan, who looked frozen. "You don't have a hat and gloves?"

Morgan shook her head. "They're in my case. I didn't think I'd need them on the plane."

It was a fair point.

And then it started to snow again. First, pretty snowflakes that swirled around them. If you squinted, it was almost like being in a snow globe. But then, the snowflakes multiplied, the wind whipped up, and soon they were both spitting out ice and shivering.

Ali made the move first, and Morgan followed. By the time they got to the services, Morgan had a layer of snow on top of her head, and her eyelids shivered.

Now she didn't just look like Ali's first love. She looked like her first love, but frosted.

"I'm not sure why snow is so romanticised. Ice doesn't get the same appreciation, does it?"

"Unless you're making a cocktail."

"I can only dream of a Negroni right now." Morgan stamped her feet as they walked into the cafe area. She clocked the stares from other people. "Do I look that bad?"

Ali laughed, leaning in to swipe the snow from Morgan's hair. "You look like you've been in a snowstorm. And let's face it, the heating is barely on in here. It won't melt any time soon." She stared into her eyes. Still deep and blue.

Morgan shivered.

"Thanks for making me look less like a snowman. It might have worked better if we still had the cabaret here, but Mrs Claus has long since departed."

They walked over to the cafe, and this time, Ali got the coffees. She added two vegetable soups and hunks of bread and butter to the order, and brought the tray back.

Morgan looked like she might cry with gratitude. "You're a lifesaver. I've only had breakfast today."

"And a gingerbread." Ali checked her watch. "Plus, it's still only 3pm. We've been in survival mode, and we've made it this far. Well done us. But we'll only keep it up with some food inside us."

"Agreed."

Ali ate the soup in silence, welcoming the warmth it provided. By the time they finished, Morgan had lost her frosting.

When she was done, she pushed away her bowl. "I've had an idea." She peered out of the window. The snow still fell, but not as fast. She stood up. "Stay here. I'll be back."

"Hang on," Ali began.

But Morgan was already out the door.

Where the hell had she disappeared to?

# Chapter Seven

Morgan blew some snow from her face and waved her hand as she walked up the side path where the Christmas trees sign pointed. She emerged into a small courtyard that seemed almost otherworldly. From here, shielded from the noise of the motorway by greenery and twinkling lights, it was a winter wonderland. She stamped her feet to make sure her blood continued to move and looked around for a staff member. Seconds later, a man in a lumberjack jacket appeared, replete with cream fleece collar. He also had a thick black hat on and thermal gloves. Envy fizzed through Morgan as she curled her own frozen fingers at her side.

"Hello, how can I help you?" The man walked over and smiled at Morgan. He wore a name badge that said 'Dave'. A solid name. Morgan hoped she could appeal to Dave's sense of community and Christmas spirit.

"Hi Dave," Morgan began. Always throw in a name when you can. First rule of negotiation is the personal touch. "I was just wondering." Morgan pointed at his nearby sign. "When you say you'll deliver, how local is local?"

Dave tilted his head. Up close, his eyebrows were so thick, Morgan half expected a family of birds to be nesting there.

"Depends how polite you are. I've delivered to Edinburgh

if I have enough trade. But normally it's more local. Where do you need the tree to go?"

"Manchester?" Morgan winced. She knew it was ridiculous as soon as it came out of her mouth.

Dave threw back his head and howled. "I think they might have Christmas trees a little closer to Manchester that you could buy."

Morgan took a step closer to him. She could see she had his interest. Either that, or he thought she was completely mad. Possibly both.

"The thing is, Dave, we're in a bit of a quandary."

"We?" Dave looked over her shoulder as if expecting someone to materialise any moment.

"Me and my friend. Well, not so much a friend. We know each other from school. Well, I know her sister more." This was not going according to plan. *Focus, Morgan!* She shook her head. "I'm going off topic."

"A little," Dave agreed with a smile.

"Here's the thing. My old acquaintance and I met today at the airport, where we were catching a flight to Devon for Christmas. But then, our plane had a fault and it snowed. We hitched a lift this far from Glasgow, but sadly for us, our driver had to turn back due to matters of the heart." She paused. "And did I mention our baggage is still at the airport?"

"You've had quite the day, and it's only," he checked his watch, "three o'clock."

It honestly felt like a year since this morning. "Exactly. We've tried hitching, but nobody's stopping, so I wondered if you would give us a lift. Even to the nearest train station so we could get to Manchester eventually?"

"You don't want to go back to Glasgow? You've not come far, and there are more trains than the local ones around here. Plus, your bags are there."

Morgan shook her head. "The bags still haven't been located." She'd hadn't received a text as yet. "And honestly, I think we'd rather go south than north. It feels a little more like we're heading in the right direction, at least."

He studied her face. "You might be in luck. I'm packing up here in around two hours, and then I'm heading home. And home is half an hour south. If you stick around and help me stash the trees in the lot in around 90 minutes, you can get in with me and I'll drop you at Lockerbie, which is on the Manchester train route. How does that sound?"

Morgan went to hug him, then remembered she must not come over as a mad woman. She was in control. She was sorting things out. She was a problem-solver supreme.

"It sounds bloody perfect. Thank you, Dave. You don't know what this means. Let me tell my friend, and we'll come back." She shivered, then clapped her hands. "Don't drive off without us." Morgan pressed her frozen fingers together, as if in prayer.

"I promise." He gave her a grin as she left.

Minutes later, Morgan skidded back into the cafe to find Ali on her phone. When she heard her, she looked up.

"You think I should cancel this hire car we have for tomorrow? I don't want to bugger up someone else's Christmas travel if we won't use it."

Morgan shook her head. "No. Mainly because I've solved our travel issues."

Ali blinked. "This I can't wait to hear."

Morgan put her hands on her hips. "You don't believe me?"

"If you've promised me to a sultan in exchange for a car ride, I reserve the right to say no."

"No sultan, just Dave, who's selling the Christmas trees. In exchange for a hand putting them under wraps at the end of the day, he'll drive us to Lockerbie, which is the next train station on the line to Manchester."

Ali stared, then gave Morgan a big smile. "You really have saved Christmas with your sweet-talking ways. Did you buy some extra chocolate to bribe him?"

Okay, Morgan deserved that. "Mock all you like, but it means we don't have to spend the night here in Bothwell services."

"And for that, you have my thanks." Ali opened the train app on her phone. "Let's see if I can get some train tickets next, shall I?"

"Even if we can't book a seat, I say let's buy a ticket and squeeze ourselves on. We're small, and we don't have luggage. I want to at least get into England tonight. This morning, that wouldn't have been my bare minimum aim, but now, it seems like an impossible dream."

Ali scrolled, made some faces, then looked up. "It says we can book them. Maybe everyone from Glasgow is getting off at Lockerbie. Maybe they know something we don't."

Morgan wriggled her fingers. They were still numb. "I say book them."

"Shall I book for both of us?"

"Yes please. How about you pay for the train, I'll pay for tonight's hotel when we get to Manchester, then we can sort the difference later? I'm good for it. And if you don't think so, you know where my family live. You can track them down and hold them to ransom until I cough up."

Ali laughed. A full belly laugh. Which made Morgan laugh, too. It felt so good to do so. Like she'd been tense and holding her breath ever since their travel disruption began. But there was still time to repair the damage and get home before Christmas. Sure, she wouldn't make it to decorate the gingerbread house, but she hoped her family would save her a section of the roof. They always had before when she'd turned up late.

Plus, she wasn't doing this alone. Much as she was self-sufficient, she was glad that was the case. Also, Ali wasn't a stranger. She was a blast from the past. A welcome one.

An attractive one.

But Morgan's fingers and brain were still too cold to process that thought. For now, she was happy she had a partner in crime.

Especially now, as Ali leaned back, held her phone in the air, and raised her gaze to meet Morgan's.

Morgan's heart boomed like a thunder crack.

She flinched, then took a deep breath in. "Did you book them?"

"We have train tickets," Ali replied. "Whisper it, but I think our luck is about to change."

Morgan clutched the hope to her chest.

\* \* \*

"I've always wanted to ask, don't you get cold? If I had to do this, I swear I wouldn't last a day. My hands would fall off, as would my feet."

Morgan and Ali hauled the last tree under the tarpaulin-covered metal cage.

Dave locked the padlock and rattled it to check.

"You get used to it," he told them in a softer Scottish accent than Morgan was used to. Was Dave considered a soft southerner when he went to Glasgow, living an hour south of the city? "I was born and bred in Scotland, so it's sunshine and warmth that makes us melt. The cold just toughens us up. Where are you from?"

"Devon," they both replied.

Dave gave a sharp laugh that pierced the air. "I don't think the Scottish Christmas tree trade is right for you. A nice office job would be best, am I right?"

Morgan bent her head, a little embarrassed. Dave had her number.

They climbed into his white van, all three in a row up front, high enough to view the traffic on the A74(M) with ease. This time, it was moving at least. Plus, the snow had stopped, although the sides of the motorway were still stacked high.

"I might see if we can get an actual tree when I get home." Ali's thoughts broke the silence.

"You don't normally?" Dave twisted his head left as he spoke.

Ali shook her head. "My family runs the local pub. We have a few trees dotted around it, but they're always fake. Too much mess with the pine needles otherwise. We buy that pine-scented oil and pipe it into the pub instead. That, and a log fire with some mulled wine and mince pies, and people think all their festive dreams have come true."

"I'm glad not everyone thinks like that, otherwise I'd be

out of a job. Me and my brother run a Christmas tree farm nearby, so it's a year-round occupation for me."

Morgan leaned over. "What's your business called?"

"Jolly Good Elf Christmas Trees. I came up with the name." Dave looked pretty pleased with himself.

"Wow. You really are Mr Christmas."

"I contemplated changing my name by deed poll, but my wife talked me out of it." Dave raised one of his excessively bushy brows. "What about you, Morgan? Are you a real-tree fan, or have I got two heathens up front?"

"We always have a real tree," she replied. "Actually, more than one. My parents go all out for Christmas. You know those houses that break the national grid with all their Christmas lights? That's ours."

Ali turned her way. "Baking gingerbread houses. Lighting up your side of town. I don't remember this from my childhood. Is this where you tell me your surname is really Claus, and Imogen is your daughter?"

Morgan snorted. "If Imogen was my daughter, I'd be super proud. Then I'd make her take a driving course." She paused. "As for my family, it's always been that way, led in the most part by my dear, departed Nan." She gave Ali a pointed look. "Don't knock it 'til you've tried it. Getting into the festive mood lifts your spirits. Having Christmas drinks. Hanging decorations and getting a tree. Buying presents. Which is why I really hope we get our luggage back in time for the big day, or all my carefully bought gifts will go to waste." But she wasn't going to think about that. "What about you, Dave? I take it a man running a Christmas tree farm has one in every room?"

He shook his head. "My wife is fed up with them by the

time Christmas rolls around. We've got one in the lounge like everyone else. And about ten thousand in the garden."

Morgan could just imagine it. A vast swathe of green trees. She'd always loved visiting Christmas tree farms as a kid. "I bet your garden smells divine. Where's the strangest place you've delivered a tree?"

"The local graveyard. I had a customer whose mum died the previous year, and she'd always loved Christmas. She buys a tree and puts it on her grave every year."

"I love that," Morgan replied. "Much better than flowers and more personal. If I die near Glasgow, can you deliver one to my grave, too?"

"We're nearly at Lockerbie, so if we swap numbers before you go, yes."

Morgan got her phone out. "I'm not really expecting you to deliver a tree to my grave. But I'd love your number so I can send you a thank you gift."

"You don't have to do that." Dave swung the van off to the next exit, and followed the sign to Lockerbie.

"I know, but I want to. You've been so kind, and you got us out of Bothwell services. For that, we'll be forever grateful."

Dave gave Morgan his number, and she saved it to her phone under 'Dave Mr Christmas'.

"We'll be sure to tell everyone we know to get their tree at the services next year, won't we, Ali?"

Ali nodded. "Absolutely. We promise to come and get both of ours from you, too."

"You just said you don't have a real tree," Dave replied.

"But I always wanted one," Ali said. "I've always thought you had to have a reason to have one. That you had to be hosting Christmas, or have kids. I never thought I could just get one anyway. But you've convinced me, both you and Morgan. From now on, I'm going to be more festive."

He gave them both a warm smile. "Here's to spreading a little Christmas cheer."

# Chapter Eight

Against all the odds, when they boarded the train at Lockerbie station, there was a spare double seat by the door. The digital reservation display said it wasn't going to be occupied until Manchester. Maybe their luck was changing. Morgan took the window seat, and Ali took the aisle. It was just gone 6pm, and they'd sprinted over the bridge to make the train. It wasn't until it moved that Ali relaxed. Possibly for the first time that day. She took off her ear muffs and put them in her bag, then rubbed her lobes and yawned.

"I thought I'd be home by now. Having a drink in the bar. Being forced to serve customers when it got busy." She smiled at the thought. She'd been reluctant to go home this Christmas, but now it seemed like the only place she wanted to be.

"Inhaling the fake pine smells. Yet here you are, starring in your own festive adventure." Morgan fished in her bag and brought out the turkey and cranberry sandwich they'd bought in the services. There had only been one left, so they'd agreed to split it. Morgan unwrapped it, got out her half, then took a bite. She chewed, made a face, then handed the other half to Ali.

"I'm going to leave mine until it's a little less cold." Ali

67

pulled down the plastic table on the back of the seat in front of her and put the sandwich on it.

"I'm not sure any amount of time is going to improve the taste." Morgan gave her a rueful grin, but took another bite anyway. "It's not Francesco's. Let's put it that way."

Ali blinked. "I love Francesco's. The one on Pollen Street?"

"Yes." Morgan frowned. "You know it?"

Ali snorted. Francesco's wasn't just a sandwich shop. It was a religion. "Of course I bloody know it! They do the best sandwiches. Have you tried their chicken, pesto, and avocado?"

"It's my favourite." Morgan's face lit up.

"Mine too."

Morgan finished her disappointing sandwich. She made a face. "By contrast, that sad excuse for a sandwich would not pass a Francesco's taste test."

"We have the same favourite sandwich bar. How about that?" How about that indeed. This wasn't just a passing comment. This was *news*. "If you'd said you preferred Pret, we might have had to part ways now."

"Dirty talk." Morgan gave an exaggerated shiver.

"Do you live around there?"

"Not far, but my office is nearby. Do you?"

They'd probably waited in the queue together. "A five-minute walk. I've often dragged my sorry hungover self down there on a Saturday for a brunch wrap, too. They're a lifesaver, literally."

"I've done that a few times."

Outside, the coal-grey night whizzed by. They were on the move, and they shared a love of Francesco's. Don't ask

Clare Lydon

her why, but somehow, that connection was important. Ali's bones eased.

"How's Nicole and her brood doing?" Morgan asked.

The announcer came over the tannoy listing the stations the train was due to stop at.

They both shut up until he was done.

"They're good," Ali eventually replied.

"I kept meaning to get in touch, but you know how it is. You move away, then the longer you leave it, the more difficult it is to do."

"I'm sure she'd still like to hear from you. Not just at Christmas."

Morgan nodded. "I will make the effort. Does she visit you in Glasgow?"

"She's visited once in seven years. I wouldn't hold your breath." Ali laughed. "Scotland might as well be the moon, according to my family. But I'll put the squeeze on her to come when I'm home. She's due a visit, and it means she gets time on her own, which I know she craves."

They knew so much of each other's pasts and their families, and yet they hardly knew anything about each other. But was it worth getting to know her when this might be a one-off thing? Morgan probably had a ton of friends and a rich life in Glasgow. Would she have room for Ali? Their paths hadn't crossed in years, which said something.

Nevertheless, they were going to be travelling together for another day, and chat was preferable to awkward silences.

Morgan obviously thought so too, as she cleared her throat.

"You said you work in apps? What are you working on right now?"

69

"A craft beer app so that people can locate their nearest pub or bar that serves different beers, and also they can track what they've drunk. Plus, they can link up with friends to see what beers and bars they rate."

"I bet your family love that. You own three local pubs, right? I remember your dad being a huge lover of craft beer."

Ali gulped. "You remember right." Her stomach lurched, but she wasn't going to be derailed. Morgan didn't know, so her chat was what normal people did. "It's the reason I developed it. Most of my apps are to do with hospitality. I grew up in the business, so I understand what pubs and restaurants need. I also devised one that simplifies booking systems, and another to help with staffing and recruitment, which the company sold."

Morgan sat back. "I'm impressed. Here's me just being a Creative Solutions Specialist. But you're the one changing the world, one app at a time."

"You've got the fancier title, though." But it still felt good to be lauded by Morgan Scott. To have her appreciate what she did. One smile from her was still enough to send Ali's pulse racing. To make her feel like she was 12 again. If Ali wasn't stuck in such close proximity to her, she'd roll her own eyes at herself.

Morgan laughed. "All smoke and mirrors. Although, when I can help my clients solve their issues and move forward in a positive way, I do feel a sense of achievement. Everyone needs help to communicate. It's the world's number one downfall. But I think everyone deserves the chance to be heard, which is why I do my job. I've got clients from all walks of life, so one day is never like the next."

"I'm sure you're great at it. Not everyone could have talked

Dave into giving us a lift, but you did. You always had the gift of the gab, and now you're paid for your talent."

"You're too kind. My sister would say I'm a blabbermouth, but I prefer your assessment."

Morgan gave her a warm smile that made Ali's toes curl. She went to change the subject to something where she'd be more surefooted, but Morgan seemed to want to stay just where they were.

"Ali Bradford. Who would have thought you'd grow up and not always be 12?" She waved a hand. "Gorgeous, intelligent, good taste in sandwiches." Morgan's cheeks blushed red. "Sorry, did that come out a bit creepy? I meant it as a compliment."

Ali's insides heated to boiling point. She hoped beyond hope she wasn't glowing. "I'll take it as one, then."

"When was the last time you were home?" Morgan asked. "I haven't managed it since July, which my mother thinks is the crime of the century."

"The summer." It had been hot as well. Too hot for any occasion, especially the one Ali had been home for. She shook the thought from her head. "I'm long overdue."

"The prodigal daughters return," Morgan grinned.

"Something like that."

The train slowed to a stop, and they stayed that way for a few minutes. Ali looked out the window, but could see nothing. She got her phone from her pocket and went onto Google maps. It showed they were in between Carlisle and Penrith, and that two miles to the right was a place called Snowton, where there was a Christmas festival and parade today. This she had to share.

She nudged Morgan with her elbow. It felt like something

you might do to a friend. She hoped they were on their way to that.

Her 12-year-old self gave her a high five.

"I've got two pieces of good news for you."

Morgan turned her head and sat up. "Hit me."

"One, we've left Scotland and are finally in England."

Morgan held up a triumphant fist.

"Second, we're just passing a village called Snowton that has a Christmas festival and parade today, and it's billed as the most festive place in the north."

"My friend told me about a town called Mistletoe in the southeast that loves Christmas. But I never knew there was somewhere in this neck of the woods, too."

The train tannoy crackled to life. Ali's body tightened. She hoped this wasn't bad news.

"Good evening, ladies and gents. This is your driver speaking. I've got some bad news, I'm afraid. We've got a fallen tree on the line up ahead that's brought down some power lines, making it dangerous to advance. There are two choices. First, wait on the train and we'll try to make you as comfortable as possible with free tea and coffee, and blankets. Second, we're pretty near a footpath to the nearest town, Snowton, which is about two miles away. If you'd prefer to get off and go there, go to carriage five. A member of staff will be on hand to escort you off the train and to the footpath. I'd say your best bet is to stay on the train as the town isn't that big, but it's up to you. Any questions, I'll be passing through the carriages now."

Ali couldn't quite believe it. She shook her head and turned to Morgan. "You ever get the feeling this trip is doomed?"

"Never. It's just throwing up problems for me to solve."

Morgan took a breath. "What do you think? Shall we get off? I don't fancy being stranded here, and I remember the last few times this happened. Trains didn't move for hours or passengers had to walk down the tracks in the dark. It happened to a friend of mine. She said it was terrifying."

Ali steepled her fingers in front of her chest. If they got off, at least they were taking matters into their own hands.

"Are you one of those people who hate waiting at bus stops, too?"

Morgan gave her a knowing smile. Ali struggled not to lean forward and touch her face.

"Hate it. I'd rather walk."

*Composure.*

"Even when the bus gets there before you do?"

"Even then. At least in my head I'm getting somewhere."

Ali twisted her mouth left and right. She didn't fancy being stuck on a train overnight, either.

She got up and hitched her backpack on her shoulder. If they were moving, it would distract her from wanting to kiss Morgan Scott, at least.

"Let's go to carriage five, shall we?"

\* \* \*

Ali waved her phone around the ground at their feet, the torch lighting some of the way. The lights of the train still cast a glow from behind, but they'd lose that soon enough. Up ahead, it was pitch black, but in the distance, there was a hazy light. The torch showed the path was wide enough for three people, flanked either side by a rough stone wall that stopped around knee height.

"It's fucking dark, and I swear I'm about to tread in cow shit."

Beside her, Morgan chuckled, as if she loved this type of adventure. Like life was better because of it. Maybe for her, it was.

"So long as this is a footpath and there are no cows on it, I'm good," Morgan said.

"We might meet the only concrete-loving cow in the country."

"Don't say that."

Maybe Morgan wasn't loving this as much as she made out. Ali shivered and pulled her scarf as tight as it would go. She dropped her phone and the night went dark. "Shit!"

"Not literally, I hope." Morgan rummaged in her bag, presumably to get her phone.

Ali crouched down, found hers, and gave them light again. "No shit attached to phone. Phone still working and acting as a torch. Be thankful for small mercies." She stopped walking, noticing Morgan had stopped, too. "Everything okay?"

"I'm sure it's in here somewhere, but I can't find my phone." She said it through gritted teeth.

"Did you have it out on the train?"

"No, I was trying to be in the moment, mindful, eating my sandwich in an aware way."

Not very helpful. "Where did you last have it?"

Morgan made a humming noise. "In Dave's van when I was taking his number down."

They both let that sink in, with all it entailed.

"But I'm sure I put it back in my bag." Morgan's tone sounded anything but sure.

"Well, you won't find it on a dark path in the freezing cold," Ali told her. "Let's walk to the town, get in the warm, then you can have a proper look."

They started walking again.

"Look on the bright side. At least I got us a room at the local bed-and-breakfast, so phone or not, we'll soon have somewhere to sleep tonight. That's enough of a win for me today." It was the first thing Ali had done while they waited for the staff to let them off the train. They were the only passengers who got off.

"Unless the bed-and-breakfast burns down before we get there."

Ali nudged Morgan with her elbow again. "Hey, you're the upbeat one of this partnership, remember? The problem-solver." She waved her phone in the air. "At least I have mine." She paused. "Although my charger's in my case."

Morgan huffed. "If it's an iPhone, I have a charger you can use. But please, remind me never to think that winter and snow are romantic again. They've brought nothing but trouble today. Romance is far more suited to summer, sunshine and beaches."

"It's romantic when you're inside in the warm with a roaring fire and glass of red."

"Does that only happen in romance books and films, though? Give me a cocktail on a beach any day." Morgan's white teeth flashed in the dark.

Ali wasn't sure if it was via a smile or a grimace.

"Have you ever had a roaring fire, a glass of red and a love interest at the same time?" Morgan asked.

The romantic periods of Ali's life flashed before her eyes.

There hadn't been many, and none had involved what she'd just outlined.

"No, but I live in hope."

"You told me there hadn't been much romance in your life, but I'm hearing flecks of a hopeless romantic in you."

Ali cleared her throat. "Don't tell anyone. I have a reputation to keep up."

"Your secret's safe with me. If we survive this path, that is."

Then a noise made them both stop walking. It sounded like a cow crossed with a wolf. The darkness creaked around them.

Ali flinched and snapped off her phone light. Whatever it was, she didn't want to startle it.

"What the fuck was that?" Morgan threaded an arm through Ali's and pulled her close.

Ali was too freaked to register the full impact of being this near to Morgan Scott.

"I thought you said cows don't come onto the path." Morgan paused, then whispered, "Is now a good time to tell you I'm *terrified* of cows?"

"Not especially," Ali whispered back.

They heard the noise again, this time a little closer than before.

Ali's brain throbbed in her skull. Of all the ways to die, she never thought she'd get trampled by a cow. She strained her eyes to see anything.

Morgan held Ali's arm with a vice-like grip.

Ali's heartbeat thumped in her ears. Normally Morgan Scott hanging onto her would be the reason. But right now, staying alive was the primary culprit. She exhaled, but could barely see her breath.

Then something up ahead flashed in the dark.

Something about knee-height.

Was that a pair of eyes?

Ali swallowed hard, and every muscle in her body tensed.

"Don't move," she whispered to Morgan. She had no idea what she was going to do next, but she knew they were trespassing on territory that belonged to whatever animal it was. This wasn't their patch.

"Is it a fucking cow?" Morgan asked, so softly it was barely audible.

"Not sure," Ali whispered back. "It looks dense. Plus, aren't cows' eyes up high?"

"They have to bend down to eat grass."

She had a point.

That tickled Ali.

This was an absurd situation. And cows had to bend their heads to eat grass.

Amusement rose up through her throat, and she let out a stifled snort.

Morgan twisted her head. "Are you laughing?" Her tone was incredulous. She was on the edge.

That caused Ali to stifle more laughs. This was a *really* inopportune time to get the giggles, but she couldn't help it. She gulped back another laugh, and a tear rolled down her cheek.

"Sorry, it's just, cows can move their heads…" Another wave of laughter sailed through her. She clamped it down, then took a deep breath.

Then Morgan shook too. "Keep it together," she whispered.

The same noise filled the air again. This time, it was definitely something akin to a moo.

"Do bulls moo, too?" Ali asked, her breath coming thick and fast now. They had to act, otherwise they'd be here all night. Standing in the middle of a field, held in place by a cow.

"What am I, an expert on bulls?" Morgan hissed. She clutched Ali tighter. "I don't know if I can walk past it."

"You're going to have to if you don't want to freeze to death and wait for his mates to turn up."

That comment made Morgan jolt. "Okay, but let's do it quickly."

The cow's eyes were on the right, now raised in the air. If they walked left, they could pass without disturbing it. Ali took a deep breath, clutched Morgan's hand in hers, then pulled her left. Together, they edged up the path, and it was only when they drew level with the cow that Ali realised it was on the other side of the wall. It was only the cow's head that was straying into the path. It was a nosy cow, come to see what the noise was about.

Whatever, she wasn't hanging around to have a chat.

She tightened her grip on Morgan's hand and pulled, breaking into a jog when they were far enough away. They didn't stop until some streetlights came into view a couple of minutes later. Then, Ali bent over, hands on her thighs, panting. Then she started laughing again. This time, she allowed herself to do so. Once she started, she couldn't stop.

Eventually, Morgan joined in.

In moments, they were both bellowing deep, round belly laughs into the night sky, rich with relief.

"Cows can bend their heads," Ali rasped. She sucked down ice-cold air and coughed some more.

"I know!" Morgan wheezed, clutching Ali's arm. "Fuck a duck, we're such wusses."

"We're city girls. Dave was right. What would our Devon families say? They're much better with animals."

Ali drained herself of laughs, then straightened up. She waited until she got her breath back before she spoke. "I'm not terrible with animals. I've got a cat, but she hates me. Spends her days covering me with fluff."

"That's what cats do, don't they?" Morgan paused, then shivered. "Who's looking after her while you're away?"

"My friend Tobias. He's threatening to bring a parade of men back to my flat, but I know he's more likely to spend the nights pandering to Snowy. He loves it when I go away, because he gets the flat all to himself."

"Sounds like Snowy wins whoever's there."

"Cats always do." Ali pulled her scarf tight as the wind whipped around them. "Tobias knitted me this scarf, actually."

Morgan blinked. "It's lovely. I thought maybe your nan knitted it, but it was Tobias. Clever man."

"He has his moments."

"Does he knit hats, too? I could do with one. And some gloves."

"It might be too late for this trip." Ali glanced up the path. "I can see civilisation. Maybe a bottle of wine with our name on it. Ready to walk the final bit?"

"Yes. And then I can see if I have my phone, or if I'm turning into my grandmother by losing it or smashing it every other day."

Ali stared at Morgan. This woman she'd put on a pedestal and held in such high esteem all of her life. But really, Morgan was just another woman. Just like her, trying to muddle through life. Plus, there was only three years between. Ali had dated women older and younger. But Morgan had always seemed light years older, wiser, hotter. That's what happened when you got stuck in 12-year-old-self thinking patterns. From now on, Ali was going to treat Morgan as she would any other hot, intelligent and available woman.

On second thoughts, maybe she shouldn't do that.

She might implode.

But more than that, her sister might kill her.

# Chapter Nine

The path led them into a cul-de-sac filled with identikit sandy-bricked houses. White picket fences surrounded their fake grass-lined front gardens.

"I don't think we're in Kansas anymore," Morgan told Ali.

In response, Ali widened her eyes. She got her phone out and checked Google Maps. "No reception."

"Of course," Morgan said. "I'm going to wait until I get inside to check for my phone. I'd rather have a breakdown in the warm than the cold." Her stomach sank at the thought. She'd just got a new screen this morning. Had it really only been this morning? She checked her watch—7:30pm. "Shall we try right and see where it takes us?"

Ali nodded and they trudged in silence.

Up above, stars studded the inky sky, lighting their way.

They rounded the first corner and walked onto a road much like the last, with minimal streetlamps. Morgan pulled her coat sleeves down in a vain attempt to keep warm. She tried her best to keep her teeth from chattering. How she wished she'd had the foresight to put her hat and gloves into her backpack. When they got to the end of the road, she tilted her head. Whooping and cheering sailed in the air.

"Can you hear that?"

"I can feel it," Ali said.

She was right. Something vibrated the ground under their feet. "I swear, if it's a herd of cows, I'm running back to the fucking train."

Ali guffawed. "You'll have to get past Maud The Nosy first."

"Maud?"

Ali grinned. "That cow looked like a Maud. My great-grandmother was a Maud. Apparently very nosy, too."

"And a bit of a cow?"

"How dare you talk of my great-granny like that." Ali backed up her words with a smile. "Shall we walk towards the noise and hope it's not cows?"

Ten minutes later, drawn towards music and lights, they found themselves on the corner of what must be the town's main street. On it, some sort of Christmas parade was taking place, with a marching band, Santa on a float and elves giving out candy canes.

Morgan blinked. She'd been to enough Christmas markets in the UK to know they were usually half-arsed. A dirty Santa's grotto, lukewarm mulled wine, smashed fairy lights. This was nothing like that. Snowton really cared about Christmas and its festivities. The elves were smiling, the band played at full pelt, and all around her, families clutched hot chocolate and gazed at the festive merriment.

Beside her, Ali's mouth hung open.

"Do you think somebody spiked our turkey sandwiches and we're actually tripping?"

Ali shook her head. "I would say yes, but I didn't actually eat the sandwich."

"True," Morgan replied. "This is like a Christmas parade from one of those cheesy Hallmark movies. That I love, by the way."

"You better be careful. You know what happens in all of them. You might meet the man of your dreams and then you'll have to move back here and bake cookies all year round." The smile Ali gave Morgan lit up her face.

It made Morgan melt. Whatever barking madness they'd walked into, at least she could finally relax.

No more broken-down trains.

No more nosy cows.

For now.

"I wouldn't mind baking cookies all year round. I'm pretty good at it."

"What about the marrying a man part?"

Morgan raised an eyebrow in her direction. "So long as it was platonic and I could shag his sister on the side, I'd be cool."

Ali cackled, just as an elf approached and offered them a candy cane.

"Aren't they for kids?"

The elf shook her head. "For everyone. It's Christmas!"

Ali took one, as did Morgan, then they looked at each other.

"Shall we find this bed-and-breakfast before this dream ends?"

* * *

The bed-and-breakfast was called Snow Place Like Home, which Morgan had to give props to for its pun-wizardry. And, despite the odds, it was a decent find. The pillows were plump, the bathroom sparkled and there was a bowl of individually wrapped chocolate Hobnobs next to the kettle. From what she'd been expecting, it was a win. The only slightly awkward glitch in the plan—could she call any of what had happened today a plan?—was that they only had one bed. A king-sized bed, but still only one.

However, it was only for one night. They could muddle through.

Morgan didn't enjoy sharing a bed with a stranger, but Ali wasn't that. What was she to Morgan, exactly? Before this morning, a vague memory. But today, Ali had made sure she was very much at the forefront of Morgan's mind. An attractive, funny part of her day. The woman who'd sorted more problems than Morgan of late, and when did that ever happen? She'd got them past the cow and got them this place to stay.

When they arrived, Ali jumped straight into the shower, ignoring the one-bed issue.

Morgan sat on the bed and emptied her bag onto it. She'd been putting this off until she was on her own, but now she really hoped her phone was here. She scanned through her life on top of the duvet. Notepad, pens, tampons (small, medium, extra-large), wallet, tissues, shopping bag.

No fucking phone.

Her stomach churned. She'd been half-expecting it, but it was still a kick in the teeth.

Morgan moved the tissues to reveal her phone charger (the irony). She blew out. There were cards from three companies she'd worked with in the past month, a little dog-eared. But no phone. She must have left it in Dave's truck. A killer blow.

She'd have to call him to ask. If it wasn't there, it was lost to the phone gods. Again. She could beat herself up, but it wouldn't change anything.

She got off the bed and walked over to the window. The main street was lit up with festive lights as the parade came to a close. At the far end, a gigantic fairy-topped Christmas tree stood tall. At least they'd landed in Christmas Central, where it was almost illegal to be glum. Despite losing her phone, she was going to put on a brave face. There was nothing she could do about it now.

The door opening made Morgan turn her head.

Ali walked out of the bathroom wrapped in only a white towel that she held in place at her side with her elbow. She glanced up at Morgan, then quickly looked away.

Morgan's senses switched to high alert. She gulped. She hadn't been expecting Ali in a towel. Her broad shoulders or her defined biceps. Did app developers work out? Apparently this one did. Morgan cleared her throat and tried to focus her eyes on anything other than Ali's body. Any part of it.

It wasn't that easy.

She stared at the bathroom doorway as steam danced in front of her.

"Did you find your phone?" Ali made sure her towel was secure, then moved to get her bag on the velvet armchair. As she leaned, her towel slipped down.

Morgan's eyes widened, and she swallowed down hard.

Ali stood quickly and pulled the towel back up.

"I must have left it in Dave's truck." Morgan smoothed herself from the inside out.

"Bugger." Ali held up her phone.

Morgan let her gaze slide down Ali's shoulders, then just as quickly away.

"Feel free to call home on mine if you remember the number." She made sure her elbow was holding onto her towel. Then Ali unlocked her phone, threw it onto the bed, and flicked a thumb back to the bathroom. "I'm going back in here to get dressed in exactly the same clothes I was wearing before." She tiptoed back to the bathroom and shut the door.

Morgan exhaled, wondering when her thoughts about Ali had jumped from 'Nicole's younger sister' to 'smokin' travel companion'. She shook her head, wiped her thoughts clean, and called her parents' number. The landline hadn't changed since she was young.

Her mum answered after three rings.

"Look, I've told you, we're not interested."

"Mum?"

"Oh, hello sweetie! Sorry, I thought you were one of those call centres trying to sell something. What are you calling on the landline for?"

Morgan sighed. "I lost my phone. It's a long story. But don't worry, I'm okay and hopefully I'll be able to get it back."

"Where are you?"

"In a town called Snowton. In the Lakes."

"And when will you be home?"

That was the million-dollar question. "Fingers crossed, tomorrow." Tomorrow was December 23rd. She had to be home by then, as it was the local secondary school's last performance of their Christmas play. Her dad had written and directed it.

"Will you make it back for the play? Your dad's very excited you're coming."

Guilt lodged itself in her stomach. "That's the plan. I'll do everything I can to make it."

Ali stepped out of the bathroom in jeans and her bra. When she saw Morgan look up, she stopped.

Morgan flinched as her breath lodged in her throat. Her skin tingled all over, and her lips were suddenly very dry. Every bit of moisture in her body travelled south at pace. She swallowed, and allowed her gaze to wander from Ali's face, down to her breasts and impossibly flat stomach, and then back up to her gaze that was now drilling into Morgan's soul.

Big mistake.

Morgan sat up quickly as Ali turned.

"I was just getting my brush," Ali muttered, then ran back into the bathroom.

Morgan jumped off the bed and slammed her left hand into the pocket of her trousers. Then she paced in front of the window, not quite knowing what to do with the thoughts that crowded her head.

*"You like her!" said one. "If she was in a bar, you'd notice her," said another. "You're sharing a bed with her tonight," said the third.*

"No," Morgan said to nobody in particular.

"Sorry?"

Morgan stopped pacing. She'd almost forgotten she was on the phone to her mum.

"Sorry, Mum," she said. "I was just talking to Ali."

"Ali?"

Shit. Her mum didn't know she was here with Ali. "You remember Ali. Nicole's little sister?" *Used to be annoying, now not so much?* "She was trying to get home too, so we're travelling together. At least, we're trying to."

Her mum paused. "Ali Bradford?"

"Yes, of course Ali Bradford." Why did her mum always irritate her?

"Okay, I was just asking. Only, she's a lesbian, too, isn't she? You keep saying you'd like to meet someone, so…" Her mum left the sentence dangling.

"Just because I'm a lesbian and so is she doesn't mean we're going to end up together. I thought I told you that when you tried to set me up with Jane Goddard's daughter?"

Her mum tutted. "She turned out to be an idiot in the end. Going out with a boy now. But Ali has always seemed nice."

"She is, but we're just travelling together." Morgan searched her brain for a change of topic. "How's the gingerbread house going?"

"Great! Josh and Annabel decorated one side, me and your dad did the other. We've left the roof for you, as instructed." She shouted to someone in the house, making sure she leaned away from the phone. "Listen, I have to go. Can't wait to see you tomorrow!"

Morgan threw the phone on the bed, then stared at the bathroom door. Ali was behind it. But something had shifted today. With everything they'd gone through together. It wasn't just because she'd seen Ali semi-naked. Today had opened her eyes to Ali altogether. Made her see her in a whole new light.

Morgan wasn't sure what she was going to do about it.

# Chapter Ten

They spent the evening wandering around the town, visiting its chocolate shop, its Christmas store and the last stop, the Snow Globe cafe-bar. There, they ordered hot buttered pretzels and homemade sausage rolls, and drank mulled cider. Ali contemplated buying Christmas gifts from the shops just in case their luggage didn't turn up in time or at all. However, she was worried they'd get stranded again and have to lug it with them wherever they went. Yes, they'd cancelled their first car, and secured another for the morning thanks to Shelley, the kind woman at the bed-and-breakfast, who'd even offered to drive them to their pick-up point. But Ali didn't want to tempt fate. She was already sharing a bed and a room with Morgan Scott. That was more than enough fate for one day.

Now, she lay in bed under a thick Scottish-flavoured tartan duvet, in just her knickers and a T-shirt, waiting for Morgan Scott to get in with her. It was all a bit too much for her brain to take. Also, had there been a moment earlier? Ali couldn't be sure, but when she'd locked eyes with Morgan, something had happened. A fizz. A swell. A stutter of her heart. At least on her part.

Morgan's face had changed, and she'd sat up abruptly. Had something changed for her, too? Ali would love to know.

Why had she come out of the bathroom in just jeans and a bra, though? When she knew Morgan was going to be there? Psychologists would have a field day working out her motives, Ali was sure. Whatever the reason, now was the moment she'd been psyching herself up to all evening.

It would be slightly more palatable if she had shorts or pyjama bottoms to wear. However, the only clothes they had were the ones they stood in. That was the same for both of them. Hence, unless Ali wanted to sleep in her jeans—which would seem a little awkward—she had to go with knickers and T-shirt. Far too few clothes for her liking. What if she leaned over in the night and threw a casual arm around Morgan? Her cheeks flamed at the mere thought. How the hell had she put herself into this situation? One that she was quaking about, but also one that fulfilled a fantasy that had flitted in and out of her mind for the past 20 years?

That thought made her stall. Had it really been 20 years? The answer was yes.

She grabbed her phone to take her mind off the situation, and tapped out a quick text to Tobias asking how he and Snowy were doing. She got one back right away, with a photo of Snowy draped across her friend's neck. She was such a tart for visitors.

*Are you home yet?*

*No, still in the Lake District.*

*You could have been having cocktails and dinner in the Big Apple in the same time*, Tobias responded with a laughing emoji.

*I'm well aware.*

*And how's it going with Morgan? Your long-lost first love. Are you married yet?*

Ali rolled her eyes. She knew she shouldn't have confided in him.

*It's going fine. We're stuck in a town in the Lakes and we're sharing a hotel room.*

Typing… typing… typing…

*Tell me you're updating me because you just had sex in the shower and it blew your mind.*

That made Ali smile.

*We're actually having sex right now as I type.*

Ali's thermostat rose at record levels just typing that.

*I always said women were better multitaskers than men.*

Ali glanced up. Through the thin door, she heard the tap shut off as Morgan finished brushing her teeth.

*She's coming back, I've got to go.*

*Okay. Don't cut yourself scissoring each other!*

*Bye Tobias.*

She put her phone back on her bedside table, then took a deep breath and sank right under the duvet.

She was going to hide.

That was the adult thing to do.

The bathroom door opened. Ali poked her head out of the duvet. She'd never been good at playing hide and seek, even as a kid. "Do you think we need to ask for extra pillows to put down the centre of the bed?"

Morgan gave her a strange look. "I think we can control ourselves for one night."

Ali sucked on her cheek. Why had she said that? It just highlighted what she was thinking. Why couldn't she keep her big mouth shut? Why was she never the cool one anywhere in her life, apart from in work meetings? Then she was in control. Work was the only area in her life where Ali had ever felt comfortable, able to be herself fully. She'd moved away from her family. She couldn't hold down a relationship. But a job? She'd never had difficulty with those. She'd just like some of that to rub off elsewhere.

As Morgan stepped out of her jeans, Ali glanced up.

Her pulse sprinted. This was really happening, but not at all in the circumstances she'd always imagined. In those dreams, Morgan pounced on the bed, and then on Ali, straddling her and promising to do all manner of things to her.

*Really not helpful.*

Fuck, why couldn't she just be normal and think normal thoughts?

Only, this wasn't a normal situation, was it?

Morgan's legs looked just as shapely and strong as Ali had always imagined. She looked away as Morgan pulled back the duvet and slid in beside her.

For a few moments, Ali held her breath and tried to stop her body from shaking. She stared up at the ceiling. This was excruciating.

What was Morgan thinking?

Probably that she couldn't wait to get home and get in her own bed.

Far away from Ali.

"This is weird and awkward, isn't it?"

Those weren't the words Ali had expected. She turned her head.

Morgan did the same.

Up close, she looked even more beautiful than usual. Yes, she might be years older than when Ali developed her first crush, but her skin had barely aged. What would it be like to touch it?

The goddess next to her was still 100 per cent Morgan Scott and all the magic that brought with it.

Okay, Ali had to shut down these thoughts, and fast.

"If we accidentally bump arms or legs in the night, no big deal," Morgan said.

Easy for her to say.

"But I should tell you, I'm not known for it. You always have one in every relationship that hogs the bed, steals the duvet and snores, right?"

Ali laughed. "Very true."

"It's never me. You can call all my exes and they'll confirm." Morgan paused. "Or at least, you could if I had my phone." She shook her head. "Let's not focus on that."

"We can get the number for Jolly Good Elf Christmas Tree Farm first thing tomorrow and call him. I don't think it's lost forever."

"Fingers crossed." Morgan smiled, then turned her head to the ceiling. She placed her arms above the duvet and linked them on top of her chest.

Ali did the same.

"Can I ask you a personal question?"

Ali glanced Morgan's way. "Sure." The word came out more confident than she felt.

Morgan's face twitched. "When did you know you were gay?"

Ali raised both eyebrows, but didn't look at Morgan. She couldn't. It might give the game away. "I don't know. From a young age, I knew I was different. That I wasn't experiencing the world the same way everyone else did. But I had no label for it. But then, when I was in my teens, I started looking at women and the world made sense."

"Were you out at school?"

Ali nodded. "In the sixth form, yes. It was impossible not to be. I had a girlfriend. It kinda just happened that way."

"You were braver than me."

"It just didn't make sense to hide." Crucially, she'd only got a girlfriend after Morgan had left to go to university in Glasgow. Ali recalled her coming back and being in their kitchen, telling them tales of Glasgow. It was where the seed of her wanting to go to Scotland was sewn. She'd gone to university in Edinburgh, and only moved to Glasgow in the past few years. But it had always been a note on her life agenda, mainly thanks to Morgan Scott.

Had everything in her life until now been connected to Morgan? That thought pulsed in her brain.

Morgan twisted, this time propping her chin in the palm of her left hand. She was almost in pouncing position.

A furnace flamed inside Ali. She wriggled her bum, then tensed her fingers.

"Who did you go out with? Anybody I'd know?"

"Tara Dooley. She was in my year. She was a terrible kisser, but she was the first girl to show interest, so I went with it. We were not the love affair of the century."

Morgan laughed. "I kissed my first girl in a toilet in Glasgow, so I win on the lack of romance. I'm not sure what I was hiding from. Probably myself."

"First kiss fantasies never quite live up to reality, do they?"

Ali's gaze dropped to Morgan's lips. They were so close.

They were so kissable. But she couldn't do that, because Morgan was not someone she kissed. Even though they were semi-naked and in bed together. Was this the definition of torture?

*Just keep breathing.*

"That's the thing. I didn't even have a fantasy of my first kiss. I just wanted to get it over with, having kissed a million boys at school. I needed to become me, and I was in a hurry to do it. I envy you knowing so young."

"I have you to thank."

Ali's brain slid sideways. Oh fuck, what had she just said? Had she just admitted something? She emptied the contents of her brain onto the floor as if it were a box of Lego, then tried to piece her thoughts and her words back together. Her brain throbbed with the effort.

It clearly hurt Morgan's, too. "Me? What did I do?"

Ali's cheeks heated at nuclear speed. If she'd been hot before, she was even hotter now.

"You just... You..."

Say something! Anything! Utter some words.

"You existed."

Not those words!

Understandably, Morgan's frown deepened. "I existed? I'm not following."

She was going to have to say it, wasn't she? "It's nothing, really. Forget I said anything." She pressed her eyes tight shut, hoping that would make the situation go away.

When she reopened them, Morgan still stared.

It hadn't worked.

Shit.

"It's kinda hard to forget when I don't understand. What did you mean, I existed?" Morgan blinked, then moved back.

Ali tried to regulate her breathing. "What I mean is, I might have had a bit of a crush on you in school. Way back when." She sat up, dragging the duvet and her dignity with her. Ali folded her arms across her chest, then brought her eyes level with Morgan. "Not now, of course! I mean, it's 20 years later. I haven't been carrying a flame for you all this time."

Surprise flitted across Morgan's face. Then her cheeks coloured pink.

Was she embarrassed?

Morgan should be inside Ali's brain, she didn't know the half of it.

She put a finger to her chest. "A crush on me? Wow."

Ali covered her face with her hands. Why had she blurted that out? She wasn't one for divulging her feelings to strangers. But that was it, wasn't it? Morgan wasn't a stranger. She knew her, and Morgan knew Ali. Plus, they'd shared something today. They'd made a connection. Maybe Ali thought by telling Morgan, she'd finally be able to frame her crush as what it was? Something from the past.

Very much not a part of today *at all*.

"And I don't know why I just told you that," Ali mumbled, still not daring to move her hands.

She felt Morgan sigh. "Ali, look at me."

It was the last thing she wanted to do, but it was also the only thing she could do. Ali swallowed down hard, then peeled her fingers away.

Morgan's kind, ridiculously gorgeous face stared back at her.

She mustn't let her gaze drop to Morgan's lips. They were already in bed together and Ali had just admitted to liking her way back when. However, as she sat up, Ali couldn't bring herself to look at any part of Morgan: face, neck, arms. It was all out of bounds. Instead, she twisted and stared at the heavy curtains, lined and blocking out any glare from the lit-up street below.

"It's not a big deal," Morgan said, telling the whopper of the century.

Her kindness did nothing to quash Ali's crush.

"We all had crushes in our youth. If I tell you mine, will you promise never to tell anyone else?"

Ali stole a look. "Unless it's too juicy."

"I don't know. It depends if you also had a thing for Ms Cherry."

That broke the tension. "Our PE teacher?"

Morgan rolled her eyes. "I know. I couldn't be more of a cliché if I tried, could I?"

"Not really. Although she had a certain charm about her in those fetching colour-coordinated tracksuits she used to wear."

"She was matchy-matchy before it was cool to do."

Ali's bum cheeks were still clenched from what she'd said, but she'd be forever grateful to Morgan for doing what she'd done. Making her laugh. Deflecting the situation.

"She was definitely queer, though."

"No doubt."

Ali glanced at Morgan again and caught her gaze. Desire rocked inside her, desperate for an exit. She took a moment to quiet it before she continued. She kept her hands under the duvet. If she took them out, they'd likely shake.

"You, though, were more of an enigma." Ali risked a smile Morgan's way.

She rewarded her with one back. "I wasn't even out to myself."

"And you had that boyfriend. What was his name?"

"Grant." Morgan's face folded into a frown.

"Yes, Grant! I hated him." Shit. Had she said too much? The truth was often a low blow.

But Morgan laughed. "If it's any consolation, I wasn't that enamoured with him either. I mean, not in the way I should have been. All the other girls had boyfriends, and they were having sex and chatting about it all the time. Whereas I never quite got it, but I wasn't ready to have that talk with myself."

"Even though Ms Cherry made you want to pop?"

Now the bed shook as Morgan let out a hoot of laughter. "Ms Cherry was far too loved up with our maths teacher, Ms Bardell, to notice me. Imagine being Ms Cherry's first, though. You really could say you popped her cherry."

Ali grinned. "I'd dine out on that for years."

They were quiet for a few moments before Morgan spoke again.

"I hope I was a decent first crush. Not too horrible to you. I remember Nicole and I making you walk behind us all the way home."

Ali shrugged. "I got to ogle your arse, so it wasn't all bad."

Morgan's mouth dropped open. "I feel used." She closed her mouth. "But also, glad I paved the way for you to have some real-life love."

Ali shook her head. "I was much better at it when I was younger. It was after university that shit got serious." She blew out a breath. "Anyway, enough chat. We should sleep because if tomorrow's anything like today, we're going to need all our strength to get through it."

Morgan slid down until she was flat. "You're so sensible."

"Tell my mother, please. She still thinks I'm rebelling by living in Scotland. Not a thought to what I might want to do with my life." Of course, after what happened in the summer, maybe her mum had a point. Life was finite. Maybe she needed to go home more often.

"Also, I need to go to sleep so I can die of shame for what I just told you. I can't wait until I wake up in the morning and remember it all over again." Ali let her eyelids flutter shut. She functioned better when she was asleep. Less able to say stupid things.

"You're going to be fine. If it helps at all, I'm glad I'm here with you. You might have been an annoying kid, but you're a pretty cool adult. Plus, getting thrown this hopelessly off course on the way home wouldn't have been half the fun alone. I'd still be stuck trying to inch past Maud the cow."

Ali burst out laughing. Morgan always had been funny. Yes, she was cute, but her sense of humour and fun had drawn the young Ali, too.

When she recovered, Ali glanced sideways.

Their gazes locked again.

All the old feelings oozed down Ali like melted butter. Hot and impossible to ignore.

Ali felt it *everywhere*.

But she stuffed her feelings deep inside. Just like she always had with Morgan. This learned behaviour would take quite the gear shift to change. Because when the glare of a Morgan Scott smile snagged Ali, all she really wanted to do was lean in and soak it up. It had always been that way.

Morgan was Ali's sunshine.

"And if you are embarrassed in the morning, I have two words for you."

"Ms Cherry?"

"How did you guess?" Morgan replied.

# Chapter Eleven

Morgan slept well, which amazed her after what happened before they closed their eyes. They'd managed the entire night in the same bed without touching each other, which was a feat. That Ali didn't snore or hog the duvet helped.

Still, Ali's revelation had caught her off-guard. But beyond Morgan's surprise, it also impressed her. Ali had always been comfortable in her identity, even from a young age. It had taken Morgan a while longer to get there. What's more, from what she'd seen so far, that played out in their lives, too. Morgan was the organised, methodical one. She had to think about things first before she acted. Whereas Ali was far more spontaneous and brave. She'd saved them from Maud last night. She'd booked this bed-and-breakfast from the train. Plus, she'd drawn back the curtain on her past. She wasn't afraid to be vulnerable. It was a quality Morgan admired, and one she taught through her work. Ali didn't need her help with that. She was in control far more than she gave herself credit for.

They'd eaten a full English breakfast to set them up for the day ahead, but Ali insisted they head back to the Snowton Gift Shop before they left.

"There's a little something I want to pick up."

So it was a short while later, Morgan found herself surrounded by more Christmas than she knew what to do with. This store might even overwhelm her Christmas-obsessed mum. What to buy? A festive hat? An apron? A Christmas loo seat cover? The whole store smelt of pine trees, and some old-school Ronettes blared from the stereo. Between that and the snow still piled up on the pavement, she couldn't help but feel festive.

Also, quite cold. She really needed a hat.

"What about this?" Ali appeared by her side, holding up a Christmas bra, replete with fur holly lining and Christmas puddings over the nipples.

Morgan held up her hand. "I can't unsee that."

Ali put it back on its hook, then held up a small bag. "I've got what I came for, so let's go. Also, just to let you know, I messaged Dave and asked about your phone, so we wait to hear."

"Thank you." Resourceful and thoughtful. Morgan was touched.

Shelley dropped them at the car rental place, which was a 15-minute drive away, and Morgan gave her a box of Ferrero Rocher as a thank you.

As Shelley drove away with a wave, Ali gave Morgan a clap.

"What's that for?"

"You and your magic sweets. Everywhere we go, you whip them out and charm the locals. I'm learning a lot this trip."

Morgan raised an eyebrow. "That makes two of us."

Ali's blush was damningly red. "I'm going to get the car." She walked off, avoiding Morgan's gaze.

\* \* \*

Half an hour later, they were on the road, Ali driving a grey Ford Focus on the same motorway they'd touched twice yesterday. Morgan had a severe case of déjà vu.

Morgan got the heating going, then put their destination into the sat nav. "It says it's only 6.5 hours away!" They could be home for dinner. That seemed like dreamland.

Until they slowed to a stop in increasingly thick traffic once more.

Ali glanced at the sat nav, then frowned. "What do all those thick red lines mean?"

"Re-routing," said the sat nav.

Morgan winced. "Let's see if the radio can fill us in." She switched it on and tuned until she found a local station. They caught the tail end of Wham's 'Last Christmas', and then the travel news followed.

"Bad news if you're trying to drive south on the M6 right now. There's a pile-up just before Penrith. It's grid locked, so be prepared to sit in traffic. Keep it here for festive tunes to keep your spirits high!"

"That's where we're heading, isn't it?"

Ali nodded. "Uh-huh. I don't know about you, but after yesterday, I just want to keep moving. We've got a sat nav, so are you okay if I get off at the next junction and try to take the back roads?"

Morgan nodded. "Of course. Like the man said, we've got festive tunes, so long as they're not East 17."

"You really need to let that go," Ali told her.

"It's been said before," Morgan replied. "If nothing else, we can sing to keep warm."

Ali leaned down and grabbed the gift shop bag. "But before we move again, I have something else to get us in the mood." She produced a pair of fluffy festive dice and hung them on the central mirror. Then she gave Morgan a grin. "You told me I needed to be a little more festive." She motioned to the Christmas dice. "Does this count?"

She was funny. Morgan loved funny. She smiled warmly at Ali, and couldn't stop her gaze from sliding to Ali's lips.

"Yeah." Morgan dragged her gaze upwards. "It counts."

\* \* \*

Even though they were on the smaller roads, the traffic was still a nightmare. They crawled through a small village, passing a sign that thanked them for only driving at 20mph. They didn't have a choice.

"Is there a reason you don't love Christmas?" It always intrigued Morgan, as it was so alien to her.

Ali shook her head. "I don't hate it, I just don't go all-out." She tapped the dice. "Apart from this year, of course." She gave Morgan a grin. "I suppose growing up, we had the pub, so it was always busy. I associated Christmas with hard work. My parents did what they needed to do. However, this year, we're shutting the pub on Christmas Day." She paused, as if searching for her next words.

"Why's that?"

Ali gripped the wheel tighter and shook her head. "No particular reason. My mum's getting older, so it's time."

Morgan would swear it was more than that. Ali's mum was younger than hers, and still very able. Had something happened to her or her husband, Tony? There was something

Ali wasn't telling her, but they had many more hours for her to spill the beans.

"Also, I've lived through a couple of terrible Christmases with my ex, so all those people who go on about it being the most wonderful time of the year? Not always." Ali shook her head. "And can I just say, I don't normally tell people this shit. I blame temporary insanity brought on by extreme circumstance."

Morgan smiled. "For what it's worth, she didn't deserve you if she let you go."

Ali glanced her way. "Thanks." Her cheeks blushed pink.

Morgan turned down Wizzard singing about it being Christmas every day. "I don't want it to be Christmas every day. We'd be in traffic jams forever." They slowed to a stop. Up ahead, bright yellow roadworks signs warned of delays. They were correct. "Was that your last relationship?"

Ali nodded. "We were together for seven years. Then she got ants in her pants and left. Just upped, and moved to Australia to be with someone she'd been having a secret online relationship with for a year. I understand they're married now."

Morgan let her lower jaw drop. "That's got to hurt."

"It did at first." Ali shuffled in her seat. "But then I realised she wasn't right, and we weren't right, so she did me a favour. But it's definitely dented my trust in other people." Ali eased the car to the end of the road. She flicked on the indicator and turned right, almost driving straight into an oncoming tractor taking up the whole road. She swerved just at the last minute, then slammed on her horn. "Fucking idiot. That is not how I want to die, either. Trampled by a cow, or flattened by a tractor."

"We're dicing with death this trip."

"What about you? No girlfriend back at the ranch? I know we told Imogen that yesterday, but you could have been lying for some weird reason."

Morgan let out a strange noise. "I wish. No lies here. My work demands a lot of hours, and I don't have the patience to swipe constantly on dating apps." She shrugged. "I suppose I'm old-fashioned at heart. I either want to meet someone in person just randomly and have that initial spark you can't get through a phone screen, or else I'd like to get together with someone I already know. Like my sister Annabel and her husband Josh. They met at school." She blinked and wriggled her bum on her seat. "Don't get me wrong, I don't want to marry my school boyfriend—"

"That would be awkward."

"Very. But you know what I mean. Someone who understands you a bit, someone you don't have to start from scratch with."

Ali glanced across and rubbed her chin. "I always think starting from scratch is part of the thrill. Although Nicole says she'd never start again with someone else, so Stu's stuck with her. She's trained him now."

"I can just imagine Nicole saying that," Morgan replied. "The belief in romance clearly runs in the family." Morgan sighed, then looked Ali's way. "I suppose I want it both ways. I wanted to leave Devon, but it'd be nice to meet someone who understands it too."

"I get that. Plus, your chances aren't terrible. It's a big county. The third largest in the UK."

Morgan pointed a finger in Ali's direction. "I love knowing that. What are the three largest counties in the UK is a great quiz question. Yorkshire, Lincolnshire, Devon. Nobody ever gets number two."

"Devon is underrated." Ali slowed the car at the next junction. Ahead were fields of snow. To their right, a graveyard and a picture-perfect stone-built church with a spire. "I don't go back enough. But I always feel less-than, and I know it's probably in my head. But so many of my friends there are already married and have kids. I feel like I'm behind. I've never even bought a Christmas tree or a TV with someone else. Am I even a fully grown adult until that happens?"

"You've bought some festive dice now, so I'd say you're on your way." Morgan grinned. "But I know what you mean. I'm a part of my family, but I'm not a part that's always there, so I'm separate. It's hard to explain."

Ali shook her head. "I get it. We're not there for the day to day. We don't understand where we're from as much as they do anymore. We don't know what's been making the local news, or what's going on at the PTA."

"And they never stop reminding us," Morgan added. "I think I left because I knew I was gay and I needed to find myself. But being gay makes me doubly an outsider when I go back."

"I prefer to think it makes us cavalier and daring. My family thinks my life is so exciting and unusual. I don't like to dispel that myth. I work in apps, I live far away, I go to gay clubs and party all the time. I mean, two of those are true." When Ali smiled, her face lit up. Had it always done that? Or was that something Morgan had just noticed?

"The go-getters of the family. I like that. Does your family get what you do for work? I can see mine glaze over when I talk about communication. It's never been their strong point, unless my mum wants to order something from a website she can't use. Then she's on the phone smartish."

Ali let out a bark of laughter. "They've no idea. I mean, they use the apps I make, but how they're devised? I might as well be selling magic beans."

A warm glow settled in Morgan's chest, and then moved to her stomach. She and Ali understood each other. Sure, they didn't work in the same realm, but they had similar family dynamics. They were from the same place. They were both gay. Maybe they had more in common than Morgan had first thought.

But Ali was still Ali. She was still Nicole's little sister. And once they were home, they'd probably never see each other again. Maybe the odd drink in Glasgow. Maybe next year, they'd rent a car together to get home, and laugh about this year. But for now, this was nice. Having Ali's company. Someone who knew Glasgow, but also her home. Someone who understood her completely.

Morgan blinked.

Completely was a *big* statement.

But she hadn't felt as comfortable in anyone else's company in a very long time.

Ali Bradford was an unexpected Christmas bonus.

# Chapter Twelve

They drove on for another half hour, singing along to Christmas music and not getting very far at all. Ali's smart plan to divert to the side roads had backfired somewhat, because a lot of other cars had done that, too. Plus, they'd had a few instances where they'd ended up going round in circles and coming back to the same set of roadworks. However, if Ali wanted to keep moving, this allowed her to do just that. Even if they'd barely moved ten miles so far.

"Okay, let's talk about Christmas. Do you have any traditions in your family? Just so I know in case we're spending the big day driving around in circles in the Lakes and I need to replicate them."

"Don't even joke." Morgan drummed her fingertips on her thighs.

Ali stared. Something fluttered just above her rib cage. It wasn't the first time Ali had noticed Morgan's legs.

Mainly because they were the kind she'd like wrapped around her head.

*Whoa. Where the hell had that thought come from?* One minute she was driving along, and the next, her mind was in the gutter. She had to sort that out if she wanted to survive the next however many hours in an enclosed space with Morgan. Luckily, Morgan was oblivious to Ali's thoughts. Which was a good thing.

"We always open one gift on Christmas Eve at midnight. Which used to annoy my nan when she was alive, as she liked to be tucked up in bed by ten."

"When did she die?" Even saying that was like someone had punched her in the gut. Ali still wasn't ready to deal with her situation. It was the main reason she was enjoying this delay getting home. Getting stranded with Morgan had been a great distraction. Something to take her mind off her very real family situation that was bowling towards her.

Particularly when it involved sharing a bed, which she had miraculously survived, wholly intact.

"It was nearly ten years ago. I still miss her. She lived a good life, but she was only 77. Nan always used to say it was better to leave before the party ended. Never be the last one standing. I like to think she died as she lived."

"A good way to look at it." Ali couldn't say the same about her dad, but she wasn't going there. Her mouth got dry even thinking about it. She needed a distraction. "Any other traditions?"

"Apart from playing charades and me always losing? Nothing out of the ordinary. Christmas dinner. The queen's speech. A cheeseboard that nobody wants. Monopoly, where my sister always steals from the bank. Me eating those Guylian seashell chocolates and realising they are the devil's chocolate. How about you?"

Ali shook her head. "None really. The pub was always open, so we always spent Christmas working. I never minded, though. I quite liked it, because everybody was in a good mood. Plus, as a child, I got to be in the pub all day, which was normally off-limits. But this year will be different." More than Morgan could possibly know.

"Maybe you'll make new traditions." Morgan glanced Ali's way as she spoke.

They were in stationary traffic, so Ali let her gaze linger on Morgan's sapphire-blue eyes with flecks of gold. She'd been closer to them in the past 24 hours than she had been in years. Yet their shape and depth were still imprinted on Ali's psyche from her teenage years. She recalled staring back then. How she wanted to kiss Morgan's eyelids. What would they taste like now?

A car horn broke her thoughts. Ali jumped, then eased her foot down on the accelerator. However, they only moved for a couple of seconds before they ground to a halt again.

"Whoever's behind is a bit trigger-happy with their horn."

Morgan turned in her seat and gave the car a glare.

Ali drummed her fingers on the steering wheel. "My cousin lives around here somewhere. I came to visit last year, but I'm not exactly sure where. It all kinda looks the same."

"Usually green, currently snowy, occasional lake?"

"Exactly that. She moved up here to open a bed-and-breakfast. I forget the name. She's always full, though. Business is booming."

The sat nav made a noise Ali had never heard before. "What on earth was that?"

"Sounded like the sat nav just burped."

Ali stared as the screen reconfigured, and then an alternative route showed up. It was suggesting going down even smaller roads with less traffic. Ali glanced up at the line of cars ahead, then back to the screen.

"What do you think? Should we follow it?" She had flashbacks of a time in Germany when the sat nav had taken her on a tour of a local housing estate for half an hour for no apparent reason.

Morgan was silent for a moment before she spoke. "It's not as if we're getting anywhere fast at the moment. Can it be any worse?"

Ali sucked on her teeth, then flicked on her indicator. Nobody else seemed to be doing the same thing, and at least this way, they'd keep on moving. It was the motto Ali lived by.

They drove down the road, which quickly turned into a lane barely wide enough for one car.

"If a tractor comes, we're toast."

"I'm well aware," Morgan replied.

Just then, the car made a loud whirring sound, the dashboard lights flashed on and off super-quick, and then it slowed.

Ali sat up straight and clutched the steering wheel, willing it to be okay. But deep down inside, she had a feeling it wasn't going to be. It had been that kind of trip so far.

"What just happened?" Morgan almost whispered the words, as if she were afraid of the answer.

"I'm not sure, but the car doesn't want to go very fast anymore, and that's steam coming out of the bonnet." Ali pulled into a nearby layby and cut the engine.

The silence and tranquillity when she did were overwhelming. For the first time in ages, they weren't surrounded by people, cars or killer cows. All that was visible were snow-covered fields with the occasional farmhouse, a clutch of hills in the distance, and almost-camouflaged sheep. Lots and lots of sheep. Did sheep feel the cold, too? Yes, they had natural woolly jumpers on at all times, but did they get cold feet and noses like humans?

Ali sat back in her seat and closed her eyes. She missed peace and quiet. She missed uncomplicated journeys. But interestingly, she was still glad she was doing it with Morgan. She shook that thought from her brain and grabbed her phone. Maybe she could see where her cousin lived in relation to where they were now?

When she clicked, there was a text from Dave, the Christmas tree man. He had Morgan's phone and if she sent him her address, he'd put it in the post today.

"Okay, so I have some good news amid every mode of transport we try breaking down." She cocked her head. "Are we the curse?"

Morgan banged her hands together and blew into them. "Maybe. What's the good news?"

"Dave has your phone and if we send him your address, he'll post it today."

Morgan's eyes went wide. "Today? Isn't he bonkers-busy selling trees? Tell him it can wait until after Christmas."

Ali shrugged. "We clearly made an impression on him."

"Well, god bless Dave."

"And all who sail in him." Ali took a deep breath. "Okay, I'm going to try this again." She hit the start button on the car, but nothing happened. She checked the car was in drive, then tried again. Still nothing.

"Not happening?"

Ali shook her head. "Let's give it a minute. My dad always said cars are like humans, sometimes they just need a little time."

Ali could see him standing over his car on the side of the M40 pretending everything was okay. Her dad had always been a positive person, right until the end. She sent up a silent prayer just in case he was listening. She could really use his help right now.

Morgan nodded, then tapped her hand on her thigh. The rhythmic beat was all Ali heard until she tried the car again, channelling all her positive energy. It was running fine before they stopped, and nothing had changed in the interim.

She squeezed her eyes tight shut, and pressed.

Nothing.

They had enough fuel, so it wasn't that. "I'm trying really hard not to feel like this is another setback, but I want you to know I'm struggling."

Morgan leaned over and put a hand on Ali's thigh. "You're doing really well for someone who's a glass-half-empty person."

Ali's leg hummed under Morgan's touch. Morgan, again, seemed oblivious. She'd clearly swallowed down Ali's lies about her crush being in the past. Ali's heart had not. It began to sprint.

However, when Ali replayed Morgan's words, she frowned.

"Who said I was glass half empty?"

Morgan's cheeks flushed red, and she pulled back her shoulders. "I deal with many people in my day job, so let's just say I know the signs."

"Really?"

Morgan had pressed Ali's buttons. Unlike the car, they

definitely worked. How many times had she heard that in her life? That she just needed to come at life with a positive attitude? Never at work, but always from her exes. She wasn't ready to put up with it from Morgan, too.

A cow might have flattened Morgan if it wasn't for Ali.

"It's not a bad thing," Morgan said. "But it is learned behaviour. I could give you some tips to flip it around if you like. We could meet for a drink in Glasgow and I could share my secrets."

This was how Morgan was going to ask her out on a date? By telling her she had faults that needed fixing? Ali may not be the catch of the season, but she was doing okay. Morgan Scott might be her first love, but that was no way for her to treat Ali.

"When did you last ask a woman out for a drink?" Ali's brain simmered, then popped.

Morgan frowned. "I wasn't asking you out—"

"Let me tell you, that's not how you do it, whatever your intention. Women don't generally respond to the line, 'You're miserable. Do you want to meet me and I can show you how to cheer up'?"

Morgan winced. "When you put it like that, it sounds terrible."

She looked so genuinely contrite, Ali's anger immediately leaked out. Maybe it was their ridiculous situation. Maybe it was thinking about her dad, or the snow that had just begun again. Perhaps she'd overreacted. Whatever, it was probably best left here.

"I used to think you were smooth when I was little. That you had all the lines."

Morgan's laugh was genuine. "I'd never say that. Yes, I know how to communicate, but I still have my floundering moments."

"I got that loud and clear."

Ali tried the car again, but nothing. She wrapped her fingers around the steering wheel and sighed. "You're the problem-solver of the partnership, so you keep telling me. Do you know anything about cars?"

Morgan's face crinkled, and she shook her head. "I know they've got four wheels and a boot?"

"Remind me never to book you for a cross-country survival course."

"Isn't that what we're on already?"

Ali unclicked her seat belt. "I know a little as my dad used to make us learn for just such an occasion. I'll have a look and see if there's anything obvious. But it could be electrical or mechanical." She got out, blew some snow from her face, then grabbed her duffel coat from the backseat. "That is, if I'm not feeling too glass half empty to try."

Morgan turned and gave Ali a forced smile. "Point taken!"

Ali slammed the back door, annoyance still buoyant inside. "Glass half empty, my arse," she muttered as she walked to the front of the car and lifted the bonnet. She secured it with the metal rod, then leaned over and pulled out the dipstick to check the oil levels. When she turned her head, Morgan was right next to her.

Ali jumped and cracked her head on the rod. She stumbled backwards. "Fuck me! I wasn't expecting you there." Ali rubbed the heel of her hand on her cheek and steadied herself. She rolled her eyes at Morgan. She couldn't stay mad at her for long. It wasn't in her DNA. "You pick your times to get interested in cars."

"Sorry about that."

When Morgan looked her in the eye, Ali couldn't look away. When she spoke, Ali watched the cold air dance in front of her face. Morgan moved closer as if huddling for warmth, then gave a shiver. Snow still fell in soft flakes all around.

Ali leaned over the open bonnet again.

Morgan followed.

"I'm just checking the oil, but it seems okay." She held up the dipstick. "Now I'm going to put the dipstick back in place." She put it back where she found it and screwed it tight. She then checked the engine coolant levels, although she was pretty sure that wouldn't be an issue today. They were hardly in the middle of summer.

"It could be the battery. It could be the alternator. It could be several things." Ali blew out a raspberry.

"Your dad was right," Morgan said. "We should know how to do this, so I thought I'd learn. Even in this inclement weather." She looked her dead in the eye. "I've only heard good things about this particular trainer."

Ali leaned in so their shoulders touched. She raised a single eyebrow. "What have you learned so far? If you had to present a deck, what would your key slides be?" She licked her lips, which had suddenly gone very dry.

Morgan thought for a moment. "I now know where the engine is. Also, what a dipstick is. It's one of those words you always hear, but I never really knew what it was." She held up her index finger. "But my key takeaway would be to make sure you take a woman who knows about cars so you can fall back on her far superior knowledge. Because problem-solving is a team activity. That's what I teach at all my workshops."

Ali took a step backwards and straightened up, then closed the bonnet. Somehow, she'd got oil all over her right hand.

"Teamwork. What's your part in this, apart from winding me up in the car?"

"It wasn't what I was trying to do." Morgan held up her palms on either side of her head. "I apologise. But I like to think my being here spurred you on to fix the issue far quicker than if you'd been solo."

"The snow and being lost in the middle of nowhere were the major driving factors." She walked around to the side and kicked a tyre. If all else failed, that was always her dad's signature move.

Morgan's gaze flicked up and down Ali's face. Was it Ali's imagination, or did it land on her lips?

Ali's internal furnace turned up a notch. Was this Morgan's idea of flirting? It certainly felt like it. On every part of this trip, with every decision made and every sentence uttered, their relationship moulded and changed. Like the snow, it was swirling and unpredictable, and Ali couldn't tear her eyes from it. Every setback tested them, but so far, they'd come through.

Ali wanted to know what happened next.

There was only one way to find out.

"Would your slide also say that said lesbian was alluring while she was leaning over fixing the car?"

Morgan gave her a look. "That goes without saying. A lesbian who can fix things is always appealing. Extra points for a tool belt."

"I left mine at home."

"Maybe we can actually have that drink when we're back in Glasgow. I can show you my techniques. You can show me your tool belt."

Outside, Ali was calm. Inside, she was screaming.

Maybe flirting was the ultimate distraction for them both. She was more than happy to play her part.

# Chapter Thirteen

Morgan wasn't sure what had just happened under the bonnet, but she knew Ali had a massive oil stain on her one and only top. Once they were out of the snow and back in the car, Morgan pointed it out. Ali looked down.

"Great," she replied. "That must have happened when I was leaning over. Just what I need. To turn up at home looking like I spent all day rolling in oil." She stretched out her top. "I think this is beyond saving. Put that on your deck: trying to save the day can be messy."

"That's the nature of risk and vulnerability."

"Okay, Freud." Ali blew out her cheeks in cartoon fashion, then gripped the wheel like she was Lewis Hamilton. "Right, we need the power of positive thought. I would guess that's your bag, seeing as you're a people person, right?"

Morgan detected a note of sarcasm. "If you believe it, you're almost on the way to making it happen."

"Do you believe this car will start?"

Morgan sat up straight, then gave Ali a solemn nod. "With every ounce of my being." She was lying, but Ali didn't need to know that. She'd enjoyed the flex of Ali's forearm under the bonnet. The stretch of her neck and the smooth skin that covered it. She'd found herself enraptured. But had Ali actually done anything to get the car moving? The jury was still out.

"Here goes!"

Ali hit the ignition and amazingly, the car sprang to life.

"You're a magician!"

Ali flexed her fingers. "Magic hands." She grimaced like she'd just eaten ten flies. "Please forget I just said that." Her cheeks flared red. She flicked on the windscreen wipers, then eased the car back onto the road.

The smaller roads were far less busy, with only a few cars passing in either direction. However, the roads weren't gritted, so they were far more treacherous. Neither of them wanted to test the car's ability to skate as an addition to their day.

Morgan pulled down the sun visor and checked herself in the mirror. Thanks to the good night's sleep she'd had in Snowton, she didn't look too shabby. She reached into her bag and touched up her lip balm. Her thoughts wandered back to the look she and Ali had shared under the bonnet. To their not-quite-necessary touching. She gulped. She hadn't imagined it. It had been both ways. She'd even suggested meeting up.

She still couldn't get her head around the fact she was attracted to Ali Bradford. Also, that she'd been Ali's first crush. While Morgan was sure Ali had moved on, there was always something that lingered. If Ms Cherry appeared at the next service station out of nowhere, Morgan wasn't sure she'd be able to form a sentence.

The car swerved a sharp left, and Morgan's heart dropped to her feet. When she glanced up, a digger bore down on them. Ali had almost driven into a hedge to avoid it, and was now swearing under her breath. The digger edged past them. Once it was clear they'd survived, Morgan let out her breath.

"I don't miss that from home, do you?" Ali glanced her way. "Also, thank god it was me driving and not Imogen, otherwise we'd currently be impaled on a digger."

Morgan let out a yelp of nervous laughter. "I feared for my life the entire way to those services yesterday." She paused. "One good thing about driving in Glasgow, on the rare occasions I do, is its lack of killer farm machinery. Unlike in Devon and here."

"I'm skilled at avoiding them. I spent my teenage years doing so. You can count on me to keep you safe." Ali gave her a smile.

"I believe you," Morgan replied. She wasn't lying. Morgan trusted Ali completely. More than she had anyone in ages. That thought pickled in her mind. She put the lid on it and flicked her sun visor to the roof. "From here on in, I see clear roads, and us gliding through to Devon, right?" She reached forward and turned on the radio.

It was East 17's 'Stay Another Day'.

Morgan bristled.

"Oh shit," Ali said.

"This one again? Honestly, it's about his brother's suicide and they added bells to it! I like the song, but I want my Christmas tunes to be upbeat, not sad."

Ali laughed. "I think you need to accept that it's played at Christmas and move on."

"It's annoying though, right?"

"I don't know. I don't mind a downbeat Christmas track. Breaks up the relentless happiness."

"I thought you told me you weren't glass half empty."

"I might have been lying."

Morgan wriggled in her seat, suddenly aware she needed the loo. She didn't want to stop the car again, but nature called.

"Ali, sorry to do this, but I need the loo. Could you stop at the next available place?"

"Sure. I could probably use it, too. If only to see if I can sort out my jumper."

Up ahead, Morgan glimpsed the top of a very tall building. Was it a castle of some sort? As they drove through the snowy narrow lanes, a massive sign came into view. "Christmas Court at Muirhead Castle."

"A Christmas Court. That sounds fancy."

"I'm sure they have a toilet there. Shall we pull in?"

Morgan nodded. "That would be great."

\* \* \*

Moments later, Ali swung their Ford Focus down a sweeping dirt drive up towards a castle that looked like something out of a fairy tale. It had turrets on either side of the main door, and someone had been busy maintaining the exterior of the building. The stonework glinted in the demi-snow shine. The snow had stopped for the moment. To the left of the main building was an enormous Christmas tree. They passed a sign for a Christmas market and ice rink, which Morgan guessed was round the back and out of view. If they had more time, she'd love to stay, have a look around and go for a skate, but time was not on their side.

"Wow." Ali cut the engine and peered out of the windscreen. She unclicked her seat belt. "There's a gift shop, so come find me when you've been to the loo. I'm going to see if they have any tops I can buy that aren't covered in oil."

Five minutes later, Morgan walked into the gift shop, which was a sensory overload. Flashing lights, Santa hats, fluffy reindeer and, in the corner, Ali riffling through a rail of Christmas jumpers. When she saw Morgan, she grabbed two hangers and held the first one up to her chest.

"What do you think? Jaunty, jingling reindeer?" Ali shook the jumper, and the bells on Rudolph's antlers jingled. "Or Santa himself?" She held up the second option, which was sadly bell-free.

Morgan gave her a shrug, like the choice was obvious. "The reindeer. Duh! Take a leaf out of Imogen's book. Jingle all the way."

Ali put the Santa jumper back. "Jingle it is." She pointed towards the hats. "You could use one of those, too."

Morgan glanced at the hats on the rack, then selected one that resembled a Christmas pudding. She put it on and puckered her lips. "What do you think? Does it make me irresistible?"

Ali gave her a grin. "Its powers are magical. I feel weirdly drawn to you. But that could be because I'm hungry." She moved towards Morgan. "Wait until you see me in my jumper for real. We're going to be a festive force to be reckoned with." Her gaze dropped to Morgan's lips and lingered there before lifting her face.

An arrow of desire landed in Morgan's chest.

It had happened again, hadn't it? Just like it had last night when she saw Ali in her bra. She was no longer little Ali. She was now a real-life adult, and one that Morgan wanted to kiss. That knowledge flickered in her chest like a pilot light trying to ignite.

She glanced up at Ali, who was giving her an intense stare. What was she thinking and feeling? This entire trip was turning into something Morgan had never expected in so many ways.

"Shall we pay for these gorgeous bits of fashion?"

Morgan blinked. "I don't even like Christmas pudding."

"But it likes you," Ali replied.

They paid, then left the gift shop. Morgan picked up a couple of tuna sandwiches, salt and vinegar crisps, and a box of Celebrations just because, while Ali got them both a coffee. Then she walked back to the car while Ali went to the loo to change her top. Morgan replayed Ali stepping out of their bed & breakfast bathroom in nothing but a bra, her taut stomach and shapely breasts on show.

That might be the last time she saw Ali semi-naked.

She wished she'd paid more attention.

Moments later, Ali hurried across the car park, coat in hand. She flung it in the backseat, then slotted herself back into the driver's seat. Her every move jingled. She frowned.

"Is this jumper already annoying? Would the more sensible choice have been Santa?" She jingled one of her four tiny bells. "Also, it's only when I put it on I realised the top two bells are positioned right over my nipples."

Morgan's laughter caught in her throat. "Santa would have been the glass-half-empty jumper choice." She tilted her head. "But you went for the festive choice, and I'm proud of you. As for the nipple bells—isn't life *always* better with nipple bells?" That wasn't a sentence Morgan ever thought she'd utter in her life.

Ali glanced down, then shimmied like she was a Brazilian samba dancer. "I guess you're right," she replied with a jingle. "The bells have it."

Morgan tried her hardest not to focus on Ali's nipple bells. *Really hard.* She pointed at the drinks' holder. "Your coffee's there if you want it."

"Thanks." Ali took a sip, then gulped down some air. "It's still pretty hot."

She jangled her bells one more time, then hit the ignition. Nothing.

"Holy fucking Santa Claus. Seriously?" Ali tried again. Same result. She took a deep breath in, then released it. "Okay, I'm not getting another jumper dirty, and my mechanic skills only extend so far." She grabbed her phone from the centre console.

Morgan tapped her fluffy Christmas dice. A little like those, they were both hanging on to their Christmas spirit by a single thread.

"Who are you ringing?"

Ali tipped her head back. "I'm not sure." She shook her head and jingled again.

That broke the mood, and they exchanged rueful smiles.

"Can we make a pact? Yes, this trip is proving difficult, but let's look on it as an adventure. Stay upbeat. You with me?"

Ali blew a raspberry. "I'm not going anywhere else, am I?"

# Chapter Fourteen

Ali squinted at the sticker on the windscreen, then dialled the number for the rental company. The woman on the other end of the line was very apologetic, but told her all their cars were booked, and their normal breakdown service was swamped with calls from cars stuck in the snow.

"I'll log you, dear, but it might not be until later tonight or even tomorrow that we can get someone to you. Tell me exactly where you are and I'll keep you posted."

Ali took a breath. Hadn't she just agreed to stay upbeat? Plus, she didn't want to prove Morgan right with her glass-half-empty summation. Ali wasn't a pessimist. She was just logical. A realist. Whereas Morgan was an upbeat problem-solver. Morgan was the kind of person Ali would normally avoid.

But that didn't factor in the star power of Morgan Fucking Scott.

Who was currently busy trying on her Christmas pudding hat. She pouted into her sun visor mirror, then turned to Ali. "What do you think?"

Ali smiled. "Gorgeous." She might not be presenting as the epitome of metropolitan cool, but she was still Morgan. Still Ali's version of perfection.

"What did the rental company say?"

"They don't know when they can come, but it might not be until tomorrow."

Morgan stilled at the news. "Okaaaaay." She took off her hat. Then quickly put it back on. "This is not me losing my Christmas spirit."

Ali pointed at the stiff grin glued to her own face. "Me neither," she said through gritted teeth.

That made Morgan smile.

"But I'm going to look up where I think my cousin lives. It's called Lower Greeton or something like that. Let me message my mum to get her address and number."

"Didn't you say she's always full at this time of year?"

Ali nodded. "Yes, but she has a spare room in her actual house. We're family, not paying clients. And then we just need to see if we can get a cab there." She glanced around the half-empty car park. "Although I don't think this is Uber territory."

"I'm guessing not." Morgan stroked her chin. "I like your plan, although I'm less enthused about not getting home again tonight." She held up a hand. "But I'm staying upbeat, don't worry. Ho, ho, bloody ho and all that."

"We will get you home to decorate that gingerbread house if it's the last thing we do. Maybe not tonight, but we will. Even if we have to hire a sleigh."

"At least it wouldn't break down like our plane, train and now car."

"Knowing our luck, the reindeer would probably go lame as soon as we set off." Ali clapped her hands. "Shall we see if we can book a cab or a sleigh, or whatever other form of transport we haven't tried yet?"

Ali slammed the car door, then pulled her jacket tight. Something wet hit her nose.

"It's snowing again," Morgan said, holding out her hands.

"I can see."

"Which is magical, apart from when you're trying to get home, right?"

Ali quirked an eyebrow. "Upbeat!"

They walked over to the court's large main entrance, two huge wooden doors festooned with Christmas wreaths. The smells of orange, cinnamon and nutmeg invaded her senses, reminding Ali of her family pub. A wave of homesickness washed over her. Yes, she was worried about what might be waiting for her, but she was excited to see her family, too.

Ali nodded at the woman on the door, then walked up to the reception desk. A fat Santa statue grinned at her.

"Can I help you?" The receptionist wore a top the colour of processed cheese, along with a smile that could power the whole estate. Her long red hair appeared freshly ironed. Ali immediately warmed to her.

"I hope so. Our car's broken down, and we need to get a cab to my cousin's place. I can't remember the address, but she lives in Lower Greeton, I think? Do you know how far away that is?"

When the woman nodded, relief washed through Ali. If they couldn't get there, at least they could have a warm bed for the night.

"It's about a 15-minute car ride." Her accent was so thickly northern, you could spread it on toast.

"Fabulous!" Ali said. "Is it walkable?"

The woman shook her head. "I wouldn't advise it on

these roads. The locals speed down them. They're not used to walkers."

"Could you call us a cab?"

The woman winced. "We only have two cab companies in the area, and they're all fully booked today because of the snow." She pointed at Morgan. "Which I can see from your hat has started again."

Ali's heart sank to her size-six boots. "Could you try them at least?" It had to be worth a shot.

Morgan stepped forward and offered the woman a box of Celebrations.

Ali did a double-take. Was Morgan a chocolate sorcerer? She never seemed to run out.

Morgan caught her stare, but studiously ignored her. "We'd really appreciate any help you can give us. I didn't catch your name?"

The woman smiled. "Liesl."

"Like *The Sound of Music*?"

The woman nodded, then blushed. "My mum's a huge fan. My brother's named Kurt."

"Better than Rolf," Ali said.

Liesl laughed. "That's what we always tell him." She put the chocolates on her desk. "It's very kind of you to give me these, but it doesn't change the fact there aren't any taxis." She looked from Ali to Morgan. "Although I might have another alternative. But I'd have to check with my manager first."

Ali's ears perked up. "An alternative?"

Liesl nodded. "How are you with cycling?"

"You've got bikes?" Ali wasn't mad-keen, but she'd done

her cycling proficiency when she was 11, and she knew how to pedal. "Two bikes would work."

"What about one bike?"

"But there's two of us," Ali replied.

"I know. But this bike has two saddles. It's a tandem. We have them so people can ride around the grounds. They're very popular for romantic weekend dates."

Ali wasn't sure it was exactly what was needed here, but now was not the time to be picky.

Liesl clicked some keys on her keyboard. "Let me just see." A few moments later, she nodded. "It's currently being rented, but it's due back in three hours. If you can amuse yourself here—there's plenty to do and the restaurant has space—I can hold the bike for you. It wouldn't need to be back until the morning, but I assume you're coming back for your car, anyway?"

Ali looked at her phone, then at Morgan. "I'm still waiting on a message from my mum with my cousin's number. For now, I think it's the best option. You up for a tandem bike ride?"

Morgan blinked. "Just when I think this trip can't get any weirder."

\* \* \*

They walked away from the desk, then sat on a pair of uncomfortable wooden chairs. Ali logged into the Wi-Fi, then typed Lower Greeton into Google Maps. The route appeared. She clicked on the bicycle option: it took 25 minutes. Would it be quicker on a bicycle made for two? She'd find out soon enough.

"What does Google say?" Morgan shivered as she spoke.

"Twenty-five minutes to the village, but then we have to find my cousin's place. Her B&B is called something clever that was in a movie, but I can't remember what. The good news is Lower Greeton isn't that big, and she lives just off the main square, so I'm hoping I remember that. If I don't, we'll knock on doors." Ali clicked on the message to her mum. She still hadn't read it. She checked her watch. Midday. Her mum would be busy in the bar for a while yet and she wouldn't answer her phone. She copied the message to her sister too, to cover all bases. Then she tried to call her. No answer.

Ali got up. "Shall we keep moving to stay warm?"

The snow crunched underfoot as they walked, following the signs to the Christmas market. However, when they arrived, Ali wasn't prepared for what she saw.

"Oh my god," she muttered, taking it all in. Five rows of Christmas stalls with wooden roofs stood in front of them, the nearest selling delicate Christmas ornaments, the next piping-hot mulled wine from a chrome barrel. The spicy, warming smell made Ali's nose tingle in the best possible way. As she raised her gaze, she spied an illuminated Ferris wheel turning in the background. When she glanced left, the promised ice rink winked at her in the midday gloom. Right ahead, there was also a sign for Santa's grotto. She'd loved going there as a kid. In fact, she'd loved Christmas as a kid. When had she got so 'bah humbug'?

"This is the most spectacular slice of Christmas in the middle of nowhere."

"I was just thinking the same," Ali replied. "If you're going to be stuck anywhere, this is not a terrible option. Shall we get a mulled wine and stroll the market? I can have a drink, now I'm not driving."

"Can they do you for drunken tandem riding?" Morgan walked towards the mulled wine stand.

"Can you get drunk on mulled wine at all?"

Morgan laughed. "Good point."

Ali ordered them both a mug of hot wine from a bearded man wrapped in so many scarves, Ali could only assume he had a neck and a chin. He handed them over, and Ali cupped her hands around the ceramic mug. She took a sip, and the alcohol warmed her through. It was better than she remembered.

"This is good," she told Morgan as they walked down the first line of stalls.

Morgan nodded. "My first of the season. I'm already kicking myself for not having some earlier."

"Me, too." Ali smiled. "You'll have to come to the pub for your next one when we get home."

"I'll drag the whole family, up your profits."

"My family thanks you."

Even so early, there was a fair smattering of people out to soak up festive cheer and do some Christmas shopping. Ali dodged around a family with a double buggy before they drew up alongside a stall selling pick'n'mix sweets.

"Talking of sweets, how did you suddenly produce a box of Celebrations at the desk earlier?" Ali jabbed Morgan's backpack. "Is this a Tardis and you haven't told me?"

"I bought another box in the gift shop for your cousin. I guess I'm going to have to restock. You can never have too much chocolate."

Ali stared at her. "You've got hidden depths, Morgan

Scott. It's the main thing I'm going to take back from this trip."

Morgan shifted her gaze left, embarrassed.

"I used to love this when I was a kid." Ali pointed at the pick'n'mix. "Can you hold this?" She held out her wine and Morgan took it. Then she grabbed some small pink tongs on the tabletop, and filled her pink-and-white striped bag with strawberry laces, cherry lips, fried eggs, bananas and milk bottles. "All the sweets from my childhood. I feel like we need a treat today. Anything you want to add?" Ali opened the top of the paper bag as wide as she could. Then she took back her wine and handed the tongs to Morgan.

Morgan added fizzy cola bottles, Black Jacks, milk bottles and toffees. "Are we just going to eat and drink our way through the next three hours?"

"Do you have a better suggestion?"

Morgan shook her head. "I should be home being festive with my family. Instead, I'm here being festive with you." She leaned in so their faces almost touched. "Whisper it, but I don't hate it."

Ali's insides warmed. "I'm glad."

They came to the end of the row of stalls, and face to face with the festive Ferris wheel. It was a classic, each carriage only big enough for two. They were lit with rainbow-coloured lights, and Christmas classics blared from the speakers. Ali glanced up, then at Morgan. "Remember the fair that used to come to Dartmouth every spring?" If Ali closed her eyes, she could still picture the layout, with the giant Ferris wheel in the middle.

"Do I? I had my first kiss on the Ferris wheel there. Unfortunately, it was with Chris Heaton. Completely the wrong gender, but I was slow on the uptake, like I told you." Morgan took a cola bottle from the bag, then took a swig of wine. "Whatever, Ferris wheels have always been romantic to me. I blame cheesy American movies where couples always kissed on them. You know we were talking about what romance is when I said I didn't get snow fitting into that category?"

Ali nodded.

"It's summer and a Ferris wheel for me."

"What about a Ferris wheel in the snow?"

Morgan smiled. "That could work. It's still a Ferris wheel."

Ali's heart pulsed. "I've always thought Ferris wheels were kinda scary. It's the height thing."

"I'm not a carriage rocker." Morgan held up her free palm. "Did you get rocked in a carriage as a child at the fair?"

"Who didn't? I think Nicole was the worst culprit for that."

Morgan laughed. "I agree. Your sister has a lot to answer for. I nearly fell out one year, she was so intense. The guy controlling the ride shouted at her." Morgan laughed at the memory. "But it was still better than getting kissed on one by Chris Heaton."

"Has nobody rectified that mistake since? No woman swooped in and kissed you off your seat?" If Ali had known, she'd have booked a Ferris wheel for just such an occasion. A vision of kissing Morgan as the wheel went round flashed into her mind, and her insides clenched. She took a deep breath.

She wasn't the one Morgan wanted to kiss.

Ali needed to remember that.

"Do you want to go on this one?" Ali really did not. She hated heights, and she detested Ferris wheels. But somehow, she was prepared to go on one for Morgan. She wasn't going to process what that meant too much. "I mean, it's practically gay with its rainbow lights. I feel like we'd do the queer community a disservice if we didn't."

Morgan fixed her eyes on Ali, her cheeks pink with cold. "We don't have to if you're scared."

Something fluttered in Ali's chest. She still didn't want to. But Morgan did, and that trumped what she wanted all ends up. "This trip is all about accidentally getting out of our comfort zones. I'll do it if you promise no rocking and no falling."

Morgan sipped her wine. "You've got yourself a deal."

# Chapter Fifteen

Morgan passed a stall selling thick woolly socks and another selling Christmas decorations.

Ali spent a few moments browsing, then bought her mum a tree ornament that was a stack of books.

"That means she'll have to get a real tree next year. Plus, she loves reading. I think it saved her after this summer."

"What happened this summer?"

"It was just…" Ali paused. "A lot."

It was also something Ali clearly didn't want to talk about. Morgan wasn't going to pressure her. She'd tell her when she was ready.

Ali shook her head, as if shaking off whatever was irking her. "Anyway, you wanted to go on the gay Ferris wheel." She looked up, then at Morgan. "Ready? You better say yes, because this is a once-in-a-lifetime offer."

Morgan's gaze dropped to Ali's lips.

If Nicole could see her now, eyeing up her little sister. Would she hate it, or would she be chilled? She and Nicole had been like sisters once.

Before she could second-guess herself, Morgan held out her hand.

The startled look Ali gave her almost made her drop it, but she didn't.

She didn't want to.

Ali took her hand tentatively, then in seconds, she wrapped her fingers around Morgan's in a surer embrace. Her gaze held a question, but she didn't air it.

Morgan stepped onto the metal platform as a carriage stopped in front of them. The man in charge had grease in his hair and all over his jeans. She stowed their backpacks with him, gave him a tenner, then got into the carriage, pressing her feet into the metal footwell. Ali slotted in beside her as the bloke secured the metal bar over their laps until it clicked into place.

"No rocking the carriage." The smell of stale cigarette smoke hit her as he spoke.

"Wouldn't dream of it." Morgan was acutely aware of Ali's presence and proximity. She was finally on a Ferris wheel with an attractive woman beside her.

Only, this was not the attractive woman she'd expected.

The wheel turned, and they rose slowly, in a backward motion. Ali clutched the bar so tight her knuckles went white.

Morgan leaned over and put her mouth to Ali's ear. "I promised I wouldn't rock it, and I was telling the truth," she whispered.

It was lucky there was a metal bar holding Ali in place as she flinched, then screamed.

Okay, she hadn't been joking when she said she hated Ferris wheels.

Morgan threw an arm across Ali to soothe her.

The carriage swayed as they made their way to the top of the wheel.

Ali blew out a long breath that lingered in the air in front of her. "Fuck, fuck, fuck! I forgot how much these scare me." She clutched Morgan's arm. "It's all Nicole's fault."

"Sorry for making it worse by whispering when you weren't expecting it."

Ali's eyes widened as they rode over the top of the wheel and began their descent. "Maybe you should do it again. Take my mind off what's currently happening!" she screamed. "Damn it, I hate these things!"

"Look at the gorgeous snow-covered forest!" Morgan motioned with her free hand. "Breathe in the pines." They went on for days. "Looks like it might even be a Christmas tree farm."

"I guess it'll soften the blow when this carriage snaps off and we fall to a prickly death," Ali replied.

They sailed round and past the wheel operator, who didn't seem bothered by their first-spin rocking. He was more interested in his phone and his cigarette.

Ali took a few deep breaths.

Morgan squeezed Ali's thigh. It flexed under her fingertips.

Ali turned her head just as Morgan did, and their gazes locked.

Ali's inviting lips were mere inches from her own.

They were stuck like this.

There was no backing away, nowhere else to go.

Morgan cleared her throat just as the snow started again. She grinned at Ali, squeezed her thigh once more, then threw her head back, opened her mouth and let the snow fall into it. She heard a laugh, and when she looked sideways, Ali had copied her pose.

Morgan pressed her body back into the seat, Ali's thigh

warm under her freezing fingertips. She should have bought some gloves, too. Then again, that would have been another barrier between herself and Ali. Right now, she wanted to strip away as many as she could.

"Is tasting snow and looking anywhere but down the perfect distraction technique?"

"Fuck, yes," Ali replied. "I might stay like this for the rest of the time. Also, I forgot my ear muffs, so my ears might be about to fall off. Another top distraction."

Ali shook herself, then glanced at Morgan. Their gazes collided again. "Stop staring." She put a hand over her eyes. "I know I've been a pathetic scaredy-cat ever since I jumped on this thing."

But Morgan shook her head. "No you haven't. You've been entertaining." She smiled, then took it all in as they sailed upwards again. "And just look at the view! Snow-covered fields, Christmas trees, the twinkly lights, you."

Morgan performed a slow blink. Shit, had that really just come out of her mouth? Ali was lovely, but she was still Nicole's sister. There was protocol to follow. Or had that gone out of the window now? When she was 15, kissing a 12-year-old would have been wrong. But now she was 38? Kissing a 35-year-old was perfectly acceptable.

Ali stared, her mouth ajar.

At least Morgan had distracted her from the view as they rose to the top of the wheel again.

Morgan opened her mouth to do damage control, but the wheel jolting stopped any sound coming out.

Then it jerked again, before stopping completely as they reached the top.

"What the…" Morgan began. She peered over the side of the carriage. Not a good move. She moved quickly backwards, pushing Ali left.

Ali screamed. "Fuck, Morgan! What are you doing?"

It was a valid question. "I was just seeing what's going on."

"Did you find anything out by hanging over the side of the fucking carriage?"

Even Morgan could detect the sarcasm wedged between those words. "Only that we're quite high up."

"Really not helping."

"Sorry." Morgan winced. "Okay, this used to happen all the time when we rode these at the funfair. They're probably just letting someone on."

"Or it's broken down. Every other mode of transport we've been on this trip has done the same."

Morgan couldn't refute that, but she'd made a promise to stay chipper. "I prefer my option. Seriously, this is what they do." She paused. "And this would also always be when your sister—"

"Stop!" Ali gripped the metal bar harder. "No more talk of Nicole."

Morgan nodded. The carriage swayed.

"And no more nodding. It shakes the carriage!" Ali added. "No wonder they got rid of these double carriages in favour of the round ones. Nobody's going to rock those."

"True. I haven't seen one of these old ones in years."

"They all ended up in the middle of nowhere." She paused. "I hope they remembered all the screws."

Morgan bit down a laugh. She didn't want to freak Ali out any more than she already was.

"I'm sure they remembered all the screws. At least the

ones they were given." She couldn't help herself. But then she instantly felt bad. "Sorry!" She squeezed Ali's thigh, then left her hand there.

Ali flinched, but said nothing.

Morgan glanced left, studying Ali. Her strong chin. Her sculpted cheekbones. Her ears and cheeks, red with cold. The way her hair stuck up adorably, buffeted by the wind and snow. Ali had told Morgan she didn't wear a hat, as she didn't want to mess up her hair. She wasn't sure that logic applied in a snowstorm on a Ferris wheel.

"Why isn't it moving?"

"Don't focus on that," Morgan said. "What can I do to distract you?" She looked at the Christmas tree farm. "How many do you think they sell a year?"

Ali gave her a look that might have been sullen, but could equally have been scared witless. Morgan wasn't sure of the difference. What she knew was that Ali was cold and working herself into a lather. Suddenly, the perfect form of distraction sprang to mind.

They should kiss.

Morgan flinched, as if someone had just punched her in the stomach. But in a warm, fuzzy way. Heat flushed through her body from her toes to her scalp. She gulped. How was she going to sell this? Would she have to? There was only one way to find out.

"Ali," she began.

"What?"

Sullen. Snarky. Okay, Ali wasn't in the best of moods.

"I have an idea. Remember I told you I always had a romantic notion of being kissed on a Ferris wheel?"

Ali gripped the bar tighter still. She didn't turn her head. "Uh-huh."

"Well, we're on a Ferris wheel, and you need a distraction. Think of it as doing me a service. Fulfilling my teenage dreams. Like Katy Perry." She paused. Should she push it further? She wasn't sure. She could hardly believe the words were tumbling from her lips, but apparently they were. "You said yourself you had a crush on me when you were 12, so maybe it's making both of our teenage dreams come true."

Morgan didn't dare look at Ali.

Not after she'd just uttered the most stupid thing she'd ever uttered in her entire life. Plus, Ali still wasn't looking at her. Had she stopped breathing?

Morgan turned her head. "If you're worried, you only have Chris Heaton as competition. And to be honest, I only remember him as a sloppy kisser. All you have to do is beat that. Piece of cake." The more Morgan talked, the more she convinced herself she was suggesting this as an altruistic act. Something to calm Ali down.

Not at all something *she* wouldn't mind. Something that had flickered on the periphery of Morgan's mind ever since last night.

Ali turned her head, eyes narrowed. Even in a snowstorm, she was still a mass of perfect angles and beauty.

"You are joking, right?" Her gaze scanned down from Morgan's face to her lips. When they got there, Ali looked away quickly, with a small shake of her head.

"I'm really not." Morgan stroked Ali's thigh again. Her pulse-rate sped up. "It'll take your mind off being stuck. Plus, we're in a snowstorm on a Ferris wheel. It's a story to tell, right?"

Ali stared straight ahead for a few moments, then turned to Morgan. "You don't have to do this. I know I'm scared, but you don't have to take pity on me. I told you, I'm over my crush." Her cheeks blared red as she spoke.

Morgan didn't believe her. But it wasn't why she was asking.

She licked her lips.

Ali's eyes followed the movement.

Morgan shifted closer. "This isn't a pity kiss. All I'm asking is that you humour me and make my teenage dreams come true." She moved her lips to within touching distance. Then Morgan flicked her gaze until it met Ali's. Up close, she had a spill of freckles over the bridge of her nose. Adorable. "What do you say?"

Ali blinked, then parted her lips a fraction.

She didn't say no. She moved her head closer to Morgan's.

Morgan did the same. Then, with a moment's hesitation, she pressed her lips to Ali's.

And just like that, Morgan's world reclined.

Ali tasted of Christmas, her mouth still warm from the mulled wine. Cinnamon, cloves, nutmeg. Snow hit Morgan's cheeks, but she hardly noticed. Ali's lips were taking up all her attention. The way they felt on hers. The shape of them, and how they jigsawed precisely. But most of all, the power they already had on her. Morgan couldn't move, and she didn't want to.

They kissed on, and Morgan melted into the moment. She closed her eyes and got whisked away to a fiery sunset beach, with sand between her toes. Her idea of romance. Although, this Ferris wheel was fast turning into her idea of romance, too. Yes, it was in the snow. But it was still a Ferris wheel.

The perfect location for a totally unexpected kiss. Morgan hadn't got on this fairground ride thinking she'd kiss Ali Bradford. That was, in fact, the very last thing she expected. However, now it was happening, it made perfect sense. They'd wasted time not doing it earlier. This something-to-pass-the-time kiss had suddenly segued into a lip-lock far bigger than them both. Something Morgan wanted to explore further. Now she'd kissed her lips, she only wanted to kiss other parts of Ali Bradford.

Ali slid her hand around Morgan's neck and pulled her closer. Then she slid her tongue into Morgan's mouth.

Morgan's breath slid away.

She and Ali were French kissing on a Ferris wheel. If her teenage self could only see her now. Chris Heaton was a distant memory, just like 12-year-old Ali. Because grown-up Ali was currently kissing Morgan into oblivion, and Morgan was here for it. She'd happily stay on this Ferris wheel forever. Kick back, relax, and offer herself up to the moment. It seemed to be Ali's plan. This was no rushed kiss. This was a warm, slow drink of a kiss. One that made every sense Morgan owned come alive. She could taste it, smell it, touch it. It was flawless but fragile. It came with a sticker that read 'handle with care'. Morgan was determined to do just that.

There was a jolt as the wheel cranked into gear again and moved forward.

Morgan's eyelids sprang open about the same time as Ali's. They pulled apart.

Morgan's heart thumped in her chest like it was sending out a warning signal. Her scalp pulsed under her hat. She already missed Ali's lips. She ran her tongue over her bottom lip and tried to conjure up some words that suited the moment. She found none. Instead, she stared into Ali's warm brown eyes, which somehow spoke a language Morgan immediately understood.

Then, before she knew it, Ali leaned back in and found Morgan's lips once more.

It wasn't words that were called for. Rather, it was action, and Ali was taking charge.

The wheel moved round, and Morgan's stomach dropped for all the right reasons.

Ali didn't miss a beat. She moved over Morgan, her lips hot and wet.

Electricity sparked in Morgan's brain as she slid her fingers into Ali's frosty hair, then her tongue into her mouth. Morgan groaned. She couldn't help it. Somewhere in the distance, she heard a wolf whistle, but she ignored it. She wasn't going to let anything disturb this moment.

This was the best kiss Morgan had ever had on a Ferris wheel, hands down.

*Scrap that.*

This was one of the best kisses she'd *ever* had in her whole damn entire life.

Full stop.

# Chapter Sixteen

H oly. Fucking. Hell.

That was the only thought rolling through Ali's mind, lit up in neon and flashing nonstop. She was kissing Morgan Scott. Scrap that. She was *snogging* Morgan Scott. Morgan currently had her tongue deep in Ali's mouth, and every nerve ending in her body was on high alert. She hardly dared to blink in case she woke up, and this was all a dream. But she knew it wasn't. She also knew that if they hadn't been in public and shackled by a metal bar, Ali would have straddled Morgan by now, and performed all manner of things not fit for public consumption.

She'd waited over two decades for this. Whatever the initial reason, this kiss was no normal kiss. It was a kiss for the ages. A kiss to tell the grandkids. A kiss that would keep her warm forever.

But that was only in Ali's mind.

For Morgan, it was purely to fulfil a teenage dream.

Ali had to remember that.

But right now, with Morgan's lips on hers, desire flamed through Ali. Dammit, she wished they weren't in public. If this was how Morgan Scott kissed for fun, what might it feel like if she actually meant it? Ali's brain shook at the thought. A few minutes ago, she'd thought her ears might drop off with cold. Now, Morgan's kisses were her own central heating system. Ali's cheeks warmed, her belly too. Even her calves heated by a couple of degrees.

Eventually, Morgan pulled away, but kept her lips within touching distance. Over her shoulder, Christmas trees winked in the distance. Then the Christmas market flashed by.

Ali stared, her breath causing small plumes of smoke in front of them. She breathed Morgan in. She smelled of bergamot and Ali's dreams.

A smile flickered on Morgan's face. "Hot damn."

Ali sucked in the biggest breath of her life. "I agree." She snagged Morgan's gaze. The wheel kept on turning. As did life, the universe. But something had forever changed in her world. Something she couldn't row back on. She now knew what it felt like to kiss Morgan Scott.

Now, all she wanted was to do it again.

"It worked, by the way." She leaned forward and pressed her lips to Morgan's once more. This time, she left them there for one, two, three seconds. Long enough for sparks to fly around every inch of her body. Long enough to make her toes flex. Long enough to know pulling them apart would be tinged with regret. But she did it anyway.

"The kiss," Ali continued. "It took my mind off the height and the wheel collapsing and us meeting an untimely demise skewered on top of a Christmas tree." She stared at Morgan. "For that, thank you."

Morgan's cheeks burned red beneath her Christmas pudding hat, and she let out a throaty laugh. "A Christmas skewer. It's no way to die."

Ali shifted in her seat. She unwrapped her arm from Morgan's neck. "But also, that kiss was... unexpected." Understatement of the century.

Was Morgan going to laugh this off? No.

She looked away, then shook her head slightly. Eventually, she turned back.

"It was very unexpected. A bit like this whole trip."

Their gazes met again.

Ali couldn't move, couldn't think. But she was 99 per cent sure there was desire in Morgan's eyes, too. Just as there had been desire in her kiss from the moment their lips had connected. It still pulsated through Ali. The wheel kept turning. The lights flashed. Ali's mind was a wasteland of previously coherent thought, now reduced to rubble. The waft of possibility hung in the air, the scorch of Morgan's lips on hers. Ali gripped the metal bar as the wheel soared over the precipice again.

But this time, she wasn't afraid of the height or the wheel. It didn't matter if the world around her collapsed now. Her own world had just shifted, and her focus was completely on that. On Morgan Scott. On when she could kiss her again.

"Did I win the prize of best kiss on a Ferris wheel? Better than whatshisname?" It was a daring question. Flirtatious, even. If you'd asked her this morning if she'd utter those words, she'd have told you not to be so ridiculous. But that was then. Now, after a kiss like that, everything had changed. Now, there were even more questions floating around Ali's brain.

Morgan's laugh came from her stomach, loud and throaty. "I would say you obliterated it. Like whatshisname never happened." Morgan's eyes focused fully on Ali's. "You are the Ferris wheel kissing champ."

Those words exploded in her like a firework, the after effects raining down and tickling her skin.

Now she was sure of it. This wasn't just one way.

Morgan Scott liked her.

When her gaze dropped to Ali's lips, she knew Morgan wanted to kiss her again, too.

The wheel spun around to the operator one more time. "Last go around if you want to get a last kiss in, ladies!" He followed that up with a knowing grin.

Instinctively, Ali pulled her mustard scarf up over her face to disappear from view.

Beside her, Morgan shook with laughter.

Ali peered right, catching her gaze.

"It seems when we're on a Ferris wheel, we revert to being teenagers," Morgan said. "I kinda like it. Being an adult is way overrated." She licked her lips, then straightened up. "What else can we do that would take us back to being 15?"

Ali flipped her head back to the sky. "Smoke a fag? Order a takeaway with my mum's credit card?"

Morgan laughed. "We could definitely buy some cigarettes. I'm not facing the wrath of your mum for anyone."

The wheel slowed to a stop when they were halfway down the front. Ali shivered and breathed in the scene. It was still snowing, and somehow, being up high now took on a magical quality. She no longer feared she was going to die. Plus, she had an extra thing to live for now. Morgan Scott's kisses and the promise of an illicit fag.

Moments later, the operator let them off with a bow. Morgan got out first, then turned and offered a hand to Ali.

It wasn't the first time Morgan had done that, but it held

extra meaning now. This time, when Ali put her fingers in Morgan's, the jolt that went up her arm was brand new. It was big, bold, alive. Just like this moment.

Ali put one foot out of the carriage and was just about to follow up with the other when her trailing leg caught on the edge. Ali stumbled. But who was there to catch her? Morgan. Her hands were tight on Ali's body as she righted her. Then their faces were inches apart.

This was so confusing. It was everything her 12-year-old self would want, and nothing her 35-year-old self could comprehend. Plus, was this even anything?

Ali shut her thoughts down. She wasn't going to figure out whatever the hell this was standing on the platform of this Ferris wheel. That was borne out when the operator cleared his throat.

"Thanks ladies, if you could step away from the carriage now. I need to let the other customers off."

Morgan blinked, then shook herself. She let Ali go and jumped down with a shy smile.

Ali followed.

They wandered into the market, neither of them saying anything.

Ali's phone vibrated in her pocket. She got it out, glad of the distraction. She wiped a snowflake from her phone screen.

*Please let it be a reply from my mum.*

It wasn't. It was from Imogen.

She clicked, and a photo of Imogen and another woman filled her screen, arms around each other. The message read: 'Back together for Christmas! Thanks for making me remember that love is worth not giving up on!'

Ali spluttered. Well, this was awkward. She'd given up on a chance of anything with Morgan long ago, but now… No, she wasn't going to go there. This was about Imogen and Sam, a couple with history who they'd unwittingly stumbled into and helped to get back together. It thrilled her they'd got their happy ending. Somebody should have one.

She turned the screen to Morgan, who blew some snowflakes from her face before steadying the phone in Ali's hand. Her fingers wrapping around Ali's once more was pure bliss.

When Morgan saw the photo and the message, a wide smile took up residence on her face.

"Did we do that?"

"If Imogen says so, then we did."

"In that case, we'll take all the plaudits. Both of us. Team Glass Half Full saved the day."

# Chapter Seventeen

The man at the bike hire place was not at all happy about them keeping the tandem overnight, despite the assurances from Liesl at reception. Morgan was fresh out of chocolate, so it took a strong charm offensive to persuade him they'd return it in time for their first hire tomorrow. That, and a credit card as collateral. They waited until they were a safe distance away before they said a word to each other. Then Morgan let out a breath.

"And they say people in the country are friendly and trusting."

"At least he didn't press us when we said we didn't want to wear helmets. Plus, I guess we don't sound like locals. He's probably been burned by tourists promising the world before."

"I guess so." Morgan went to put a hand on Ali's arm, but thought better of it. She was still processing that kiss, but ignoring it, too. If she gave herself time to process and analyse her actions, she knew where that would lead her. Down a long road named What The Fuck Were You Thinking? Kissing any woman in the snow on a Ferris wheel was something she never thought she'd do. But kissing Nicole's little sister had broken some rule or other in the friend world, she was sure. This was the little girl she'd robbed of a toy trumpet, after all. A little girl who'd been in the background of Morgan's life for years, and then, nothing. But she would always be Nicole's little sister. That would never change.

However, after that kiss, Morgan wasn't sure of anything anymore, never mind some arbitrary rules that might have been in the friendship code 20 years ago. Did friendship rules have a use-by date, after which lines blurred?

She pushed that issue to the back of her mind. Right now, she had a tandem to master. The perfect distraction. So long as it didn't break down. Could a bike break down? Morgan squatted by the chain and poked it with her finger just to make sure.

"What are you doing?" Ali dangled her ear muffs on her fingers, retrieved from the car for this part of the journey.

"Making sure the chain is fully attached. With our luck with transport of late, I want to check it won't fall off five minutes down the road." Morgan looked up at Ali, and something scrunched in her chest. It almost knocked her off her feet, but she stayed upright. She gulped. She had to keep a lid on this, or it might explode.

"Oh god, it can't go wrong again, can it?"

Morgan snorted, then stood up, coming face to face with Ali. More specifically, Ali's lips. Her insides pulsed. This was going to happen every time now, wasn't it? She gulped, then ploughed on.

"Famous last words." She patted the back saddle. "Are you going up top, or bringing up the rear?" Oh fuck. She hadn't meant for it to sound so flirtatious.

Ali's eyes glinted. "I was going to ask you the same

question." She raised an eyebrow. "But seeing as I need to steer because I'm the one who sort-of-but-not-really knows where we're going, I should go up front, right?"

Morgan hadn't thought of that. "I suppose that's true."

"You know what your job is?"

"Looking pretty at the back?"

"And singing that song 'Daisy Daisy'. It mentions being on a bicycle made for two."

Morgan wrinkled her forehead. "Never heard of it."

Ali rolled her eyes. "In that case, can you manage looking pretty and not falling off?"

How the tables had turned. When they'd first met, Ali had seemed a little prickly about seeing Morgan again. Then bashful when she'd revealed her childhood crush. But now? Ali was the one calling the shots, the one with the cousin and the local knowledge. Also, it appeared to Morgan, she was quite enjoying it.

Strangely, Morgan didn't mind. She was happy to let Ali take the lead. The little girl who'd once been an annoyance had turned into a capable, strong woman Morgan had faith in. Also, one Morgan was attracted to more by the second. But she wasn't about to divulge that. At 3pm, it was still snowing, the light was dimming, and they had a cousin to find.

Ali checked her phone and swore. She tried calling someone, then blew out a sigh when nobody picked up. "Why are none of my family answering their phones? I've messaged mum, Nicole and Stuart."

"What about your dad?"

Ali flinched, then focused on her phone. "He won't answer either," she mumbled. Then she checked her bag was secure in the back basket, kicked the bike stand and got on the front saddle.

Had Morgan said the wrong thing again?

She adjusted her backpack, got on the back saddle, then realised she'd done nothing like this before. Morgan was a team player, but if there was an opportunity to do something solo, she'd always choose that. Today, she didn't have that option.

Up front, Ali twisted, then let out a yelp of pain.

"What was that?"

Ali winced. "Just some muscle in my neck waking up and punching me in the face." She twisted back. "I'm going to look up the village on my map. I'll send a couple more urgent messages to my family, and then we'll set off. If I see my cousin's house, fingers crossed, I'll recognise it."

Morgan rang the bell on her handlebars. "Ready when you are." She paused. "Before we go, I just need to know. Are you a super-expert biker? Because if you're about to speed off like Laura Kenny, we might have an issue. I haven't ridden a bike since I left Devon."

Ali tipped her head back, then blew out a raspberry as snow battered her face. "I am not Laura Kenny, so don't worry," she shouted. "You really haven't ridden since you lived in Devon?"

Morgan shook her head, even though Ali couldn't see her. "Nope."

Ali sat up and fixed her ear muffs in place. "Try to forget that. On three. Right pedal first. One, two, three!"

The bike wobbled as they set off, but they kept it upright. After a few moments, though, they were in a rhythm. Ali steered them out of the car park and down the long drive, flanked by snow-covered trees. If everything hadn't gone so wrong for them on this trip, they might have appreciated the winter wonderland they'd been dropped in. But staying upright and not face-planting on the concrete was now the first thought in Morgan's head. So far, so good. However, this long driveway was clear of snow, with no other traffic. It was the smaller roads she worried about.

Up ahead, Ali signalled with her arm, then pulled out onto the road. Two cars flashed past them in the opposite direction.

"Just keep pedalling at the same pace, and holler if you want to slow down. Stopping is not an option!" Ali shouted.

The snow had momentarily stopped, so Morgan could speak without ingesting a mouthful. "Not even for the loo?" She shivered as a gust of wind whistled by her face. Not for the first time this trip, she was glad she'd brought a thick jacket.

"I'm afraid you'll have to wet yourself!"

That brought a laugh from Morgan. "We better not run into any cows either!"

"Especially cows that can move their heads," Ali bellowed.

Morgan grinned. "The very worst kind!"

Over the next ten minutes, her fears about narrow roads turned out to be very real. On December 23rd, everyone had somewhere to get to fast, and a slow bike in their way wasn't popular with anybody. It didn't help either when the snow started up again, and began driving right at them.

After a couple of minutes, Ali flagged with her hand and they pulled into a layby. The cars behind them revved their motors and sped past, sending arcs of grey sludge their way.

Ali got off and kicked the bike stand. Her face was the colour of a pillar box, her lips blue, her hair frosted.

Morgan wanted to hug her, but that wouldn't get them anywhere fast.

"I bet you're glad you bought that hat now, just as I'm glad I got my ear muffs." Ali squinted, then rubbed her palms up and down her face. "I just hope my cousin's home, otherwise I might cry."

Morgan reached out and touched her arm. "I think she'll be at home, making a gorgeous dinner with just enough for two extra people." Every fibre of her being hoped that was true. "I'm also picturing hot chocolate, wine and spin the bottle."

Okay, now she was just plain flirting again. With a woman whose face was nearly falling off she was so cold. Bad Morgan.

Luckily, Ali saw the funny side. Even when the snow appeared to fall thicker. "I've never hoped for anything more in my entire life." She grinned, then pulled her scarf tighter.

"You're doing a great job."

"I need to do it for another 15 minutes according to Google Maps." Ali patted her saddle, then got back on. "You ready to annoy some more drivers in this picturesque biking nightmare?"

# Chapter Eighteen

Ali had never been more grateful to see a sign in her entire life. 'Welcome to Lower Greeton! Please drive carefully.' Now, all they had to do was find Helen's cottage in a snow storm. After the past 15 minutes, her opinion of snow storms had changed. They were great when you were inside. But when you were in them, they were brutal. Small lumps of ice that pummelled her face until she wanted to cry. But Ali wasn't going to cry in front of Morgan Scott. Plus, there was enough water already in the air. She didn't need to add more.

"Lower Greeton!" she heard Morgan cry from behind.

Ali put a thumb in the air. "Nearly there!"

Morgan's reply was drowned out by the roar of a car engine. The bike wobbled. Ali threw out her left arm, and they pulled up by the kerb. A red Audi blazed past, horn blaring.

"Happy Christmas to you, too!" Ali shouted, then twisted to Morgan. "I'm riding until we hit the village green, then I know where she is. Ready for the final push?" she shouted.

"Lead the way."

They wobbled back onto the road. They rode past the village post office and The Black Bear, the larger of the two village pubs, and then down a slope in the road. Thankfully, there was a lull in the traffic. Ali didn't even want to look at her jeans and how muddy they were. Along with her snow-frosted hair, she was sure she looked a sight. Thank goodness she'd at least seen Helen in the past year and wasn't showing up as a complete stranger. The first thing she was going to do was fling herself in the shower.

They swung down the hill, Ali applying the brakes in a pumping motion. When they turned the corner, the village green came into view. Ali's Christmas spirit soared: she could see Helen and Jamie's house beyond the Christmas tree on the green, all lit up even at mid-afternoon. The oak trees on the green were lit with white fairy lights, too. Ali guided the tandem onto the semi-circular road that lined the green, and pulled up outside her cousin's house.

"Kellermans' B&B," Ali said, reading the sign. "I really should have remembered that, right?"

"From *Dirty Dancing*?" Ali felt Morgan get off the bike. When she turned, Morgan was beside her.

"Of course! We watched that film about 200 times when we were kids. It's the one that our mums and us all loved." Ali's phone vibrated in her pocket. She took it out. A message from her sister with Helen's number and the name of the B&B, along with a Patrick Swayze gif. Ali rolled her eyes. A little late in the day.

With Morgan's help, she pulled the bike off the road and they wheeled it onto her cousin's driveway.

"You never told me your cousin lived in a picture-perfect village in a picture-perfect house."

Ali looked at the place with fresh eyes. The house was made of old local stone, but they'd done it up so it shone, both inside and out. The doors looked freshly painted, the black-framed windows gleamed, and the front gardens were worthy of gracing any gardening show.

It *was* pretty cool. When she'd rocked up here last November, she'd been fresh out of a fling she'd hesitated to even name as such. Ali and Cath had met, had a lot of sex, and then when Cath had come out with a group of Ali's friends in Glasgow one night, she'd dumped her the following day, telling her their lives were on different paths. Ali had been stunned, and when she'd got a message from Helen to come visit the following weekend, she'd grabbed it with both hands. However, being newly dumped, she'd been too wrapped up in herself and hadn't truly appreciated how well Helen had done for herself. Now she saw it through Morgan's eyes, she did.

Ali was just about to reply when the front door of the main house opened, and her cousin stepped out of it, carrying a black bin bag. She glanced up and stopped when she saw them approaching. Helen's fair hair was tied up in a tight ponytail, and she wore a pair of faded jeans ripped at the knee, along with a T-shirt the colour of hot sauce. It must be warm in the house, because it wasn't out here. Plus, Ali remembered from their childhood that Helen didn't feel the cold.

Ali whipped off her ear muffs and waved.

"Hey Helen, it's me!" The most unhelpful comment of the year by far.

Helen did a double-take. "Ali?"

Ali nodded.

Helen dropped the bin bag where she stood and walked over to her. Then she took Ali in her arms. "What the hell are you doing on my drive?" She eased Ali back to arm's length. "Not that it's not great to see you. But you're about the last person I expected to turn up two days before Christmas looking like an icicle." She glanced at the tandem behind them. "Tell me you didn't just pedal all the way here from Glasgow?" Helen's face was rightly confused as she glanced from Ali, to Morgan, then back.

Ali laughed, then a heady mix of relief and warmth rushed through her. They were going to be okay. They wouldn't freeze in a bus shelter, be found as blocks of ice on Christmas morning and be the talk of the local news. After all the setbacks of the past two days, arriving here to somebody familiar was the best feeling she'd had in the past 48 hours.

*Okay, second best.*

"We didn't, although it kinda feels that way. We set off from Glasgow yesterday morning, and this is as far as we've got. So far, we've broken a train and a plane, and our hire car is currently conked out in the car park of the Christmas Court at Muirhead Castle. I was half expecting the bike chain to fall off, but no, we made it here. A Christmas miracle!"

Helen rubbed her hands together. "You'll have to tell me all about it over a coffee. Jamie might help. He's good with cars, but he's not due back until this evening, so it might have to wait until the morning."

"I thought I was good with cars, but apparently not." She pointed to where Morgan had propped the bike onto its stand. "Hence, we have a bike, loaned from the Christmas Court. We have to get it back to them by midday tomorrow. If we don't, the man has my credit card. From the look on his face, he might book himself and his whole family a trip to Lapland if we're a minute late."

"I think he's counting on it," Morgan added with a grin.

Ali gave Morgan a smile, then turned to Helen. "This is Morgan. We're trying and failing to travel together."

Helen stepped forward and extended a hand. "Helen, pleased to meet you." Then she gave a little shiver. "But enough chat in a bloody snow storm!" She looked skywards. "Come in and get out of the cold. Jamie can put the bike in the back of his van when he gets in."

"You've no idea how happy those words make me," Ali told her.

Helen led them into their part of the house, which was far less festooned with Christmas than the outside. However, the kitchen was still a welcome hug. Ali fell into it, letting out a contented sigh. With its midnight-blue cupboards and copper handles, teamed with orange tiles on the wall and two giant skylights, it was a modern ode to stylish cuisine.

"Sorry for not calling ahead, but I got a new phone since we last spoke and I didn't have your number. I've been messaging mum and Nicole all day, but they only just got back to me."

Helen waved a hand. "Don't be silly, we're family." She sucked on her top lip. "Although you look a little like the rat in *Muppet Christmas Carol* after he falls into that ice barrel." She walked forward and swept a strand of Ali's hair from her face. "Do you want a coffee first, or a shower?"

It was a good question. Ali glanced at Morgan, her coat already off, but she couldn't ask her to make this decision. She wanted both at once. Preferably with Morgan. But that would be a little rude. Today had been eternal, and it wasn't even 4pm, according to the clock on Helen's bright orange kitchen wall. This morning, they'd woken up in Snowton. But now, at least, they were somewhere familiar.

"A coffee first, but then a shower would be very welcome." She glanced at Morgan. "Do you want to go for a shower first?"

Morgan blinked, then nodded. "I would love to." She looked at Helen. "This might be cheeky, but do you have a washer/dryer? We've been in these clothes for a couple of days now, and I feel like getting them clean would cheer me up, too."

Helen nodded. "We have both. I'll pop a wash on when you both give me your clothes."

"That would be brilliant." Ali stared at the bottom of her jeans, covered in mud and grime. "Cycling on country roads is unforgiving."

"I'm impressed you made it in one piece." Helen walked to the other door in the kitchen. "Follow me, Morgan, and I'll show you the guest room. I just made it up for Christmas last night—Jamie's parents are coming to stay—so the sheets are fresh. You're in luck."

Ali's stomach floored. Oh shit. One bed again. One bed last night had been torturous. But one bed tonight might be impossible. Being that close to Morgan and not kissing her again was totally out of the question. Once the kissing started, she knew where that would lead. She blew out a breath as her mind filled in the blanks in a blur of skin and heat. She closed her eyes to get rid of the image. Really not helpful.

For now, she had to stay in this moment. Not worry about the future. Isn't that what this trip had taught her? You could plan all you liked, but in the end, life would have the final say.

\* \* \*

Once Helen and Morgan left the kitchen, Ali walked through to the lounge and pressed Home on her phone. It needed another charge soon, but she had just about enough juice left to call Tobias.

"Hello, Glasgow City Cat Adoption Centre. I'm afraid I just shipped the last cat out because it peed in my shoe, so we're all out."

"Very funny." Ali collapsed on Helen's super-squishy cream sofa. Thoroughly impractical colour choice, but cushions that meant she might fall asleep at any moment. That would be one way to deal with tonight.

"How's Snowy doing, apart from fulfilling my brief to pee in your shoe?" Ali paused. "She didn't really do that, did she? Now is not the time to be teaching her new tricks."

"I swear she started to, but then I distracted her by vogueing. We all know how mesmerising I can be when I do that."

"She does love a dance." Ali could just imagine Snowy's transfixed face. That her cat loved dance was a well-worn joke between the two friends. Once *Strictly* was on, there was no way anybody was distracting Snowy. "Everything good in the hood?"

"Gorgeous, darling. I bought a nut roast yesterday, along with some of those meat-free pigs in blankets. I daren't look at the ingredients to see what they really are. I also bought a bottle of champers, and a bottle of red for a tenner. Splashing out this Christmas. Me and Snowy are going to have a great time. I even bought her a new toy. Santa is going to come to this part of Glasgow, even if he never does in the movies." He paused. "How are things in Devon?"

Ali closed her eyes. She'd checked in last night to see how

Snowy was, but not given him any other details. Of course he thought she was in Devon.

"We're still not there."

"Whaaaaaaaaat?" Tobias was a fan of drama. It's why he was addicted to the *Real Housewives* franchise.

"Remember I told you the plane was delayed? Then it became cancelled, then our train broke down—"

"Yes, and you were travelling with your first love and it was like the most romantic thing in the world!" He was screeching now.

"Lower your voice. You'll scare Snowy."

"I'll just vogue a little more. She'll be putty in my hands." He paused. "Where are you now?"

"Were we in the services when we last spoke?"

"You were."

"We hitched a lift, our train broke down, as did our hire car, and now we're staying the night with my cousin before trying to get to Devon tomorrow." When she said it out loud, it sounded even more ridiculous than it had been living through it. However, she knew that when she looked back on the past few days, she'd remember the ups and the downs. Getting to know Morgan again. Dave, the Christmas tree man. Hanging out in Snowton.

The Ferris wheel.

*That kiss.*

"Where exactly are you right now?"

"Sitting on one of the most comfortable sofas in the world at my cousin's place in the Lakes."

"You've only made it as far as the Lakes? You can drive that in three hours."

"If you've got a car that works. Which we hopefully will have by tomorrow. Otherwise, we're spending Christmas with my cousin." Which wasn't the absolute worst plan in the world. But then again, it really was. It was the whole point she'd said yes to going home this year, because it was the first Christmas without Dad. The first one her mum had actually closed the pub for the day. The first one where it was just going to be the family, and nobody else. Ali sat up. She had to get home tomorrow, there was no two ways about it. She knew Morgan was just as keen.

"And you're still with the dreamboat that is Morgan Scott?"

Ali grinned like a cat of the Cheshire variety.

"You're bloody grinning, aren't you? I can hear it!" He let out another squeal of excitement. "Is she still gorgeous?"

Ali conjured Morgan in her mind. Then she thought about her right now, naked in the shower. Every hair on her body stood to attention.

"She still has a certain allure."

"Hang on." Tobias paused. "Has something happened? As I recall, she's on the lady-loving bus. You haven't climbed aboard, have you?"

That single question took Ali right back to the kiss.

She paused long enough for Tobias to know the answer.

"You fucking hussy! I love it! Something's happened, hasn't it? Have you stumbled upon a one-way ticket to love-town rather than just going home for Christmas like normal people?" He could barely contain himself. "Just so you know, I'm covering Snowy's ears, because this is strictly on a need-to-know basis." He paused. "Of course, I need to know, so you have to tell me."

Now that Tobias was interested, Ali found she was desperate

to tell someone. She'd been pondering who, but her family was out. She couldn't tell Nicole. Not yet. Not that she thought her sister would mind, but it would just be… awkward at first. But that was supposing there was anything to back up that blistering kiss.

Fuck, she hoped there was.

"Hello, are you still alive?"

Ali sat up. "Yes. Sorry, I'm a bit thrown by it all." Especially now it was in sharp focus. She'd spent the past two days trying to contain herself, but she wasn't capable after that kiss. "Nothing happened, but then, everything did. We kissed on a Ferris wheel in a snowstorm, then we rode a tandem bike to my cousin's, and now we have to share a bed for the second night running. The first one was bad enough. I don't know what the fuck I'm meant to do when my first crush—my first fucking love, let's not beat around the bush—"

"Although you'd like to—"

Ali let out an enormous laugh. "I would. Especially when she's currently in the shower. Naked." Her entire system revved at the thought.

"Why aren't you in there with her?"

"Because it would be a bit much to turn up at my cousin's, then disappear to fuck my travel companion."

Now it was Tobias's turn to roar. "*Travel companion?* Could you sound more Radio 4 if you tried? I've heard it called a lot of things."

"You know what I mean. But now I'm thinking about it, I'm panicking. I've been wearing the same clothes for two days, my hair's a mess, and yet I'm contemplating sleeping with someone for the first time in forever."

"Over a year, but who's counting?" he replied.

"You, apparently." Ali leaned her head back on the couch. "Fuck, I'm out of practice. I can't be out of practice for Morgan Scott! I have to be ready. Hit the ground running. What if I've forgotten how to do it? What if I'm a really terrible lover and all my past conquests have been lying through their teeth?"

Tobias didn't snigger. "Don't be so ridiculous. You're a love goddess, I'm sure of it. Plus, I reckon the sight of her naked might sort you out."

"Don't say that! I've been pushing it all down, and now I'm thinking about it, I'm freaking out." Fear pulsed through her body, pursued by a frenzy of excitement. All her fantasies might be about to come true, and she really wasn't ready.

What was it they said? Never meet your heroes? Perhaps never fuck your first crush was on the same ticket.

"Ali, you're overthinking it. Go back to not doing that. You've let this sizzle, which is good. She's someone you're still attracted to. She's clearly attracted to you if you already kissed. I'm assuming you didn't trip up, fall onto a Ferris wheel and accidentally land on her lips?"

The kiss lit up in her mind. "There might have been swooning, but definitely no falling."

"Okay then. My advice is to go with the flow. See where tonight takes you. But if you're sharing a bed, you're bound to kiss again. Then it depends if you're feeling like Maria von Trapp before that dance with the captain, or after."

Ali laughed. "Does everything come down to *The Sound Of Music*?" It was Tobias's favourite film.

"I just watched it, and I still say it was that dance that clinched it. When he holds her and they look into one another's eyes, Maria wants to jump him. Before that, she's happy to dream. You've had your lightning bolt moment. I assume the kiss was good?"

This time, Ali didn't have to work hard to summon the image or the feeling. It had never left.

"It was fucking incredible."

Tobias whistled down the phone. "You don't use words like that very often. You're normally the master of understatement. I'm going to give you some sage advice now, and you will listen. You ready?"

Ali waited. "I'm ready."

"Do not push this off. This is your chance to go after what you want. Your first love. Even if it is terrible fucking timing with you leaving the country next month. But don't think about that. You deserve this. You're fabulous. Have some fun. Live a little."

Fuck. In all the mayhem, she hadn't expected anything to happen. For any feelings to be involved. But she was moving to New York next month. That was an irrefutable fact.

"But what if she doesn't want to have sex?"

"Then she'll tell you."

"And what if we do? What happens afterwards? Should I tell her I'm leaving?"

Even worse, what happened if it was good—*great, even*—but that's where Morgan wanted to leave it? Ali knew it couldn't go anywhere because of her job, but she wanted it to be on her terms. Putting herself out there made her vulnerable. Morgan Scott might stamp on her heart. She wasn't sure she could take that.

"For once in your life, Ali, take a chance. Just do it, sod

the consequences. Go with your heart. Sort everything else out afterwards. What would your teenage self say?"

Ali conjured an image of her younger self in her mind. "Her mind would be blown."

"There's a joke in there, but I'm not sure it works for lesbians," he replied.

She had to smile.

"Just fuck her, Ali."

She heard Snowy meow in the background.

"Snowy agrees with me. If nothing else, do it to make yourself smile. Do it for the moment. If it all goes tits up, at least you'll have a night to remember."

# Chapter Nineteen

Morgan sat back and rubbed her stomach. "That was delicious. Thank you so much, you're both life-savers." She picked a crumb of garlic bread from her jeans—strictly speaking, Helen's jeans—and slipped it into her mouth. "I can't believe you made that pasta from scratch, too."

"I enjoy doing it." Helen's husband Jamie—a 6-foot rugby type who'd made the divine carbonara they'd just devoured—took a sip of his wine. "Helen bought me a pasta-making course for Christmas last year, and now I see the method behind her cunning plan."

"I bought it because you love cooking, dear husband." She gave him a wink.

Next to Morgan, Ali's cheeks had a tell-tale Rioja glow, her chestnut hair back to normal, frost-free and styled thanks to products provided by their hosts. Ali had showered right after Morgan, and then, as if they were staying in some five-star hotel with a laundry service, Helen had collected their clothes and chucked them in the wash. She'd also given them some old jeans and a couple of sweatshirts to wear while their clothes dried. Helen claimed everything they were wearing was destined for the charity shop. Morgan wondered if there was a way she could smuggle the lot back to Devon. Yes, the jeans were a little tight, but Helen had impeccable taste.

"What are your plans for Christmas?" Ali asked Jamie.

"The last guests check out tomorrow, my parents arrive tomorrow night, and then we're having Christmas dinner down the road at The Black Bear. When you've catered for guests the whole year round, a holiday is someone else cooking and washing up for you."

"We're definitely on washing up duty tonight," Ali added.

Jamie shook his head. "Nonsense. Take your drinks through to the lounge and I'll clear up while you catch up. I'll bring dessert through when I'm done."

Helen was up in a flash. "Let's go before he changes his mind." She gave him a wink, and Jamie rolled his eyes. She followed it up with a kiss and led the way through to the lounge.

Morgan loved how easy Helen and Jamie were. The relaxed banter, the loving looks, the way they worked seamlessly together as a couple. It was what she wanted for herself. What her parents and her sister had in their relationships. None of them could quite understand why Morgan didn't have it, either. It was a puzzle that Morgan herself had yet to work out. However, being in this cosy, warm environment made her want it even more. Perhaps there was more to life than work. This couple worked hard, but they did it together, and saw each other all the time. It had been the main gripe of all Morgan's previous relationships that she always put her work first. The trouble was, she hadn't met anyone in the past couple of years that made her want to change that.

In the lounge, Helen squatted and opened the small door on the log burner. She grabbed some logs from the wooden box to her right and stacked them neatly.

"Please, sit," she said, indicating the large squishy sofa on the left.

Ali made an 'after you' gesture with her arm, squeezing Morgan's own as she walked past.

Warmth rolled through Morgan at Ali's touch. Yes, it had been a while since she had a connection with a woman, but in less than 48 hours, Ali had staked her claim. But Morgan wasn't about to go there. She didn't have the brain space, especially not after pasta and wine. Right now, she wanted to sit and relax for the first time in the past two days. Jamie was driving them to their car in the morning. The hire company was sending a replacement. Whisper it, but it looked like they might finally get home for Christmas.

"You've no idea how amazing it is to have a good meal and to sit on a couch, so thank you again." Morgan paused. "You said you didn't live in Devon when you were younger. Did you and Ali see a lot of each other growing up?"

Helen put some kindling between the logs, added a few twigs and small pieces of wood, then lit a long match.

They all watched the fire catch, and Helen blew on it before closing the door. "We'll add a couple more logs when it gets going." For now, it was down to the flames and heat to work their magic.

"My family live in Surrey, but we always made the effort to meet up over summers and Christmas. We went on holiday a lot when we were kids to Bournemouth, didn't we?" Helen said.

Ali nodded. "I have really fond memories of those times. Even though you and Nicole used to bury me in the sand every year. I had a recurring dream I was buried alive throughout my childhood."

Helen laughed as she sat down on the sofa opposite. "Poor Ali. You were always smallest, so always the one to get picked on. But the adults thought you were the cutest."

"I'm still younger than both you and Nicole, so who had the last laugh?" Ali gave her cousin a grin.

"You, clearly. Although Nicole will always be a year older than me, and I cling to that." Helen swilled her wine around her glass. Through the door, glasses clinked as Jamie cleared up. "He's a keeper, that one," Helen added.

Morgan nodded. "Any spouse who likes to cook is one to be cherished."

Helen glanced at Ali, as if weighing up her next sentence. Morgan caught the hesitation.

Next to her, Ali clutched her glass that bit tighter.

"A little like your dad," Helen said eventually.

Ali visibly flinched.

"I remember his amazing lasagne, which he always cooked every summer, even when it was boiling outside. 'It's always lasagne weather', Uncle Tony would say." Helen smiled. "And he always joined in with the sand-burying antics." She paused. "How are things with everyone now?"

Ali cleared her throat. "They're okay. I haven't been back since… since everything."

"Understandable," Helen replied. "I was so sorry when I heard, and even sorrier we couldn't make the funeral. It happened so quickly and we were still on holiday."

Funeral? Morgan twisted to look at Ali, but she didn't meet her gaze.

"It's fine, really. He had many people there to see him off. It was a lovely service and a great turnout. And yes, he was buried within ten days, which is unheard of. There was obviously a dearth of deaths this summer. My dad led the trend into autumn."

Morgan flicked her eyes from Helen to Ali, then back. She didn't want to say anything right now. This was a family moment, and she should shut up. But Tony Bradford was dead? This was news. She remembered him with great fondness.

Why hadn't Ali said anything? They'd talked about going home, about the pub, about their families, and Ali hadn't mentioned it once.

"Getting home this year is a big deal, then. Being with your family for Christmas?"

Ali gave the most noncommittal shrug. "I guess." She gathered herself, then looked directly at Helen. "I mean, yes. It is. I know they're probably thinking I engineered this travel chaos to limit my time at home, but I really didn't."

"Do you need to call them?"

Ali shook her head. "I've been messaging Nicole, she knows we're here and we're leaving tomorrow." She flicked her gaze to Morgan. "She probably wants more details on me travelling with Morgan, to be honest."

Morgan reached out and put a hand on Ali's knee. The electricity was palpable. "I'm really sorry." She hoped her face conveyed her sincerity.

"Thanks," Ali whispered.

For just a moment, it was the two of them again, inside their cocoon. Morgan caught Ali's wounded stare. She wanted to reach out and make it all better. Wrap her arms around Ali and take the pain away. Even if just for a few moments. But now wasn't the time.

Helen's voice broke the spell. "But Uncle Tony wouldn't want us to wallow. Plus, I know he'd be thrilled about you two. How long have you been together?"

Morgan blinked, stared at Ali, then turned to Helen. "We're not together."

Ali shook her head. "No."

Helen raised both eyebrows in an unspoken question, then fixed her gaze on Ali's thigh, where Morgan's hand still rested. "You're not? I just assumed…"

Morgan snatched her hand back, then shook her head. "No, we're just old friends, as we said at dinner. I mean, we sometimes see each other when we both go home, but we've never hooked up." Why was she over explaining? "When I say hooked up, I don't mean *hooked up*."

*Oh god, make it stop. Somebody put a plug in my mouth.*

But no, Morgan wasn't done. "More, we've had a drink, said hi. Whenever I see Ali, she's behind the bar or in the pub. We've never really had a conversation on our own, have we?"

As soon as Morgan said it, she realised how stupid that was. All these wasted years, when actually, they got on. They coped together in a crisis. Plus, Ali was kind, resourceful, hot. Why had she never seen that before? Because she'd never looked. That was the stupidest thing of all. But she was looking now, and Morgan liked what she saw.

Ali shook her head, a sad look in her eye. "You were always Nicole's friend. I was the kid sister. We had our roles."

A silence descended on the room as everyone digested that. "But now?"

Helen's question was cut off as Jamie walked in with a tray of Bailey's and a round of homemade tiramisu in individual glass dishes. "I was up at the crack of dawn making these, so I hope you enjoy, ladies." He put the tray on the coffee table with the precision of a gymnast. "Now, what or who were we talking about?"

"We were just discussing how Ali and Morgan are definitely not a couple." Helen could barely contain her smirk.

Jamie sat beside his wife and cast his gaze on the two of them. "Aren't you?" he asked.

# Chapter Twenty

One Bailey's had turned into two, and then into cheese and port, and before she knew it, they were playing a card game with no boundaries, and sharing another bottle of red. By the time they tripped up the stairs to bed, it was gone midnight, and they had to be up at eight to get going.

However, it had all been worth it. Ali loved Helen and Jamie, and it had been fabulous to finally relax after two days of what-the-fuck. She'd probably have said no to that last glass of wine if she was at home or in a normal situation. But she wasn't. Accepting that last glass of wine meant she had another half hour delay to the inevitable moment of going to bed with Morgan. It also meant she had another layer of liquid confidence to take with her. In the morning, she'd think that was a mistake.

But tonight, it was everything.

Ali rolled over in the bed. Her phone was on the side table. She picked it up. There was a message from Tobias that simply said, 'Don't overthink it.' Easy for him to say.

She also had one from Nicole. 'Is there something going on that you need to tell me?' Ali's heart flipped. The family inquisition was going to be worse than anything the Spanish had ever faced. For now, though, she tuned that out and focused on what Tobias had said.

In the guest bathroom, she heard the light go off, then the bedroom door open.

Then there was Morgan.

Every delicious ounce of her.

Ali gulped, suddenly overcome with nerves. This wasn't a sure thing, but then again, she felt like it was the surest thing ever.

They hadn't had a date. They'd just had a single dreamy kiss in the snow, on a Ferris wheel. Where the stars had aligned and the world had seemed brighter. Time had stood still. Possibilities seemed endless. But she had no idea where they were with each other. This was the first time they'd had alone since that kiss. And now, they were about to sleep in the same bed again.

Maybe Morgan would get in and they'd go right to sleep. She'd be absolutely fine with that. They had a big day tomorrow, and getting home in time for Christmas was the most important thing. Plus, there was New York.

And yet somehow, in the past 48 hours, Morgan had crept onto her list of most important things, too.

What had Tobias told her? 'Don't overthink it. Live in the moment.'

Easy for him to say, sat at home vogueing with her cat.

Morgan clearing her throat made Ali look up.

"We meet again." Could she have come up with a dumber line? She didn't think so. Even though Ali had known Morgan's emergence was imminent, she wasn't ready.

She had to remind herself to breathe.

Morgan gave her a shy smile, then put the clothes she was holding on the chair by the dressing table, neatly folded. Morgan was a neat person. After 48 hours together, Ali knew this already. She glanced at her clothes, thrown on the floor.

Morgan would have to take her as she was. There was no masking the truth on this trip.

Ali tracked Morgan's path to the bed, her legs long and lean, her stomach flat. She wore black knickers and a black T-shirt (courtesy of Helen). A tickertape ran through Ali's mind: 'What's underneath???'

When Morgan slipped under the covers, Ali took a sharp intake of breath.

*Subtle. Really subtle.*

They lay in silence for a few moments, the only sound the low rumble of Helen and Jamie's voices from along the hallway. It was Morgan who broke first.

"I'm really sorry about your dad. I always liked him."

The muscles in Ali's jaw clenched. "Thanks. Everyone said the same."

"Because it's true." Morgan paused. "How is your family doing with it?"

Ali steadied her breathing as much as she could. What was the answer? She didn't know. She'd steadfastly avoided going back since his funeral. She didn't want to deal with the fact he was dead, so she'd swept it under the carpet. She'd left Nicole, Stuart, and her mum to pick up the pieces and carry on. She'd gone back to her life and pretended like nothing had happened. That charade would have to end soon.

"Honestly? I have no fucking idea. I call them, they call me, we message. We even have the occasional Zoom. But we don't really talk about it. I'm sure they do without me. They must do. And sometimes Nicole calls me and tries to talk, but I always have some place to go, something to do. I always have an excuse. Because I don't want to deal with it." She shook her head. "I know that's wrong of me. I know it's not what my family needs, but it's how I cope."

Morgan reached under the covers and took Ali's hand in hers.

It was warm, comforting.

Ali let her.

"Everyone copes with grief differently. I know that was the case when my granddad died. Same with my nan. Mum fell to pieces, we all picked up the slack. Don't be so hard on yourself."

Ali tipped her head to the ceiling. She admired the cornicing on the central light before she replied.

"True, but I had a choice. I could leave. They couldn't. They had to stay and deal with everyone knowing. Be in the place where he'd lived his life every single day. I couldn't stand that. Even being there for the week after his death leading up to the funeral was stifling. I could leave, so I did. I'm sure that makes me a terrible person."

Morgan squeezed her hand. "I think that makes you a normal person." Her thumb stroked the palm of Ali's hand.

Ali felt it everywhere. Suddenly, the room became louder, just like her heartbeat inside her. She turned to face Morgan, and she could see it all in Morgan's eyes. The sympathy for her dad's death, the understanding of how she'd reacted.

Ali didn't want any of it.

She'd run away from her family, run away from what had happened. She didn't deserve understanding.

Right now, she certainly didn't want Morgan's sad puppy eyes on her. She wanted Morgan's lips.

Ali's brain and body agreed.

"You know, I'm always here if you need a sympathetic ear. If you want to talk. I knew your dad, but I'm not directly involved, so maybe that makes me the perfect person?"

Ali had heard enough.

"Morgan." She twisted her body to face her. She had no idea where to start. No idea where this was going. But all she knew was she wanted to get off the topic of her dad. If the only way she could do that was to cover Morgan's lips with her own, then so be it. Ali moved forward until their lips were within inches of each other. "I just want to pretend we're back on the Ferris wheel, back in that magical moment. I don't want to talk about my dad. Not when I'm in bed with you. I want to kiss you again. You think we could do that instead?"

There was a moment of hesitation on Morgan's face before her features relaxed. She nodded. "I think that can be arranged."

Morgan's smooth fingers glided across Ali's cheek; her scorched gaze lasered Ali's soul.

Ali took a steadying breath. They hadn't even kissed yet, but this was already a level up from the Ferris wheel. That had been surprise, shock. This was not. But it was years of Ali's dreams on the line.

Morgan's nose slid next to Ali's, her mouth tantalisingly close. She looked into Ali's eyes, silently asking the question.

Ali's gaze didn't waver, giving Morgan her answer.

But even though Ali knew the kiss was coming, she still wasn't prepared. When Morgan's lips met hers, a cannon of gold confetti exploded inside her, and her mind and body soared. Everything else in the room fell away, apart from Morgan's lips. She'd had her eyes on the prize for two decades. Finally grasping it in her hands was almost dreamlike.

Morgan moaned into Ali's mouth, then her tongue parted Ali's lips and slid inside.

Ali sucked her in. She wanted every part of Morgan Scott. She'd wanted it when she caught her gaze earlier in the card game. She'd wanted it when their fingers had accidentally collided when they reached for the pepper grinder. She'd definitely wanted it this morning when she woke up with Morgan lying next to her, but strictly out of bounds.

This morning, she'd had to grin and bear it. Soldier on.

What a difference a day made.

Now, Morgan's sure hands were on her hips, pulling her close, and her lips were brush strokes to Ali's soul.

"You sure about this?" If Morgan's voice was faint, her fingers were anything but.

Ali couldn't find the words, but she'd never been surer of anything in her entire life. In reply, she simply kissed Morgan even more furiously than before.

Morgan's hands were a blur as they stole over Ali's skin like moonlight.

They both pulled back in unison to throw off their T-shirts and shed their underwear. Tonight wasn't the night for tiptoeing. Maybe that night would come. This wasn't about luxury or five-star service. Tonight was about vital pleasure, and Ali was determined to be in the driving seat. So much so, when she pushed Morgan onto her back and climbed on top of her—exactly the way she'd dreamed Morgan might do to her—Morgan's face spelt surprise.

"I wasn't expecting that." A satisfied smile crossed her features.

Ali leaned down and ran her tongue slowly along Morgan's

top lip. "I'm full of surprises." Ali didn't know whose voice was coming out of her mouth, but it was husky and knew what it wanted. She nibbled on Morgan's lip, and felt her shake beneath her.

Ali sat up.

Morgan stroked both hands up and down Ali's sides, her focus fixed.

Ali wanted to drink in the look on Morgan's face forever. It was as if Ali was a work of art, and Morgan simply couldn't stop staring.

The feeling was mutual.

Ali ran her hands over Morgan's full breasts, just as she'd dreamed of doing when she was a teenager. If you held on long enough, dreams could come true. When she leaned down and took Morgan's right nipple into her mouth, Morgan gasped.

Ali sank into the lush sound. Into Morgan's bergamot scent. She made sure she gave Morgan everything she had. She'd never forgive herself otherwise.

"I can't believe this is really happening," she rasped, before she could even think about what she was saying. She should have been embarrassed. But there was no time.

Before Ali could process another thought, Morgan slid her hand between Ali's legs and slipped a finger into her.

Electric wonder shot through Ali, then her eyes went wide. She'd nearly sprained her fingers a few times trying the same trick, but Morgan was a natural. Ali rolled her hips, then gently ground down on Morgan.

Taking the encouragement, Morgan slid another finger inside.

Ali let out a sound she'd never be able to name. One she'd

never uttered before. It was the one she'd been saving for 20 years. The one reserved for when Morgan Scott finally fucked her. Ali's insides roared as she melted into her.

She fell forward, crushed her mouth to Morgan's once more, and let the moment wash over her. If she was riding Morgan Scott, she was going to do it in style. Low and slow. Every part of her pulsed as Morgan's fingers eased around inside her. Ali could feel how wet she was.

When she'd imagined this in her younger years, it had never been like this. Then, Morgan had taken her against a wall, crushed her to a bed. She'd dominated Ali. But that was a fantasy from her youth. Now she was up close, a private audience with Morgan Scott was more than living up to its billing. The later-life version of Morgan was more rough around the edges, but that only added to her charm. A charm that had sparkled for Ali ever since they met.

Now, Morgan had Ali in the palm of her hand.

Literally.

They stayed like that for a few more exquisite moments, Morgan locking Ali in with her intense sapphire gaze. Her blonde hair was mussed, her cheeks red. She looked absolutely, intensely, momentously gorgeous. As Morgan's stare drilled into her, a crush of lust looped between them, holding Ali in place with its force. She swirled her hips, desire drenching her from the inside out. She'd never felt so filled, so satiated in her life. She stilled, never wanting to leave this bubble. Euphoria bubbled inside. Ali had to hold it together.

Which she did. Right up until Morgan shifted under her. She gently nudged Ali off her and got to her knees, mirroring Ali's stance, twisting her hand with crazy skill. Morgan stared into Ali's eyes, her own irises dark pools of want, before kissing Ali's lips with the lightest of touches.

It made Ali's head spin. Then she was on her back as Morgan straddled her, her breasts tantalising, her lips wet. Morgan's hands were all over her, sliding, fucking, driving Ali on. She didn't need much encouragement.

"You feel so good." Morgan's thick, honeyed voice nearly tipped Ali over the edge.

She was so close. Ali opened her eyes, and they locked gazes again.

Morgan thrust into her and held it. Then she leaned down again, her fingers steady.

Her hot breath tickled Ali's ear.

"Come for me, Ali," Morgan whispered.

Ali didn't need a second invitation. As Morgan pressed home her advantage, sparks flared inside. Seconds later, years of pent-up desire rattled through her, and Ali came undone under Morgan's sure, smooth touch. She spread her legs and threw back her head, revelling in the moment. Then she hooked her arm around Morgan's neck and pulled her in for a kiss that shook her very bones.

Morgan kept her fingers just where Ali needed them, and in seconds, with Morgan urging her on, she came again.

Ali clung to Morgan, heart pounding, everything she possessed hot and raw.

This was a night Ali would never forget, even if this was the extent of it. Of them. The last glass of wine had been worth it. The heart palpitations had been worth it. Every moment of the past two decades that she'd lived through had led to this. She didn't want to go to sleep, but she knew it wasn't far off.

She certainly didn't want to wake up tomorrow, just in case the spell was broken.

Whatever happened next—and she hoped that involved fucking Morgan Scott into the night—they'd always have tonight.

For now, that was all that mattered.

# Chapter Twenty-One

Morgan cracked an eye open and took a moment to work out where she was. Still very far from home. With the world's most genial hosts.

Naked in bed with Ali Bradford.

She couldn't help but smile at that last part.

She glanced right and revelled in the warmth of having Ali beside her. Another living, breathing human. It'd been a while since it'd happened.

Morgan flicked through the sex cards in her head. When had the last time been? Edna Shelly. Morgan remembered that name, because who their age was called Edna? It was the name of your great aunt, not the name of someone you ended up in bed with. But Edna Shelly had been hot. Also very married to a man, a tourist for the night. Which, judging by how much she knew her way around a woman's body, was not the first time she'd played away. She'd asked Morgan if they could carry on as fuck buddies. Romantic as the suggestion had been, Morgan had told her no. That was the last time anyone had touched her until last night.

Even though Edna had been good, she had nothing on Ali.

For a first time, last night had been incredible. There had been such an ease between them, even though it had sprung out of Ali avoiding talking about her dad. But the sex had been... more than just sex. They'd connected. When Ali had fucked her, Morgan had responded in a way she never had before. As if Ali could see right through her. As if her fingers had unlocked something inside.

They had. An almighty orgasm, which Morgan's whole body responded to when she replayed it in her mind. The smile that followed was so broad it made her jaw click. But it was more than just physical. There was something else there. Maybe it was because she knew Ali.

Morgan shook her head. Just because she knew where Ali went to school, why would that make the sex great? Whatever it was, the connection they had stunned her. When Ali was inside her, Morgan never wanted her to leave. Had Ali felt it too?

She wasn't about to ask. Last night was one night. She wasn't about to build a future on it.

A movement beside her made Morgan look down.

Ali's tousled walnut hair stuck to her peachy cheek. Morgan wanted to reach down and kiss it, but that wasn't first-morning behaviour.

"Morning, sunshine." Morgan turned and propped herself up on her elbow. "How you feeling?"

Ali made a noise, then covered her face with her hands. "Embarrassed. Did I make a fool of myself last night?"

Morgan blinked. "From my memory, no. You did a lot of things, but making a fool of yourself wasn't one of them."

"Right."

"You remember last night, yes? I'm not alone in remembering the hot sex?"

Thankfully, Ali smiled. "No, I remember that. I was talking about before. When we were playing games. I think I was asking too many questions of Helen and Jamie."

Morgan shook her head. "They're old enough to cope. Plus, we'd all had wine."

"It seemed a good idea last night."

"It *was* a good idea." Morgan gulped, then snagged Ali's gaze. "I don't regret what happened one bit."

Ali's cheeks flushed. She shook her head. "I don't, either."

And then Morgan didn't care how she came across. She needed a kiss from Ali, and only her lips would do. She leaned down and acted on impulse. Just like that, she was transported back to last night. To how right it felt, to the bliss of getting to know Ali up close and personal. This morning's kissing mirrored last night. It was too perfect. Also, far too fragile. She wanted to tiptoe around it, but also to show them off to the world.

Moments later, they came up for air, but stayed within striking distance. The only sound their shallow breathing, plus the thud of Morgan's heartbeat in her chest. If she leaned forward, she bet she'd hear Ali's heartbeat, too. Was she wondering where this went next?

There was, of course, an easy way to find out. Morgan could just ask. But it wasn't that easy. 'Hey, was this just a one-off thing for you, or could you see us repeating?' Morgan had no idea what this was herself, so it was unfair to ask Ali. Even if she desperately wanted to.

*Do not be needy.*

Instead, she focused on Ali's lips. It was so much easier to kiss them, and leave the talking to another time.

Ali had thought so last night, too, when Morgan had asked about her dad.

Sex was always easier than talking.

Morgan ran her fingertips over Ali's slim waist.

Ali shivered.

Outside, a door slammed.

Ali cleared her throat, but held Morgan's gaze. Morgan could almost see the thoughts racing through Ali's mind, because they were racing through hers, too. Even if they both wanted to talk, get answers to their questions, they didn't have time.

Morgan blinked, then stretched her arms above her head. "I guess we should get up. It's Christmas Eve, and we need to drive home, hope our luggage arrives, and turn up at our childhood homes before Santa does."

"Do you think we're on the naughty list?" Ali raised a suggestive eyebrow.

"After last night, I certainly hope so."

\* \* \*

The hire car company called soon after to let them know they'd meet them at Christmas Court at midday. All of which meant they had some time to kill before they had to leave to drop off the bike and pick up the car. Jamie shooed them all out, telling Helen to drive Ali and Morgan to the nearest village to do a spot of last-minute Christmas shopping.

"Are you sure? We've got guests to check out and the rooms to clean."

"It's four rooms. I've done it before. Plus, when do you ever get to spend time with your cousin otherwise?" Jamie flapped his hands at them all. "Go, before I change my mind and have you all cleaning the loos."

That brought a smile to Helen's face. "You heard the man."

They parked the car at the top of the main street, and Ali pulled her mustard scarf tight. She was in clean clothes for the first time in a few days, which felt amazing. She wasn't sure how the chat was going to roll once she was alone in their car with Morgan, but she'd worry about that when she got there. For now, she was going to revel in what was in front of her. And that was a picture-perfect Christmas village.

The main street swept down before them, a blaze of independent local shops selling gifts, plants, clothes and walking gear, along with a variety of pubs, cafes, restaurants and bakeries. The streetlamps were hung with festive lights, the snow cleared and the pavements gritted. However, even with the morning sun low in the milky blue sky, the cold still lingered in the brittle air.

"I want to show you these gorgeous gingerbread houses they do at the bakery. I always thought gingerbread was for American Christmas movies, but it turns out, rural Cumbria is mad for them too!" Helen walked them over to the bakery, its windows covered in glittery Christmas signage. But what truly drew the eye were the gingerbread houses on display in the window. Not just houses, but also shops, hotels, and even a gingerbread pub.

The pub was named The Rising Sun. Just like hers back home. Ali's eyes filled up when she saw it. She could still picture her dad behind the bar, even though she knew he wasn't there anymore.

Morgan pressed her nose to the shop's glass. "Does that pub sign say what I think it does?"

Ali went to nod, but only smacked her forehead against the glass as she peered too close. She let out a yelp and held her head.

"Are you okay?" Helen asked.

"You should ask the glass that." Ali gave a wry grin as she took her hand away. Her forehead still smarted. "But it says The Rising Sun, doesn't it?"

Morgan nodded. "You think it's a sign?"

"That there are a lot of pubs called The Rising Sun?"

Morgan's Christmas pudding hat tilted. "That I should buy it for you?"

"What? No, don't be silly. How would we carry it home?"

"We're in a car. Did your dad like gingerbread?"

"Hated it." She was being awkward, but she couldn't stop herself.

Morgan paused. "What about the rest of your family?"

Ali relented. "They like it."

"Then I think this is a must-buy. You said it yourself, this Christmas will be a different one for you all. Wouldn't it be nice to turn up with this?"

Ali rubbed her forehead, then eyed Morgan. She'd been avoiding thinking about going home, but this brought it all back. Where she came from. What had changed. What she was going to have to face. She took a deep breath. Her mum would love it, as would Nicole. Plus, it was brilliantly intricate.

"You were the one who wanted to make a gingerbread house. Now you're buying me one?"

"Christmas is all about sharing and giving." Morgan

winked, then disappeared into the bakery. She pointed at the gingerbread pub, and the woman behind the counter gently removed it from the window, then put it in a box.

Beside Ali, Helen tapped the window. "You're lucky. I was speaking to Laura who runs the bakery yesterday, and they've already sold most of these. The pub was the only one still available. Maybe Morgan's right and it *is* a sign. I forgot that was the name of your pub, too."

Helen stared at Morgan as she paid, then turned back to Ali. "Are you sure there's nothing going on between you two? Because I'm definitely picking up a vibe. Plus, you don't rush into a bakery and buy someone a gingerbread pub if you don't care for them. Especially when the recipient isn't the most amenable."

Ali tried as hard as she could to keep her poker face. "We're just friends."

The look Helen gave her told Ali she didn't believe a word of it. However, for now, Ali wasn't ready for whatever they were to be public knowledge. Because if she said it aloud to someone else, that made what had happened true. Then, when it inevitably went nowhere, she'd be doubly sad. If she just kept it inside for now, she could manage it. Especially as she had enough to contend with when she got home.

Only now, Morgan stood in front of her, holding out a white cake box with a transparent lid, the gingerbread pub inside.

Ali blinked back tears. What on earth was going on? It was just a stack of biscuits with icing. But Morgan had bought it for her. Morgan knew what the original Rising Sun meant to Ali. Home. Family. Even though that was forever changed, this gingerbread pub was still standing, still making people smile. Just like the real thing.

A lump formed in Ali's throat. She wasn't going to get emotional. Not in front of Helen, or in front of Morgan.

Instead, she gave Morgan a tight smile. "Thank you. Mum's going to love it."

"And she'll try to eat it at the first opportunity if I know my aunt," Helen added.

Ali bit her lip. *Keep it together.*

"Can I have the car keys so I can put this in it? I don't want to risk it getting broken."

Helen nodded and handed Morgan the keys. "We'll either be in the Paddings Gift Shop, or else Jen's Boutique."

Morgan took the keys and turned towards the car.

Ali watched her go. Buying her that was a super-sweet gesture. The more time she spent with Morgan Scott, the sweeter she became. Sweet and hot, the very best combination.

She followed Helen's lead, walking along the pavement as the cold air needled her face. She spied the gift shop up ahead, and they dodged a slew of last-minute shoppers before they went in.

"There's some great local gin in here I want to buy for Jamie. He loves it," Helen told her.

The shop sold a mix of clothes, things to eat and drink, and high-end gifts. It was just the sort of place Ali loved. She stopped near the candles and picked up some rosemary and lavender pillars for her sister. If their luggage didn't make it in time with Ali's original gifts, Nicole would love these. She grabbed a rich orange cashmere scarf for her mum, and a bottle of expensive olive oil for Nicole's husband Stuart, who loved to cook. As Morgan said, they had a car that hopefully worked. They should make the most of it.

She headed to the cash desk, but stopped when she saw some gorgeous dark green leather gloves. Morgan. She needed a gift for her, too, and these were just the thing.

A loop of Morgan's hands running across Ali's back last night made her zone out. She sank into the moment. Morgan was great with her hands, but she was severely lacking in accessories for them. Next time she got stranded, Ali was determined Morgan would be fully equipped. She grabbed a basket, put her purchases in, then picked up the gloves: they were as soft as Morgan's backside.

*Baby soft.*

Ali couldn't help but beam again. She had presents for everyone who was important in her life. Mum, Nicole, Stuart, Morgan. Morgan had made the headline list. She wasn't going to dwell on what that might mean.

"Are you buying the entire shop?" Helen's face appeared by her shoulder.

"Looks like it," Ali replied. "Just in case our luggage doesn't show up. I can't turn up empty-handed, can I? Luckily, Mum already bought my gift for Harrison. Not sure he'd be impressed with a candle and a tea towel of the Lakes."

"I doubt he would." Helen stilled. "Any of those for Morgan?"

Heat rushed to Ali's cheeks. "Just one. I had to buy her something after what she just bought, didn't I?"

Helen gave her a knowing smile. "I'm not sure why you're trying to deny there's something between you. Did something happen before? Like, in the past?"

Ali shook her head. "No. But maybe it could." Damn it, she was terrible at keeping secrets. "She's Nicole's friend, so it's tangled." Even more so after last night, but Helen didn't need to know that.

"Sometimes things get tangled for a reason. Maybe tangled is good. It means she knows what she's getting into, and vice versa. One thing I know from spending time with you both? The feelings are mutual. I could light a match with the chemistry between you."

Ali chewed on that for a second. Had they really been that obvious even before anything happened? What was it Morgan had said in the car? That she wanted to meet someone who she already knew. That she didn't want to meet someone on a dating site, she wanted to do it the old-fashioned way. Ali wasn't sure a disastrous Christmas trip home counted as old-fashioned, but the two of them did. They'd known each other forever, but never actually stopped and considered what had always been there.

Now, maybe they should?

Ali might, if it wasn't for New York.

"Any of that for me?" Morgan's voice startled both Helen and Ali.

Ali clutched her hand to her chest and shielded the basket. "No, but it would probably be better if you didn't see. Just in case you tell my mum I've bought her a chrome rabbit and spoil the surprise." Ali nodded at Helen. "Why don't you put that bottle on the counter and I'll pay for it as a thank you for everything."

Helen shook her head.

Ali held up a palm. "I don't want any arguments. How

about you take Morgan across the road while I pay? See you in the boutique?"

Helen nodded. "If you're sure." Then she put an arm around Morgan and steered her out of the shop.

# Chapter Twenty-Two

Morgan gave Helen and Jamie an enormous hug. "You've no idea what your hospitality meant after the 48 hours we had before. I feel like whatever happens on this leg of the journey, we can deal with it now. Particularly since the Nurofen Plus have finally kicked my hangover and I'm ready to roll."

That got a laugh from everyone.

Ali followed it up with a bear hug for her cousin and Jamie, glancing over Helen's shoulder at the impressive Christmas Court. Behind the stone castle was the Ferris wheel where her and Morgan's story had begun, less than 24 hours earlier. Of course, the full story started way before that. You could call them a slow burn. She still couldn't quite believe they'd only kissed for the first time yesterday. Now, they were back in the car park with their new grey Ford Focus—a carbon copy of the old one, albeit with a working engine.

"I echo everything that Morgan said," Ali told her cousin. "Staying with you has been a real bright spot on our ill-fated journey."

"You're welcome anytime. Both of you." Helen sent a pointed stare in Ali's direction. "We're not that far if your transport works."

They waved until their hosts were out of sight, then got into their new hire car. This afternoon, the sky was overcast, with the sun breaking through intermittently. It was a vast improvement on the last few days. Critically, there was no snow forecast.

"They have to be one of the most welcoming couples I've ever met. If I could meet a partner like Jamie, but female, that would be perfect. Someone who's funny, charming and cooks like a dream." Morgan glanced Ali's way. "What are you like in the kitchen?"

Ali wanted to melt into her seat.

"I make a mean tortilla." Her stomach lurched. The words 'New York' flashed in her mind.

"Tortilla is a good start."

Ali's phone buzzed in its holder before Morgan could say anymore. She'd never been more relieved.

She leaned in, pressed a few buttons, then clenched her fist in triumph. "Our luggage is due to land at Exeter airport this afternoon and will be ready to pick up between 4–7pm."

Morgan leaned forward and keyed in the details to their sat nav. "It's 12:15, and sat nav reckons it'll take five and a half hours to get to the airport. What are the chances?"

"We're going to make it. I need my case." Ali adjusted her seat, then her mirrors. "Only essential loo breaks, otherwise we'll just drive. Then another hour to get home after that."

"So long as we don't break down again."

"Don't jinx it!"

"You think this trip isn't already jinxed?"

"Fair point." Ali smiled, then settled her hands on the steering wheel. She nodded to the imposing main building on their right. "This is where it all began. The Ferris wheel. The snow. That kiss." Ali paused. "I know it's been a clusterfuck of bad luck, but there's been some good, too, wouldn't you say? Plus, I might not be Christmas-crazy like your family, but I've always loved Christmas Eve. A time when anything is possible. I think this Christmas Eve is living up to that billing, don't you?"

"Yes, I do." Morgan licked her lips.

Ali reached out and put a hand on Morgan's thigh.

Morgan trembled under her touch.

As amazing as that felt, she knew they had to talk. That she had to tell her. Morgan had bought her a gingerbread pub and nearly made her cry, after all.

"But while I love your nostalgia, I'm hoping one of those possibilities is that we can get home today. You think we can give it a go?" She brought Ali's hand to her lips and kissed it. "I've no idea if that's allowed, but I just did it. Shall we see if we can find some festive songs on the radio and style out the awkwardness?" She gave Ali a shy smile.

In response, and even though her mind screamed at her to stop, Ali leaned over and planted a smacker on Morgan's lips. So quick and so sure, it was almost like it didn't happen.

But Ali's body knew. She sucked in an unsteady breath before she dared to look Morgan's way.

"There are many things I find awkward, but kissing you isn't one of them."

*Way to go muddying the playing field, Ali.*

She tapped the furry festive dice, rescued from the old car, and started the engine. "Let's go home, shall we?"

\* \* \*

Ali cut the engine and unclicked her seat belt. Her tongue felt furry and her eyes tired. They'd made it to the airport in five and a half hours, just like the sat nav promised. Incredibly, traffic had been light, and they'd amused themselves with the radio and a little light chat. But nothing heavy. No mention of last night, of her dad, of their future. The weight of the unspoken hovered in the air, but they both skilfully avoided it. Morgan had even slept through some of their journey, while Ali had run through every ending they might have. None of them came out with the word 'happy' stamped on the front. 'Wrong place, wrong time' was the verdict in all of her disappointing day dreams.

But for now, with transport on their trip finally working, she was going to put a brave face on it. They just had to collect their luggage and get home. Then she'd deal with whatever came her way. One hour at a time.

"Everything okay?" Morgan's gentle, concerned voice broke into her thoughts.

Ali blinked, then nodded. "All fine." She stared at Morgan, gulped, then got out of the car.

A gust of icy wind whipped through her. She shivered and got her duffel coat and scarf from the backseat. She waited for Morgan to get her coat before they both scuttled to the terminal. Once inside, they stamped their feet as if shaking off the cold. It wasn't snowing like it had been up north, but it was still the kind of cold that burrowed into your bones. Ali glanced around and located the luggage desk in seconds.

The bloke behind the counter was dressed in what looked like his school uniform. He scowled when they approached. It was 6pm on Christmas Eve. He probably wasn't best pleased to be at work. "Can I help?" His accent was pure Devon, and immediately made Ali relax. She knew this place. Despite not living here anymore, it was still home.

"We're picking up our cases from the delayed Glasgow flight. Loganair LM4015?" She tried to put as much pep in her speech as possible to show the man she appreciated him still being here at six o'clock on Christmas Eve.

"You're lucky. I was just about to close up and go home." He eyed them over his glasses. "Do you want to come and identify your luggage?"

They followed him through and immediately saw their cases. Relief swept through Ali. Maybe things on this trip had turned a corner.

"You've both got the same case?"

Ali nodded. "We do."

"Two-for-one deal?" He gave Ali a knowing smile.

Did he think they were a couple too, just like Helen and Jamie? It seemed like everyone did bar them.

Morgan's cheeks were red as they wheeled their suitcases back onto the main concourse.

Ali headed back the way they came, towards the main door. An elderly man walked by with his trolley, and she stopped to let him through. When he looked up, his face broke into a broad smile.

"It's you! My Devon travellers. You weren't on the plane. How did you get here?" It was the man from the plane. His broad Glaswegian accent coated the air like honey.

That made Ali smile as well. Devon might be home, but so was Glasgow. He still looked like the sort of man who might star in a Werther's commercial, and then sit on the porch with a glass of sherry. Very unlike her granddad, who was far more at home sipping pint after pint of wine.

Morgan stepped forward, a smile on her face. "Good to see you again. Did you say you were on the plane? Were you in Glasgow all that time?"

"I was," he continued. "They offered to put me up in a hotel, but I went home instead. Two-day delay, but I got here eventually. Although my daughter's car isn't working, and there are no taxis would you believe, so I've hired a car with a sat nav. My daughter says it's easy to work, but she would, wouldn't she?" He gave them a broad smile, then pulled his grey scarf tighter around his neck. "Just bracing myself for the cold."

They could have just stayed in Glasgow. Ali had to laugh. Although, if they'd stayed in Glasgow, they'd have missed out on so much. Getting reacquainted with each other. Having an adventure. Riding a bicycle made for two in a snowstorm. Ali glanced at Morgan, and she could see a smile at the edges of her mouth, too. She was glad they'd done it the hard way. Because it had led to them, and the past 24 hours. Whatever happened next, that had been worth it.

"Where are you headed?" Ali asked.

"She lives in a place called Dartmouth."

Morgan put a hand to her face. "That's where we're going. We could have given you a lift. You've already hired your car?"

The man nodded. "Bought and paid for. I don't mind, it'll give me a bit of independence when I'm there. My daughter seems to think now I'm 70 I need to be treated with kid gloves." He leaned forward. "Spoiler alert: I don't." He grinned at them. "Anyway, I better go. I want to get there before it snows again.

It was lovely to see you both." He put a hand to his chest. "I'm Walt, by the way."

"If you're in Dartmouth, pop by The Rising Sun for a drink. It's my family's pub." Ali gave him a grin.

"I might just do that. Especially now I can drive wherever I want." He gripped his trolley. "You both have a lovely Christmas." He tilted his head. "You make a great couple, if you don't mind me saying. My daughter's partner is a woman, and they've got a couple of smashing kids too. I was together with my wife for 45 years and I loved every minute. I carry on living well on her behalf, but I'd give it all up to have more time with her. You've both got time, so make the most of it." He leaned over and patted Ali on the arm. "But now it's my time to do battle with a sat nav."

Ali watched him go in silence. It wasn't until Walt was out of sight that she turned to Morgan.

Her face was pensive.

"How come everyone we meet thinks we're a couple? Do we scream 'couple'?"

Morgan ran a hand through her blonde hair. "Apparently, we do." She paused. "Do we need to have a chat about that?"

Ali nodded.

It was time.

# Chapter Twenty-Three

Morgan lifted both suitcases into the boot, shrugged off her coat, then threw herself into the front seat. She rubbed her hands together and blew on them. Still cold. She glanced over at Ali.

The frost wasn't just in the air. It was in this car, too. Morgan had a foreboding feeling about whatever it was Ali was about to tell her.

Ali started the engine, then cut it. She unclicked her seat belt and turned to Morgan.

Morgan took a breath, then mirrored her movement.

"Why do I get the feeling you don't feel the same as everyone else about how we should move forward with whatever this is?" She moved her hand between them as she finished her sentence.

Ali licked her lips, then sighed. "It's not for the reasons you think."

Morgan waited for her to say more. Outside, it started to snow again. It had been the soundtrack to their journey from the start.

"There's something I haven't told you about me."

Morgan's stomach sank. She gripped the sides of the seat and braced. "You've got a girlfriend? A wife? Three children?"

She tried to say it as lightly as she could, but it wasn't how she was feeling. Darts of pain sank into her brain as a carousel of scenarios played out in her head. Not one of them good.

Luckily, her words brought a smile to Ali's face, and she shook her head. "No, I am one hundred per cent single. Available."

"Phew."

"But."

"I was waiting for the but."

"I'm leaving the country in three weeks."

A punch in the gut. She hadn't been expecting that.

"I got a work placement in New York. Six months to start, but then it might go longer. It depends on the job, but also on me. I wanted to shake things up. I arranged it before my dad died. After he did, I tried to bail, but Mum didn't want me to stop doing what I wanted just because of that. She didn't realise what a shit daughter I was going to be in the interim, never going home, but that's another story." Ali exhaled. "Which is why, when it comes to us being a couple—and I've no idea if that's what you want—I don't know how it might work. And I'm really sorry about that, just for the record."

Disappointment anchored itself in Morgan's stomach. "But you're coming back eventually?"

"Yes, but I don't know when that will be." Ali leaned forward and peered out the window. The snow was getting heavier. "Shall we get going?"

Morgan nodded and tried not to stare at Ali's fingers as they gripped the wheel. The same fingers that had gripped her last night. The ones she'd hoped might do so again. But now, she learned it might be a one and done. Something bubbled up inside her and her eyes stung. She blinked.

Fuck, she would not cry.

She took a deep breath and looked away from Ali.

One night. If that was all this was, so be it. She wasn't going to come across as a loser. She had to be cool. She could totally do that.

"I'm not going to pretend I'm not disappointed." Morgan's voice cracked on the final word. She cleared her throat and composed herself.

Ali kept her eyes on the road as they made their way out of the airport and onto the road home.

"Because it feels like we could be something. We both live in Glasgow. We like each other. We're very good at kissing. We're even better at sex."

Ali let out a strangled laugh as she guided them off a roundabout and past a sign that told them they were 32 miles from home. "I can't argue with that. We were all those things."

"Is it because of who I am? Because if it is, Nicole will get over it. Don't believe a word of what she tells you, by the way. I was only terrible to the men I went out with. I'm far nicer to women."

"Good to know, but it's nothing to do with that." She glanced Morgan's way.

Morgan heated from the inside out.

"I've had a thing for you for longer than I care to remember. Nothing Nicole might think would deter me from seeing where this goes if it was an option. But it's not." Ali shook her head. "And before you say we could make it work, we can't. New relationships need care and attention. We can't do that if we're thousands of miles apart. Believe me when I say I would love to see where this goes, but I don't want to ruin it before it's even begun. This is just a case of right place, wrong time."

Morgan's insides twisted once, twice, three times. There had to be a way around this. She didn't want this to be the end. It was really just the beginning. But even as she thought that, she knew what Ali said was right. If she was leaving the country, it wasn't fair to put ties on either of them.

"I could come and see you. I might even wait for you. It might work. Is this you being glass half empty again?"

Ali turned her head. Her smile was so sad. "This is me being a pragmatist, which I always claimed to be. It's in my DNA. It's what developers do. However, my teenage self is gagging right now. Morgan Scott is saying she'll wait for me, like we're in a fucking Austen novel and the wind is whipping round my ears—"

"Will snow do?"

"—and I'm telling her no." Ali snorted at her own words.

"What if I want to wait?" Did that sound desperate? Probably.

But Ali shook her head. "There are too many obstacles, too many things standing in our way. Let's just call this what it was. What it *is*. A glorious, ridiculous, crazy adventure. We got to see each other in the worst of circumstances. We laughed, we cried, we kissed, we had off-the-scale sex. But it was just for now. Something we can look back on and smile. I don't want things to be awkward with us in the future. I want you to come into the pub next Christmas and have a drink with me."

The traffic up ahead made them slow until eventually, they came to a standstill.

Morgan ground her teeth together. She hoped the traffic wasn't a huge issue. Unlike the one Ali had just unfurled in the car. She couldn't imagine having a drink with her in the pub next year. Unless she sat in the corner, crying into her beer.

The air in the car grew tense, despite them trying to keep it light. Morgan would remonstrate more if Ali wasn't driving. Maybe she'd planned it this way.

"There's really nothing I can say to convince you? I at least think it's worth giving some thought. Not simply chucking it out right away." Now she definitely sounded desperate.

Ali pulled up at some traffic lights. She reached over, took Morgan's hand in hers, brought it to her mouth, and kissed her knuckles.

The effect made Morgan close her eyes. It transported her back to Ali doing exactly the same thing to her last night. It really wasn't helpful.

"If this was last year, I'd be asking what you were doing for New Year and beyond. But I'm just trying to make it as painless as possible for us both up front." She kissed her hand again, then put it back in Morgan's lap. Ali eased the car forward as the lights went green.

"It doesn't feel that painless to me." Morgan's shoulders slumped as she spoke.

Ali nodded, never taking her eyes from the road. "If it helps, it doesn't for me, either."

\* \* \*

An hour and 15 minutes later, they finally pulled up outside Morgan's family home, the same one she'd grown up in. Plus, true to form, you could probably spot the house from outer space.

"Is that a full Santa and six reindeer all lit up on your roof?" Ali peered out of the window. When she couldn't quite see the whole thing, she undid her seat belt and clicked the button to lower the window. "Wow, it really is." Her breath stained the nearby air.

Morgan saw their house through Ali's eyes, someone who wasn't expecting it. Every piece of greenery in the garden was lit with fairy lights. The black iron railings were strung with huge lit candy canes. Plus, there was a giant inflatable snowman in the front garden.

"It's not subtle, is it?" Morgan laughed, then glanced out the window around their close. All the houses were similarly festooned. "It's a neighbourhood thing. They all spur each other on, and every time I come back, there's something different to admire." She pointed at the roof. "Santa and his reindeer only arrived two years ago."

"They make it. Tell your parents good call."

The car was quiet for a few moments.

Morgan turned to Ali. "I guess this is where we say goodbye."

Ali nodded but wouldn't meet her eyes. "I think it is. We're already late back. We need to spend time with our respective families."

Morgan gulped, then sucked on her top lip. "We do. I have a gingerbread house to decorate and a phone to pick up. I need to know what I've missed in the past 48 hours I've been without it."

"So much," Ali replied. "The world of communications has blown up without you."

"I sense some sarcasm." Morgan smiled, then held Ali's stare.

Their gazes danced in the air between them, and the car grew warm. There was so much to say, and they both knew it. However, Morgan didn't know where to start. All she knew was she wanted to spend more time with Ali when they weren't in a crisis. To see where this might go. But Ali had already made her feelings clear.

"There's nothing I can say to change your mind? You won't at least consider another option? Because they could be on the table."

Ali closed her eyes, sighed, then massaged the bridge of her nose with her thumb and index finger. "It's for the best. I don't want you waiting for me for a year. What if I meet someone and then I feel guilty? What if you do?"

"Because that happens all the time in my normal life. Women just throwing themselves at me on the street."

"You might meet the love of your life on New Year's Eve this year. You never know."

"Then again, I might not." Morgan's brain pulsed as she shuffled her thoughts, trying to get them in order. But she'd make a terrible croupier. Her thoughts refused to be ordered, instead lying on the floor of her mind and refusing to budge.

She took a deep breath and made a final plea. "What about if this is the moment we're meant to grasp? What if we've met each other and got together en route home for a reason? We could have been like Walt, gone home and been none the wiser. Maybe this is the change we're meant to notice and act on."

But Ali either didn't want to hear what Morgan had to

say, or she wasn't ready. She shook her head before Morgan had even finished speaking.

"If it is, then fate will play out how it's meant to. But I can't start on my new adventure with conditions. It's not what my dad would have wanted. He wanted me to travel and see the world, because he never did. I've got to honour his wishes and not get tied down."

Morgan was about to point out she never wanted to tie Ali down, but then she thought better of it. This wasn't just about Ali's new start. This was about her dad, too. From the little Morgan had gleaned on this trip, Ali hadn't dealt with his death yet. Which meant Morgan had to tread carefully.

Ali wasn't going to listen tonight. She'd made up her mind, and she wasn't going to bend. But maybe tomorrow. Or the next day.

Morgan would keep trying.

This wasn't over.

"Will I see you for a drink at least one day? It seems weird if this is it."

Ali's smile that greeted those words was at least genuine. "I hope so. Come into the pub. We're not open tomorrow as you know. Tonight and tomorrow, I need to spend some time with my mum. But Boxing Day, let's have a drink." She let out a heavy sigh, and finally let her gaze settle on Morgan.

All the blood inside Morgan rushed south, and her vision swayed. Ali had that effect on her.

"I'm going to miss being in a mess with you." Ali's smile was soft and sincere.

"I'm going to miss *you*," Morgan replied. Then she winced and shook her head. It was the truth, but it wasn't what Ali wanted to hear today. She held up a hand. "Sorry, it just slipped out." She paused. "I take it you're not going to say anything to Nicole? What happened on the road stays on the road?"

Ali smiled, but it didn't quite reach her eyes. "I think so. It makes everything easier, doesn't it?"

Morgan swallowed down the flash of anxiety that flared inside. "Whatever you want." She flicked her thumb to the boot. "I'll get my case and you can get home."

She tore her eyes away from Ali's beautiful face, then got out of the car and stretched, her back clicking after so long in one place. She grabbed her backpack from the backseat and slid into her coat, the chill acute in the country air. Up above, the stars twinkled in the village darkness. She'd always loved that about living here, not in the city. The stars always brought her home.

When she reached the boot, Ali was waiting. She pulled it open, checked the luggage tags, and got out Morgan's case. "Can you believe we bought the same case from the same place?"

Morgan shook her head. "Excellent taste, clearly."

"I'd say so, wouldn't you?"

Ali held her gaze, and it took everything Morgan had not to sweep Ali into her arms and kiss her into next week. But that wasn't on the cards. She'd forgotten this part of meeting someone and getting to know them. The not knowing. The stomach-churning uncertainty. Especially when the significant other was moving thousands of miles away imminently.

"Morgan, I—" Ali began.

"There you are!"

Morgan blinked, then turned to see her mum walking towards them.

Something flashed across Ali's face, and she stepped back. Really, Mother? Now?

Morgan slipped on her exaggerated smile, when really she wanted to bundle her mum back into the house, lock the door and then rush back to let Ali finish her sentence. What had she been about to say? Morgan would never know.

"You're later than you said you'd be. I've been looking out the window waiting for you." She reached Morgan and pulled her into a hug.

Morgan went with it, her mind a blur of emotions.

She'd forgive her mum. Eventually.

Her mum kissed her cheek, then let her go.

"And Ali, how are you?" Now it was Ali's turn for a hug.

Her mum was terrible at reading a room.

"What a palaver you've had getting home, eh? Such good luck you found each other and could do it together." Her mum pulled her cardigan close. Her dyed golden hair was shaped into its usual bob. She often got mistaken for a younger version of ex-tennis pro and TV presenter Sue Barker when they went shopping. Usually in Sainsbury's.

"It definitely was, considering the time it took." Ali turned on her high-beam smile.

Its glare dazzled Morgan.

"But Morgan and I made the most of it, didn't we?"

"It was an adventure," Morgan agreed. "An illuminating adventure." There was so much more to say. Maybe she'd finally find what she wanted to say on Boxing Day.

"I better get going," Ali said. "I'll see you around?"

Morgan nodded. "You will."

"Say hello to your family, won't you?" Morgan's mum told Ali.

Then, just like that, Ali got in the car and drove away.

Morgan felt like she'd lost a limb, but she couldn't tell her mum. However, watching the red lights of the car fade and turn the corner, Morgan wanted to run after it. Tell Ali to stop and come back. To rethink everything she'd said. To stop and see what was right in front of them. A seed of something that could be pure fried gold.

Her mum's arm wound around Morgan's shoulder as they headed back to the house.

Morgan grabbed her suitcase with the other hand, and the wheels rattled along the ground, breaking the neighbourhood's silence.

"Thank goodness you made it home for Christmas Day."

"Sorry I missed Dad's play. How was it?"

"Terrific. Not a single one of those kids fluffed their lines, and nobody threw up in the wings like the past two years. Truly a Christmas miracle. Don't worry, you can watch the video. Plus, I made sure Annabel saved you the gingerbread house roof to decorate."

Morgan thought of the gingerbread pub on the backseat of their hire car. She couldn't hope to do it as well as that, but she'd try her best.

Had she tried her best to tell Ali what she was feeling?

No.

But she would.

# Chapter Twenty-Four

Ali parked the car in the street round the back of the pub, but sat for a few moments before going in. Leaving Morgan and being strong about their future had been hard, but necessary. She couldn't go to New York and start afresh with a girlfriend in tow. That wasn't the deal she'd made with herself.

Even if that girlfriend was Morgan Scott.

Could she?

She shook her head to clear her thoughts. Coming home was all about reconnecting with her family, and already Morgan had impacted that promise. She didn't want that to happen. She was going to be strong and focus on being present with her mum and her sister and everyone else. She was going to talk about her dad, and be in the space where he used to be. She wasn't going to moon over Morgan.

In fact, if there was one thing Morgan had taught her, it was how to be excited about coming home for Christmas and spending time with her family. Ali should be, too. However, it didn't stop the nerves creeping up her spine as she stared at the back of the pub. At their adjoining house, and her parents' bedroom, now just her mum's. She had to get over it. The only way to do that was to step inside the pub and say hi to her family and friends.

Ali unclicked her seat belt, then checked her hair in the mirror. The bags under her eyes weren't a surprise after the past two days. She smoothed them upwards and smiled at her reflection. Because even though she was tired, she couldn't deny Morgan had put a smile on her face. Their night of passion still pulsed in her veins. It had given Ali a tantalising taste of what might be available if she met someone when it was the right place, right time. Morgan had shown her what she was missing. Once she was settled in New York, maybe she'd meet someone out there who made her feel the same.

Or maybe she'd come home and meet Morgan. Was it only Ali who'd wanted to push Morgan into the toilets and fuck her in a cubicle when they'd stopped for a loo break at Keele Services on the M6?

She closed her eyes. That was not for now. Today's mission was to get back into the bosom of her family. At least, what was left of it.

Tears welled inside, but Ali clamped them down. She would cry this holiday, she knew that. But she didn't want to arrive with red eyes. There had been enough of that last time she was here. This was a new day, and Ali was going to present her best self. Her real self. The self she'd been daring to think about again ever since Morgan had tapped her awake. Had made her think there could be a happy life again in her future.

Ali blinked. Morgan again? It had only been three days and one steamy, incredible night. Why couldn't she get her out of her head?

She snapped the mirror back to the car roof, then got out. Ali shivered as the cold air hit her. Then she grabbed her coat and paused, a hand over the gingerbread pub. Should she take that first, or her case? For maximum impact, she chose the gingerbread pub. She didn't have a front door key, so she'd have to walk through the main bar while carrying this piece of art. She glanced down at The Rising Sun sign on the biscuit pub, then up to the real-life one. She tipped her gaze to the sky.

"This one's for you, Dad."

Ali pushed open the wrought-iron gate and stepped carefully down the six large steps into the pub garden. Even though it was December, there was still a smattering of smokers and drinkers. One couple near the door were already slamming tequila shots, and it wasn't even 7.30pm. The Rising Sun was fitted out with many gas heaters, a huge stretch tent to keep the warm air in and the cold air out, along with bunting, flowers and fairy lights. Plus, now it was Christmas, there was a life-size Santa at the door to the pub, along with mistletoe and paper snowflakes suspended all around. Ali couldn't help but smile.

She missed this place.

She missed home.

She pushed open the side door with her bum. The warmth hit her like a brick. She breathed in the scene of fake pine trees and smiled. It was a far cry from Dave and his Christmas tree farm. Inside, the bar was packed, and the atmosphere crackled with festive cheer. Anticipation leapt from everyone as they contemplated the next day, and those to come. It was the Christmas Eve magic she'd told Morgan about. A time of hope, the calm before the Christmas storm. Before you burned your turkey and had a row with your sibling, before you opened the disappointing present and drank too much port. A time when Santa really might turn up with exactly what you wanted.

She glanced down at the gingerbread pub. Her mum might not know she wanted this, but she would when she saw it.

Ali nudged her way carefully through the busy pub, the volume turned up high. When she reached the L-shaped bar, she slipped behind it. It only took a few seconds for her sister to spot her. When she did, Nicole's mouth turned into a huge, all-encompassing smile and she let out a little scream. Her sister was dressed in mind-bending pink, as usual. Her spirit animal was a prawn.

"You made it!" Nicole finished topping up a pint of Guinness, took the payment, then walked over and wrapped her arms around Ali.

A flush of love worked its way from Ali's toes to the tips of her fingers.

Yes, she'd missed this. Now she was here, she wondered why she'd stayed away so long. She was an idiot. Her dad might not be here, but the rest of her family was. She had a lot of time to make up for. Starting now, as she hugged her sister hard.

When she came up for air, Nicole gave Ali's cheek a squeeze.

Ali even excused that.

For now.

Then Nicole moved her head sideways, her gold hoop earrings glinting under the pub lights. She peered into the white box Ali had set on the bar just before she was crushed. "What's that?" she asked, moving closer and lifting the lid. "Oh my days, it's a gingerbread Rising Sun. Where the hell did you get this?"

Ali grinned, but the truth died on her lips. *Morgan bought it for me.* She couldn't say that, could she? That would admit too much. To herself, if to nobody else.

"I got it up north, in Helen's village. A bakery made it. Isn't it perfect?"

Nicole stuck her head in the box now, inspecting it fully. "It's absolutely perfect. Mum's going to love it."

Ali looked down the bar, but could only see Sheryl and Brian serving. "Talking of, where is Mum?"

"Talking to customers somewhere. She was here a minute ago." Nicole grinned, then pointed. "And now she's behind you!"

Ali swivelled, and in moments, her mum deposited a leaning tower of pint glasses on the bar, then took her youngest daughter into her arms. She squeezed Ali until she could squeeze no more, before moving her out to arm's length. "My littlest daughter. You made it! Where's Morgan? Did she go home?"

The mere mention of Morgan's name made Ali's stomach churn. "She did. She's with her family, and I'm with mine." Her tone was light, like it didn't matter.

She ignored the way her heart flip-flopped when Morgan's name sat on her lips. That was an inconvenient truth.

"What are you doing out collecting glasses? I thought you had staff to do that?" Ali asked.

At 60, though many of her friends had retired, her mum refused to do the same. "Working keeps me young," she always said, even before Dad's untimely death. "What would I do otherwise? Watch TV and wither?" Ali could never imagine that happening. Her mum was far too full of life. She was also slathered with fake tan, her skin tone the same colour as a blood orange. Nicole had warned Ali, but seeing was believing.

Mum laughed, then moved her silver-framed glasses up her nose. She was shorter than her two daughters. They'd both gained a few inches from their dad. "They need to be collected, so what's the harm?" Her eyes fell on the box. "What's that?"

Ali's heart pumped that bit faster as she picked it up and held it up to her mum. "I got it in the Lakes. It's a gingerbread Rising Sun."

Her mum's eyes widened as she flipped the lid, then gazed at the model. "It's incredible. It even has tiny iced people and lights in the window!"

"And snow on the roof, like a proper Christmas fairy tale. Maybe that will happen on Christmas Day too. It never normally does, but this year feels different," Nicole added.

"It always did when you were little and your dad was alive." Mum glanced at Ali, then Nicole. "Maybe if he's up there looking down on us, he'll send some down for Christmas morning."

Ali's skin prickled at the thought. She didn't believe in the afterlife, nor that her dad was floating somewhere up above. But she'd glanced to the sky earlier when she arrived, and she did it again now. If it helped them all to think he was watching over them, there was no harm at all.

"He'd have hated the gingerbread pub though, wouldn't he?" Ali said.

Her mum laughed, then squeezed her arm. "He'd have loved the craft of it, but he wouldn't have eaten it for love nor money. Which is why it's perfect for us. I love it." She kissed Ali's cheek. "We should let everyone else see it, too." She carefully lifted it out of the box. "Nic, grab one of those wooden boards from the back. I want to show this off."

Moments later, the gingerbread Rising Sun was on the end of the bar, and getting the attention it deserved.

Nicole leaned into Ali. "I'm not sure I want to eat it after the whole pub has breathed on it, but it looks amazing." She nodded towards their mum, chatting with customers about it. "Look how proud and pleased she is. You did good, little sis."

*Morgan did.*

"It's about time, isn't it?"

\* \* \*

A while later, Ali's suitcase was safely upstairs and she sat with Nicole at the end of the bar, both nursing half a cider. Mum insisted they take a break after Ali stepped in to help with a drinks rush. She'd then disappeared into the garden, handing out candy canes as Christmas treats. She took her responsibility as the landlady seriously. Plus, candy canes at Christmas were a pub tradition. Mum was determined to keep those up, even with Dad gone. Ali had forgotten to tell Morgan about that tradition, hadn't she? Maybe her family had more of them than she realised.

"How's she been? First Christmas without Dad?" Ali still had her Christmas jumper on. It seemed fitting in the pub.

Nicole pondered the question. "Okay. I think the pub has been a great constant. I wondered if it might be too much for her to do on her own, but she's risen to the challenge. She's always liked to keep busy, so it suits her. She misses Dad, but we talk about him and I've insisted she take time off. Brian has been terrific, too, really stepping up and sharing the load." Brian had been full time for a few years. When Dad died and Mum needed some time, Nicole promoted him to pub manager.

"Sounds like I'm the one who hasn't dealt with things." Ali gave her sister a sad smile as the truth escaped from her lips.

Nicole shook her head. "Don't be too hard on yourself. Live your life, just like we all do. But our lives are here, which means we can't avoid dealing with Dad's death. This pub is where he always was." She paused, then shook her head. "Where he *still* is. It's probably strange for you, first time back, right?"

Ali glanced around the space. On a nearby wall were photos of customers through the years. Her dad holding aloft a darts trophy the pub team had won. The huge painting of a rising sun expertly done by one of their old regulars. She shook her head. "I think I've built it up in my head to be bigger than it is. But when I stepped into the garden, it felt like home."

"That's because it is, stupid." Nicole nudged her shoulder.

"You know what I mean. I wondered if it would feel the same without Dad. But it does, because you're all still here." Why hadn't she realised this before? "I'm sorry I haven't been back. I've left you to deal with everything."

Nicole shook her head, then put an arm around Ali and kissed her cheek. "It's what big sisters are for. You're here now, and that's the main thing. Although I was wondering if the whole issue with getting home was another ruse not to come. That you'd be spending Christmas in the Lakes with Morgan and Helen." She paused. "Talking of which, how was that? How the hell did you and Morgan end up travelling together? Helen called earlier to see if you were back yet. She said it was lovely to see you, and that she really liked Morgan."

Ali blushed, not daring to hold Nicole's gaze for fear she'd see right through her. To the truth that she'd slept with Morgan. That she liked her.

It didn't matter anymore.

But the question now flashing at the forefront of her mind

was, had Helen said anything? Ali curled her toes in her shoes. She'd love to ask, but that would only tell Nicole everything she needed to know. Instead, she stayed calm and answered Nicole's question.

"It was just one of those strange coincidences. We were on the same flight that got cancelled, from there we shared a car journey together with Mrs Claus…"

"Mrs Claus?"

Ali laughed, remembering Imogen and Sam. The face of romance and hope. Was she the opposite? Morgan had accused her of being glass half empty.

Was that true?

"It's a long story." Ali waved her hand. "One that if I said it out loud, you'd struggle to believe. Anyway, we travelled together after we got stranded at some middle-of-nowhere services after Mrs Claus buggered off." She shivered as she recalled the snowstorm. "But in the end, I'm glad we did." She paused. "Plus, it was nice getting to know Morgan."

Nicole tilted her head and narrowed her gaze.

Was it Ali's imagination, or did her sister seem like she could read Ali's mind?

"It's just, you know, weird," Nicole added. "My sister and my oldest friend. Together."

"We're not *together*. I mean, not *together together*."

Ali's words stumbled out of her mouth like terrible drunks. They'd witnessed a few in this pub. "We were obviously *together* as in we were travelling home with each other."

Her stomach twisted as she prepared for the inevitable reaction.

Or perhaps Nicole would let it slide.

"I didn't mean you were *together*." Nicole gave her a confused look. "Unless I'm missing something here?"

Or perhaps she wouldn't.

Her sister moved her bottom jaw from side to side, then rested her chin on her palm, elbow on the bar. Her conker-brown gaze didn't move from Ali. "Tell me, darling sister, whose cheeks are going redder by the second. Did something happen between you and Morgan on this trip home? Mum mentioned it, but I waved it off. I told her you wouldn't be that obvious. Two lesbians, stranded, obviously they're going to have sex, right?" She raised a single, pencil-thin eyebrow in Ali's direction. Her sister always over-plucked. "Was I wrong to defend you?"

"It wasn't like that. We just enjoyed each other's company. Despite the issues, we had fun."

Fun? Fun was an impromptu afternoon in a pub on the river. A gig where you knew more songs than you thought. It was not three days trying to get home with your first love and then sleeping with her.

Or maybe Ali's definition of fun had suddenly changed.

Still Nicole stared. "Now I know something's up. 'We enjoyed each other's company'. When you talk like a BBC presenter from the 1970s, Houston, we have a problem."

Ali pulled out her 'don't be so ridiculous!' face, then shook her head. "Nothing happened." The lie burned her throat. "I just got to know her a little better, and I realised that I've probably never had a proper conversation with her in my whole life until the past few days—"

"It's like you're rambling to cover something up."

"I'm not!" Just like that, they were quarrelling teenagers

again. But even Ali knew her cheeks were the colour of deceit. The warmth she felt could probably power the pub. At the very least, boil a kettle.

Nicole leaned so close, her breath tickled Ali's face. "I remember the crush you had on her when you were younger. These things don't just go away."

Ali almost stopped breathing. "You knew about that?" She'd never breathed a word to anyone apart from Tobias. Those long, hot, tortured years were ones she thought she'd endured alone. Now, apparently, she'd had an audience. Which only made it ten times worse.

But not as bad as telling Morgan they didn't have a future.

*Glass half empty.*

"How did you know?"

"I've got eyes," Nicole said. "That, and you were always tongue-tied around her. Always clumsy. I hope these past few days have cured you of that, at least. I know Morgan and I don't see each other much anymore, but I still have a lot of time for her." She pressed the tip of her index finger to Ali's forearm. "Just so you know, if anything happened, it wouldn't be the worst thing in the world. I love Morgan and I love you. Although Morgan was a bit of a player back in the day, and leopards don't usually change their spots."

"Leopards might not, but maybe lesbians do." She was defending Morgan now. Not the smartest move. Time to course-correct. "But that's beside the point. Nothing—"

"—happened, I know. But I wanted to let you know, just in case anything changes." Nicole kissed her cheek, then gave her a wink.

How could her older sister be so lovely, and yet so annoying all at the same time?

"Oh my god, look at this dinky gingerbread pub!" A woman who'd clearly had far too much to drink stuck her hand out to touch it, but Nicole jumped in.

"Gorgeous, isn't it? I'm going to move it behind the bar for its own safety. I'd like The Rising Suns—both of them—to still be here on Christmas morning." Nicole disappeared with it, then came back right away. A crush at this end of the bar meant they were back on duty.

Ali rolled up the sleeves of her top and served an older couple a pint and a half of lager. She took their payment, jingling as she moved, then stabbed the receipt onto the metal pin. When she turned back to the bar, she took a deep breath.

Because there, on the other side, looking just as delicious as when she'd left her, was Morgan Scott.

# Chapter Twenty-Five

It wasn't the first time Morgan had seen Ali behind the bar, but it was the first time she'd done so since they'd had sex. Now, everything about Ali was different. She noticed the flex of her forearm when she reached for a glass overhead. The way her fingers wrapped around said glass. Her easy smile to the customer.

It was nothing like the suggestive smile Ali had given Morgan just before she kissed her lips. Or the way Ali had wrapped her fingers around Morgan's neck before she slipped her tongue into her mouth. The jolt of that memory made Morgan slide into a temporary trance where Ali was surrounded by a ray of light. Right up until the bald man to her right elbowed her in the neck as he tried to muscle his way to the bar.

"Hey!" Morgan turned to the bloke.

"Sorry love," he said, clearly not sorry at all.

When she looked back up at the bar, Ali's eyes were on her, a mix of confusion and something else on her face. That was fair enough. Ali had told her nothing could happen. They'd agreed not to see each other until Boxing Day. Now, here she was.

Ali gave her a small wave as she poured two pints of Moretti for the woman at the bar. When the woman paid and left with her drinks—coming perilously close to dumping half of one down the front of Morgan—Morgan squeezed to the front.

"Did you forget something?"

Many answers swam to the front of Morgan's brain, but she didn't utter one. "I think we've got the wrong cases."

"But I checked the tags when we unloaded yours."

Did Ali sound peeved?

"Plus, I saw them put my luggage tag on mine."

"I know." Morgan's gaze dropped to Ali's lips, and she forced herself to focus. "I have a theory about how it happened, but you're busy."

Ali gave her an embattled smile. "Do you want to wait at the end of the bar and I'll try to be done as soon as I can?"

"Sure."

Her gaze lingered on Morgan a few seconds more than necessary. Then Ali blinked and served the next customer.

Morgan edged out of the crowd that was still three-deep and walked around to the end of the bar. She sat on a spare bar stool and took in The Rising Sun, still packed despite the absence of Tony Bradford. Morgan wasn't surprised. The pub had always been a pillar of the community, because Ali's family made it so. As Ali's mum always said, you walk in a stranger, you leave a friend. Morgan had walked in a few times and left with a variety of friends. She'd even picked up a woman in here six Christmases ago when she was on the rebound and took her home to have sex, before sneaking her out before her mum realised what had happened. Those were different times.

"Hey, stranger."

Morgan looked up to find Nicole beside her, resplendent in pink like a stick of Blackpool rock. Morgan grinned, got off her stool, and gave her friend a hug.

"How long's it been? Three years? I thought you were avoiding me until you kidnapped my sister."

What had Ali told her? Morgan laughed all the same.

"Your sister was willingly kidnapped. You need to tell her not to talk to strangers in airports. You never know what can happen."

Nicole's smile was still the same one that had lit up Morgan's whole life. She'd always been a bundle of positivity, and Morgan was pleased to see nothing had dimmed her wattage. Not even the death of her dad.

"I'm not going to ask you what happened, but my sister has been acting strange since she got back. Like she's hiding something. You wouldn't know anything about that, would you?"

*Don't give anything away.*

"Don't you always think that about your little sister?" She placed a hand on her friend's arm. "I'm sorry I haven't seen you in so long. The last couple of years I've only done a flying visit, but I should have stayed long enough to pop in and have a drink with you."

"Damn right you should have. Good job I'm the forgiving sort."

"Also, I wanted to say I was so sorry to hear about your dad. He was a great man."

"Thank you. And yes, he was." Nicole's eyes glistened as she spoke.

"But it looks like the place is doing as well as ever."

Her friend nodded. "It is. We're lucky. We have a very loyal customer base."

Morgan squeezed Nicole's forearm again. "Luck's got nothing to do with it."

Ali walked up behind her sister, her face pensive. "Whatever she's saying, don't believe it. That's a blanket rule."

Morgan's heart swelled in Ali's presence.

"Nicole was just accusing me of kidnapping you, and it's a fair cop." Morgan snagged Ali's alluring gaze. "I also kidnapped her suitcase. Which is why I'm here. I wanted to check you had mine, too. Have you opened it yet?"

Ali shook her head. "I got back and was put to work behind the bar before I could blink." She stood back. "You want to come through and I'll check?"

Morgan nodded, then followed Ali through the small plating-up area—with the gingerbread pub sat on the side—and into the family hallway.

"I haven't been in here in years." Not since she was in her mid-20s, if Morgan had to guess. "Nicole and I spent many nights in our late teens sneaking drinks from the bar. I've no idea if your parents ever knew."

"I suspect they did. They weren't stupid." Ali nodded towards the stairs. "You want to come up?"

Twenty-four hours ago, that line would have signified something completely different. Now, she ignored the heightened anticipation on her skin as she followed Ali up the stairs. She bit down her smile that Ali still jingled.

"The place looks great, by the way. I love what your parents did with it." The walls were covered in crisp, patterned wallpaper that looked straight out of a magazine. Plus, the light fittings were a copper-inspired triumph that was all back in vogue now, as it had been in her great-grandparents' era.

Ali paused on the landing. "Yeah, my parents have a way of making places feel just right." She paused. "*Parent*." She drew her mouth into a straight line.

Morgan went to grab Ali's hand, but stopped. That wasn't in the script anymore. "I'm sure your dad had a hand in it, too." She pointed to the right. "Definitely in hanging that Mexican hat over the hallway cocktail cabinet." Ali's dad had always been obsessed with Mexico, along with its food and drink. Tequila had been his drink of choice.

"That has Dad written all over it."

Ali led Morgan through to what had been her bedroom, now the guest room.

"This has had a makeover, too. It looks like a boutique hotel room." The walls were a cool midnight blue, the skirting boards and ceiling crisp white, with splashes of chrome and gold on the accessories. Morgan was impressed.

"It's not bad, is it?" Ali put her code into her case lock, but it didn't budge. She glanced up. "Okay, what's your code?"

"1234." Morgan would fail sleuth school on the first day.

"Seriously?" Ali put it in and the lock opened. "How the hell did that happen? I hope you've got mine."

Morgan crouched down, unzipped the case, and checked the items. Yes, it was hers. "The only thing I could think was, we took the wrong cases from when we got out of the taxis. Remember that was the first time we met on our doomed trip?"

Ali nodded, her face inches from Morgan's. "I do." She exhaled. "That must be it, right?"

"Uh-huh." Morgan gulped. Ali was so close, her instinctive reaction was to kiss her. But she couldn't. No matter how much every hair on her body craned towards Ali. No matter how her brain screeched inside that they were meant to be. That this was right.

Ali didn't agree.

"There you are!"

Morgan jumped at the interruption, jerking forward and head-butting Ali instead. Smooth work. Now, rather than kissing her, Morgan clutched her head and toppled sideways. The pain in her skull was acute, but it had nothing on her embarrassment, currently running red hot through every cell of her body. She looked up to see Ali's mum in the doorway. Had she always been orange, or was Morgan seeing things?

Ali got to her feet, rubbing her head with a frown. She still jingled. "I'm going to change this bloody jumper," she muttered.

"Did I interrupt something?"

Ali shook her head. "We were just checking cases because ours somehow got mixed up." She pointed. "That's Morgan's, so she must have mine."

"These airlines and their mix-ups. Did I tell you about the time your gran went to Paris and her case flew to Athens? Spent the first three days of her trip with the same clothes on, including pants!"

Morgan got to her feet. "Hi, Mrs Bradford."

"Don't be silly. I'm Elaine, you know that." She paused. "Could you give us a hand for another ten minutes, love?"

Ali nodded. "Of course." She glanced at Morgan. "You okay to wait and we'll sort the cases out?"

Morgan nodded as her head throbbed. "I already told

you I'm prepared to wait." Shit. She hadn't meant to say *that*. "I'll get your case from the car in the meantime."

Ali stared, then nodded. "That would be great, thank you."

\* \* \*

Morgan put the front door on the latch, then took her case out to the car and brought Ali's in, making sure for about the tenth time the padlock didn't open and it was indeed Ali's case.

It was. She shivered as she returned. Fuck winter. Summer was definitely more her vibe.

However, she'd do romance in the winter if that was what Ali wanted. Red wine, snow, roaring fire, the works.

She put Ali's case on the floor by the front door, then stuck her hands in the pockets of her jeans and glanced around the hallway, her teenage years playing in her ears like a tinny speaker at a bad party. She'd had fun here with Nicole. Back then, Ali had been an afterthought. Very much in the background, a tiny speck on Morgan's watercolour of life. Never once had she figured in Morgan's thoughts or daydreams. How times had changed. She was very much figuring now.

Morgan spied a photo of Ali and Nicole when they were kids. Nicole was around eight, and Ali grinned up at her, the tell-tale home-style wonky fringe in full view. It was around the time Morgan stole Ali's trumpet. To make amends (albeit 30 years later), she'd bought her another one from the gift shop in Lower Greeton. She wasn't sure she'd get to give it to her now. They weren't on their trip anymore. They'd gone off road.

A cheer went up from the bar. Morgan strode towards it and peered through the plating-up area. Ali dashed past, serving someone, not looking left. Out of sight, she heard Elaine cackling, her laugh as loud as her skin tone.

Maybe Morgan should just leave. They'd agreed this would be family time, and this was Ali's family home. But she should hang around to say goodbye at least.

The gingerbread Rising Sun was still on the side. Morgan hadn't seen it up close, so she carefully picked it up, held her breath, and put it down on the counter in front of her. She leaned in, marvelling at the lit windows, the gingerbread bar, and the biscuit bar stools. She'd never have the skill to make something so intricate. Gingerbread biscuits and bigger cakes, she could do. She'd love to have the patience for the fiddly things, but it wasn't her style. She reached out a finger to the outdoor table and the gingerbread umbrella, painted bright pink. The level of detail was off the scale. She leaned forward a little more. How had they done that?

She poked the tip of her finger onto the top of the picnic table. It was softer than she'd imagined, but still sturdy enough. It didn't need to take much weight, so she guessed that made sense.

"How's it looking?"

The words jolted Morgan. It also jolted her finger unexpectedly and suddenly forward.

Right into the picnic table.

It caved under pressure. Then, like the absolute best episode of the Great British Bake Off where one cake falls off a stand, it snapped in half with consummate ease.

"Shit!" To rescue what had just happened, Morgan tried to pick up the two halves of the table to stick them back together again, but only snapped off the benches, too. Which then also split into a few uneven pieces. As a final insult, the umbrella toppled left and broke, too.

Admitting crushing defeat, Morgan took her hand away—her fingertip now adorned with pink glitter—and stared.

The model had looked beautiful. Now it looked like a drunk had gone on a rampage in the garden. The whole sequence probably only took ten seconds, but it felt like the longest ten seconds of her life.

In moments, Ali stood beside her.

Morgan didn't dare risk a look at her face. This wasn't doing anything to help her cause.

"I did ask 'how's it looking?', didn't I?"

Morgan nodded. "You did, and I'm sorry. I was just admiring it, but you coming in made me jump. Not that I'm saying it's your fault." She risked a glance right.

Ali caught her stare and sighed. "We have to fix it before my mum sees it."

Morgan's brain ran on overdrive. A thought popped into her head. She turned to Ali. Whatever was or wasn't happening between them, at least Morgan could fix this.

"I have a possible solution."

Ali's brow furrowed. "Go on."

"We could take it back to mine and bake a new table and benches there? I've baked gingerbread before, and my mum will probably have the ingredients." She paused. "I assume your mum wouldn't?"

Ali snorted. "I told you, we're a strictly no-baking family."

Morgan gave a slow shrug. "It's worth a try. Even if we just bake a normal biscuit table and stain it brown with nail polish, nobody will know, right?"

Ali covered her face with her hands. "I can't believe we got it all the way back from up north, then break it in the pub kitchen." She peeled her fingers away. "You were joking about the nail polish?"

"Either that, or your mum's fake tan. Although it looks like she might have used it all." She put a hand on Ali's arm briefly. The touch stilled them both.

"Harsh, but fair," Ali replied.

Morgan stared at her fingers, still connected to Ali. Her heart swelled. How she wanted this connection back. However, it wasn't hers to ignite.

"One way or the other, we'll fix it. I've already brought your case in and put mine in the car, so we're good to go."

Ali gave her a nod, then carefully placed the pub inside its box. She grabbed their coats from the bottom of the stairs. "I'll just let my mum know I'm heading out for a little while." She gave Morgan the gingerbread box with the words, "Don't drop it!" then grabbed some keys from a hook on the hallway wall.

"You don't need your keys, by the way. I'm driving my dad's car."

"I thought you didn't drive?"

"I do here."

# Chapter Twenty-Six

Driving with Morgan at the wheel was a novel experience. Throughout their journey back to Devon, Ali was in charge. Now, the tables were turned. She'd be a liar if she said she wasn't pleased to be spending more time with her, but it wasn't what they'd planned.

They'd agreed to have more time apart, so that Ali's plan could bed down in her heart and her mind. Some time away from Morgan to see this as what it was. A random three days together, an illusion. Once she was back in the real world, and off to New York, she was sure Morgan would fade from reality. But that wasn't going to happen if Ali kept looking over at her long fingers currently wrapped around the steering wheel, as well as breathing in her bergamot smell.

Moments later, they turned into Morgan's road, the jollity in stark contrast to the tension that hovered in the car. Morgan pulled into her parents' driveway, and they got out in silence. Ali got the pub from the backseat and slammed the door. Morgan retrieved her suitcase from the boot, then gave her a weak smile in the illuminated air as they walked across the drive and up to the front door. They stopped beside a frosted Christmas tree.

"I assume you have one inside as well?"

Morgan nodded. "Main one in the lounge, one in the dining

room and a small one on the side in the kitchen. If she could, my mum would have one in every room along with a Santa's grotto in the garden, but my dad put his foot down at that. She lets him put his foot down when she thinks he needs it."

"Smart woman." Ali stared at Morgan. At her smooth skin. Her full lips. Ones that Ali would not focus on one bit. However, when she glanced upwards, a sprig of mistletoe was stuck above the front door. She took a sharp inhale of breath, then let her gaze wander back to Morgan's face.

"Don't worry. I'm not going to insist on a kiss."

"I wondered if it was one of your many traditions." A shimmer of anticipation worked its way from Ali's heart to her throat. Kissing Morgan wouldn't be the worst thing in the world. But she pushed that thought from her mind.

Morgan opened the front door, and they walked into a hallway decked out in tinsel, with Christmas cards strung from the white picture rail. A wooden nativity scene was lit on a side table, and through the open door to the kitchen, Ali saw a tiny countertop tinsel tree. Morgan hadn't been kidding when she said her family took Christmas seriously. She left the case at the bottom of the stairs and took Ali's coat.

Ali jingled as she shrugged it off. "I swear, I'm about to murder my jumper." She followed Morgan through to the kitchen, and they put the gingerbread pub on the marble-topped island, one of the biggest Ali had ever seen. When they turned, Mrs Scott stood in the doorway, a questioning smile on her face.

"Hello Ali, didn't expect to see you here so late on Christmas Eve. Not that you're not welcome, of course."

Luckily, Morgan hijacked the conversation before too

many questions were asked. "If we wanted to bake some gingerbread, do you have the ingredients?"

Morgan's mum frowned. "You want to bake gingerbread *now*?"

It was a fair question.

But Morgan styled it out. "We had a bit of a gingerbread malfunction. Plus, it's Christmas Eve, Ali's never baked any, and I promised her in the car on the way down. I'm going to decorate my part of the gingerbread house roof while we're at it, so I thought, two birds, one stone."

It almost made sense to Ali when she put it like that.

Mrs Scott turned to Ali. "I can't believe you've never baked gingerbread. You're in for a treat. All the ingredients are in the baking cupboard in the island. There's some icing already made in bags. Just remember to clear up after yourselves."

Ali watched her go, then turned to Morgan. "Where's your gingerbread house, then?"

Morgan disappeared, then came back with it. The house had a white picket gingerbread fence, gingerbread bushes in the front garden and resembled a kid's drawing of a house. Four windows, a sloped roof, crazy luminous paving and the front door even had a wreath on. However, the roof was starkly plain, and needed some attention.

"Did you say your sister did the paving?" It was quite the statement.

"She was feeling hormonal at the time."

"I can tell. Pollock-esque."

"In her defence, she is very pregnant. And very mad at her husband for putting a baby inside her. You know some people say that pregnancy is just the best? My sister would disagree."

Ali grinned. "I think every woman I know would say the same." She raised an eyebrow. "Are you going to show me your baking skills, then?"

Morgan held up both hands and waggled her fingers. "These hands have many uses. Prepare to be wowed."

\* \* \*

After checking them on her phone—"Look, Dave sent my phone back unscathed!"—Morgan weighed out the ingredients for gingerbread, then set about making it. She beckoned Ali over with a crooked index finger.

Ali shuffled along the counter obediently.

"You want to do this first bit?" She pointed at the pan. "We need to get the dough made so we can chill it." She paused.

"Baking and chill is not the same as Netflix and chill, right?"

Morgan raised an eyebrow. "It would be a bit awks with my parents in the next room. Besides, I thought that was out of bounds?"

Ali sucked on her top lip. That wasn't the question of a woman who wanted boundaries. She pulled back her shoulders and fixed Morgan with a stare. "I know I'm giving mixed signals." She put her hands on her hips to create a boundary. "What I said earlier still stands. We can't work because I'm moving countries. Nothing's changed."

Something in the side of Morgan's jaw clicked as she gave Ali the faintest of nods. "You've made yourself very clear. This is just about gingerbread. Nothing more."

A thick silence settled on the space. Ali didn't dare take a breath, in case it lodged in her throat and choked her.

Perhaps this wasn't the best idea, after all. Because she knew just as well as Morgan that this was *never* just about gingerbread.

Morgan, however, was on a mission. She put the butter, sugar, and syrup in a small pan. "Stir this until it's melted, then take it off the heat."

Ali blinked, then nodded. "I think I can do that."

Morgan then mixed bicarb, ginger, cinnamon and flour in a bowl. She tested the butter mixture for heat, then added it to her bowl. "Okay, now I just want you to bring it all together. Don't be shy. Get your hands in there."

A landslide of wrong responses formed on Ali's lips, but she chewed them up and swallowed them down before any escaped. She didn't want to leave any room for doubt with them.

Namely, that there wasn't a 'them'.

Once the dough was mixed, Morgan put it in the freezer to chill. "And now, we get the piping bags to do the roof of our family house. You want to help?"

Ali shook her head. "I don't really think that's appropriate. It's a family thing and, well, I'm not part of the family, am I?"

Morgan stared, then took a deep breath. "Strictly speaking, no. But I feel like you should have a go. After everything we've gone through this week. Plus, you didn't expect to be here tonight. Decorating the roof will be an excellent distraction from any tension. It's art, and art is therapy."

Ali laughed. "You're offering me therapy on Christmas Eve?"

"It's normally when it's needed most."

Ali couldn't argue. "Okay. I'll play."

Morgan beamed. "The golden rule to remember is, if you bugger it up, you can always smudge it and pass it off as snow." She filled a few small china bowls with Jelly Tots, Smarties, mini marshmallows and Midget Gems. The sound of them hitting the bowls made Ali's mouth water and her stomach rumble. She hadn't eaten since she arrived home, and it was only now she remembered she was hungry.

"Don't be shy with the sweets or glitter either. When it comes to gingerbread house roofs, the gaudier, the better. Make it so my sister's paving looks tame."

Morgan got some pre-made icing from a deep drawer in the island, then cut the bag around the nozzle. Then she stepped up to the roof, squeezed the bag, and expertly coaxed the icing out until she'd piped a row along the apex of the roof like it was an everyday occurrence.

It wasn't in Ali's world.

"That's impressive."

Morgan hadn't been lying about her baking skills.

Neither had Ali.

Morgan held up the bag. "You want to give it a go?"

Ali's response was instinctive and immediate. She shook her head. "That's a big fat no. I'll just mush some sweets on the side of the roof. I feel that's where I could shine."

"You need some icing to stick them to." Morgan fixed her with a warm smile.

Ali wobbled under its glare.

"Wouldn't it be good to learn a new skill this Christmas Eve?"

"I just wanted some food and a cup of tea." It was the honest truth.

"I'll get you a mince pie when the gingerbread's in." Morgan paused. "What do you say?"

Ali went to say no, but instead said, "Okay." She walked up to the roof, and Morgan made way for her.

What was she doing? It was as if her body was acting independently of her brain.

Once Ali was settled in front of the roof, Morgan stepped up behind, her body warmth pressing ever so slightly into Ali.

Flashing red danger signs lit up all over Ali's body, but she didn't move. She couldn't. Mainly because she liked it and she didn't want to. She felt Morgan's hot, sweet breath on the back of her neck, and then Morgan's breath hitched. Was she trying to gauge Ali's reaction?

Ali should say something, tell her to stop.

Only, she was too busy trying to regulate her breathing and her thoughts.

Moments later, Morgan wrapped her hands around Ali's waist and shifted closer behind her.

Ali's heartbeat thudded in her ears.

The bells jingled on her front. She bit down a smile.

"Pick up the piping bag."

Morgan's voice brought the mood back. It was liquid silk in her ear. Smooth, just like her baking skills. Plus, some others Ali had tried desperately hard to forget.

She gulped, then did as she was told.

"Take care when you're working with the gingerbread. As we know, it's fragile and easily broken."

A little like Ali's boundaries. She turned her head, caught Morgan's smile, and her mind scrambled.

*What the hell was she doing?*

But Ali stayed static, as her mind jammed with panic. However, this was the good panic. The kind of panic she could bottle and sell all over the world.

"Remember, I'm a communications expert, so follow my lead. I know just when to press and when to stop."

Something deep inside Ali rumbled at that. After the night they'd spent at Helen and Jamie's house—was that only last night?—she wasn't going to argue. With Morgan, her insides were still molten lava, however she might fight it.

Morgan's fingers closed around Ali's.

Ali's mind flailed.

"Now, gently squeeze the piping bag. You won't get this the first time, but consistent pressure and confidence are the key to good piping."

She tried to focus on what Morgan was saying, but it wasn't easy. When she focused on Morgan's fingers, she remembered them inside her. How they filled her exquisitely, as if Morgan's fingers were made just for her. How just a simple movement had set off an intoxicating shock wave of wonder and lust inside her. A feeling she could conjure up at will. As she was doing now.

*Must focus on piping.*

But holy hell, that was hard when her insides pulsed and her heart rocked.

Ali squeezed. Hardly anything came out.

Morgan's fingers pressed around hers.

Ali's insides pulsed some more. She gulped.

Another squeeze. Finally, some icing appeared on the roof. In a splodge, yes. But there was icing.

However, Ali was far more focused on Morgan's breath

in her ear. Her arms that were still wrapped around her waist.

Until they weren't. When Morgan stepped back, Ali wanted to turn and grab her. She wanted to fix Morgan's arms around her and demand she never let her go.

But again, boundaries.

New York.

*Glass half empty.*

But fuck, she wanted to top up the glass. Fill it to the brim. She wanted Morgan to fill her more than anything in the world.

Morgan stood beside her. "Hold the icing in the palm of your hand, squeeze with your fingers, and do it consistently and with confidence. It's the same with most things in life you want to get good at."

Ali glanced left, watched as Morgan ran her tongue along her top lip, then returned to the roof. A flash of Morgan as she came pressed into the front of her mind. Then it was gone. She took a deep breath.

Confidence and consistency. She could do this. She squeezed. Another splodge. It wasn't going to be a masterpiece, but it wouldn't be naked, either.

The word 'naked' lodged in her brain then, as she recalled Morgan this morning. Naked in bed beside her. Why was she saying it couldn't happen again?

Because of a non-existent future.

"Two splodges already. You're a natural."

Ali snorted, but produced another splodge.

Morgan reached over and retrieved a pink-and-white-filled icing bag, cut the bag around the nozzle, and piped neat, uniform swirls across her roof.

"Did your mum teach you this?"

Morgan shook her head and paused. "My nan. She taught my mum, and then she taught my sister and me. It was one of her Christmas traditions." She swept her arm around the kitchen. "Everything you see and smell in this house all stems from her. She was the Christmas queen, and she was the one who always had to bake her own gingerbread."

Warmth swept up Ali. She loved that Morgan was so connected to her family.

"Nobody in my family bakes. It's a badge of honour. But we keep the local bakeries in business."

"In that case, we're going to make some gingerbread stars and gingerbread people for you to take home, too. You can splodge until you can splodge no more. Your family will be amazed."

"They'll also think I'm lying."

Morgan walked to the baking drawers and pulled out some cutters in the shape of stars and people. "I'll tell them, and they'll have to believe me."

"You forget my sister knows you."

An arrow of happiness pierced Ali's heart. That was the thing here, wasn't it? It was a crying shame this couldn't work, because they didn't just have a mutual attraction and chemistry. They had history. Foundation to build on. They were a solid gingerbread house that simply needed decoration. Ali stared at Morgan, then shook her head. Morgan already decorated the world just fine.

More than fine.

Morgan narrowed her eyes. "What? Do I have something on my nose?"

A shake of Ali's head. "Nope. I was just thinking, this is not how I expected my Christmas Eve would go. Baking gingerbread. With you. Here. Not after everything." She glanced down at the piping bag in her hand. "Who knew I could feel so much contentment being a shit baker?" Her hand shook as she spoke. "You know what? Ignore me. I'm a bit addled from all the travelling, and the lack of food. Plus, walking back into the pub was overwhelming. As is being here with you."

*What on earth was she saying?*

She fully expected Morgan to take a step back. Literally and metaphorically. They'd spent a few days together, had one hot night, Ali had brushed her off and now she was redrawing their boundaries every five seconds? Even she knew she was acting a little crazy.

But Morgan didn't move. Instead, she reached out a hand and placed it on Ali's arm.

That was all. Just one tiny touch. But it was enough to make Ali's pulse sprint. Enough for her cheeks to heat to nuclear. Enough for every nerve ending she had to fling itself open, waiting for more.

With Morgan, she'd flipped the switch.

Ali flicked through her mental notebook for an emotion that fitted what she was feeling. Aroused. Alive. But also, *comfortable*. Ali flinched as the final one hit her. Yes, that was what it was. With Morgan, she felt comfortable. Like herself, but alive. If she was brutally honest, she hadn't felt like that with anyone else that mattered for a very long time.

It was a crime they couldn't be more.

"It's okay." Morgan's words were low, almost whispered. "I get it."

250

Ali's arm shook under Morgan's touch. "Do you?" Was she about to have a breakdown in the middle of decorating a gingerbread house? It was so out of character, it was almost comical.

But Morgan's steady gaze on her made her feel seen. Reassured. Safe. Ali breathed through it and steadied her nerves.

"I do."

Ali's heart thudded like a kick-drum. She hung on Morgan's every word.

"We could have a future. A great one. But it's up to you to change your mind. I'm all for it." Morgan's blue eyes shimmered as she spoke. "Whether you like it or not, we make sense. We're not typical, but that's a good thing. We are precisely who we need to be and where we need to be, and I wish you would see it. I'm not saying we're destined, far from it. But I think we might be if you'd give us a try." She put a hand to her chest. "I feel it here. Every time you're near me."

Ali gulped, then stepped towards Morgan. Her chest ached with want. She still didn't think they could work in the long run. But maybe another short run would get Morgan out of her system.

She glanced at Morgan's soft, full lips. She was desperate to feel them pressing against hers once again.

"How's the baking going?" A male voice sliced through the moment, killing it dead.

*For fuck's sake.*

If it wasn't Morgan's mum, it was Morgan's dad.

Ali jumped back, as did Morgan. Her heart clattered to the floor, so much so, she almost felt winded. Ali picked up

251

the piping bag and tried to remember how to hold it, but it was useless.

She was useless.

Morgan made her useless.

In the best possible way.

"Going well," Morgan replied. "Just getting the chilled dough."

She heard the freezer opening, but Ali didn't dare turn around. She couldn't face Mr Scott right at this second. Not with all the illicit thoughts about his daughter still whizzing around her brain.

"We're just about to bake, so shouldn't keep you up too long."

"Nonsense," Mr Scott replied. "I love it. Reminds me of your nan." He paused. "I'll leave you to it. We're going to bed soon. See you in the morning, love. Will we see you tomorrow as well, Ali?"

Okay, she couldn't ignore him forever. She didn't want to appear rude.

"Not tomorrow." She turned her head. "Merry Christmas for then!"

He wished her the same, then disappeared. As if by some unspoken agreement, they kept quiet for the next few moments, until Morgan's mum appeared and said good night, too. Only after a decent amount of time had passed did Ali dare to look at Morgan. When she did, Morgan was staring at her, too. She gave Ali the widest grin in her armoury.

"I remember now why I left this village, and particularly why I moved out of my parents' house. It's lovely, but it's limiting."

Morgan rolled the dough, then offered Ali a cutter in the shape of a star. "You do the stars. I'll do the bench to replace the one I broke."

"What about the umbrella?"

Morgan raised an eyebrow, looking very pleased with herself. She pulled out a kitchen drawer and produced a cocktail umbrella. "My plan is to stick this in the still warm dough, et voila, instant umbrella. What do you think?"

Ali shook her head. "That you're a communications expert with a solution for everything."

"It's my job."

"I can see why you're in demand."

Morgan licked her lips. "You might never see my best moves."

# Chapter Twenty-Seven

A while later, Morgan stood back and surveyed their handiwork. The pub garden furniture was restored, and the new-look table and umbrella even added a little extra kitsch that she was very much here for. Plus, they'd also made a plate of gingerbread stars, which Morgan and Ali had iced the edges of. A solid evening's work.

"Not bad, even if I say so myself," Morgan said. "For emergency baking, we did a lot of extras." She glanced at the clock. 10.45pm. "You must be starving. How about a mince pie and a glass of Bailey's before you go?" What's more, they'd boxed up any sexual tension. For now. What might have happened if her parents hadn't been in the house was anybody's guess. Morgan sensed a wavering on Ali's part, but that was all. They hadn't chatted in any depth. All she knew was if she lit a match in this room, it might go up.

Ali eyed her. Now the baking was done, there was no more distraction. Was she thinking the same thing?

"You've been promising me a mince pie all evening. I'd like two and a Bailey's, please." Ali paused. "So long as you warm them in the microwave for 15 seconds and serve them with cream."

"I'm not a monster."

Ali laughed.

Morgan's heart swelled. How she wanted to keep that laugh in her life. Morgan wasn't sure how she could negotiate that deal, but her mum's mince pies were a good way to start.

She grabbed two from under their glass dome, heated them, and squirted whipped cream on top. It melted immediately.

In seconds, Ali was by her side. She bit into one pie, made a sound that Morgan would like as her new ring tone, then turned to face her. "You didn't warn me your mum's pies were a new religion."

"Now you understand why I have to come home. Mr Kipling mince pies, while lovely, simply don't cut it."

"I might have to come round every day now on some flimsy pretext just to have one of these." Then Ali winced. "Which isn't what I should say after everything I said. I know that." She blew out a long breath. "This is why I wanted us to have a break from each other. It's been very intense over the past few days, and I wanted to get some distance."

Morgan let her finish, and didn't fill the gap in conversation. Instead, she let Ali's words hang.

The surrounding air throbbed with red-hot uncertainty mixed with possibility. Morgan wanted to wrap them both in it, squeeze out any doubts Ali had. But Ali had to work it out for herself. Morgan couldn't force her to do anything, no matter how much she wanted to.

Ali ate another mince pie, then gave a satisfied sigh. She licked a bit of stray pastry from her lip.

Morgan followed its trajectory. She'd never been jealous of some buttery pastry before, but she was now. Ali's face was a work of art she wanted to stare at for days.

"Can I steal some to take home with my gingerbread stars?"

If Ali kissed her again, she could take the family jewels as far as Morgan was concerned. "Of course." She paused. "Shall we go to the lounge for a quick Bailey's?"

When they walked through the door, Ali gasped behind her. Morgan understood. Her parents' lounge was like a picture-postcard of Christmastime. A fully decked-out tree with presents spilling out from under it. An enormous fireplace with six stockings lining it for her parents, her sister and brother-in-law, Morgan, and her upcoming niece or nephew. The fireplace itself was a work of festive art, topped with greenery, candles, pine cones and ribbons. What's more, the log burner still burned, giving the room a gorgeous focal point and a warm glow. A large cream rug nestled in front of it.

When Morgan turned to look at her, Ali shook her head.

"I mean, I know places like this exist, but it's normally in a magazine. Your house *bleeds* Christmas." Ali walked over to the mantelpiece and breathed in the scent of pine. She ran her fingers across the top of some red ribbon, then looked up.

Morgan did, too.

A sprig of mistletoe hung over the fireplace.

She lowered her gaze. "Is that what I think it is?"

Morgan nodded. "Mistletoe."

When their eyes met, something clicked inside Morgan. Something that hadn't clicked before. In that instant, she knew she couldn't let this go. That it was too important. That *they* were too important. She had to fight. She *wanted* to fight.

Ali stepped towards her, her gaze lasering Morgan's skin

with its intensity. She reached out an arm and pulled Morgan towards her.

Everything Morgan owned pulsed.

Electricity crackled in the air.

Morgan swallowed down, steadied her hand, then rubbed her palm up and down the outside of Ali's shirt before slipping it underneath.

Ali sucked in a sharp breath.

Morgan closed her eyes as she continued to stroke Ali's back. She was right back to last night. She couldn't remember the last time she felt like this. The last time she'd touched someone and never wanted to stop. She couldn't fight this. She didn't want to fight this. And by the look on Ali's face when Morgan opened her eyes, she was having trouble fighting it, too.

"Morgan," she began.

Tension rippled between them, so thick Morgan could almost see it and taste it. Anticipation patrolled her skin. Excitement thumped in her brain.

Morgan had never felt this turned on in her life.

"Yes?"

"What am I doing? What are we doing?" Ali reached up a hand and slid her fingers around the back of Morgan's neck.

The bells on her jumper jingled.

Ali took a step back, ripped it off, then resumed her position.

She smelled of gingerbread, of sugar, spice, and all the things Morgan had always wanted.

"I'm not jingling the rest of the night," Ali said. "Also, I'm trying so hard not to want you. But you're killing me looking like that."

They were the last words she uttered before she closed the space between them and pressed her lips to Morgan's.

If she was asked later in kissing court, Morgan would point to this action.

Orchestrated by Ali.

She kissed her first.

She didn't stop, either. Ali's lips were like painted gold on Morgan's. They kissed her furiously, the same way Ali rode a tandem. Full on, no fear. Ali's arms wound around her.

Morgan's mind unwound in crazy time.

They still didn't make a sound. Noise would taint the moment, which was all fast lane, warp speed.

Eventually, Morgan pulled back, panting.

When they stopped kissing, broke their lips apart for a few seconds, Ali's pupils were dark with questions. Her fingertips stumbled as she flicked open the buttons on Morgan's shirt, pulled back her lacy black bra, then took Morgan's nipple into her mouth.

It wasn't just Morgan who wanted this.

"I fucking love your breasts, have I told you that?" Ali's words were husky, tangled.

Morgan stared, not able to form a coherent thought. "Not in so many words, but in actions…"

Ali sucked her left nipple in reply. "I didn't want you to be in any doubt." She ran her hands over them once more, then tugged on Morgan's fingers until she followed her down to her knees and onto the fireside rug.

Desire dripped down Morgan like a slow waterfall. It came in unhurried, deliberate drops that slid along her skin, their slick trails leaving steam in their wake.

Ali eased off Morgan's shirt, and she shrugged off her bra. Before she knew it, Ali was topping her, grinding into her. She slipped a thigh in between Morgan's legs before travelling south, kissing Morgan from her neck to her navel.

Morgan glanced up at the Christmas stockings, the names on the front blurring into one. She closed her eyes. Now was not the time to be thinking of family. She didn't want to think about anyone but Ali. The two of them, and this moment.

Seconds later, Ali made sure that was going to happen when she undid the buttons on Morgan's jeans, slid down the zip, and shuffled Morgan out of them.

Morgan should have felt exposed, lying on her parents' rug in her briefs. But she didn't. Ali hadn't promised her anything. But Morgan didn't need any promises. The only thing that mattered in this moment was action. By the intense look on Ali's face, she knew that, too.

Seconds later, Ali was beside her, fingers soft as sunlight on Morgan's skin. They skimmed her stomach, danced on her thighs. Ali kissed her way to Morgan's belly button, before her hot breath settled at the top of Morgan's thighs.

Thunder roared inside her. Morgan needed something to hold on to, but there was nothing. Not a bed frame. Not a pillow. Not even her dignity. It was overrated, anyway.

She glanced south just as Ali's teeth lifted the edge of her pants. Ali's index finger slid to hold the material up. Then her tongue worked its magic as she licked her way along Morgan's pant line.

Morgan closed her eyes as pure lust rolled through her. A second wave crashed down when Ali slid off Morgan's underwear. Her breathing hitched, and every part of her went onto high alert. She'd imagined this moment happening again ever since it happened for the first time. She spread her legs, making herself an invitation for Ali. Then she got onto one elbow, hooked an arm around Ali's neck, and pulled her in for a steamy kiss. As she slid her tongue between Ali's lips, Ali slid two fingers into her.

Morgan moaned into her mouth as a desire bomb detonated inside her. Lust took all its clothes off and streaked around her system. And why not? If there was ever a time for it to happen, it was now. She was naked and Ali was inside her. What it all meant, Morgan didn't know. Right now, she didn't care.

As Ali's fingers slipped slowly in and out, Morgan tried not to think of more nights like this. Because she'd love there to be more. All Morgan had ever wanted was to find a partner who got her. Who understood the rhythm of her heart. Rhythm was certainly something that Ali was no stranger to, as she showed Morgan now. If this were a dance, Ali was adept at the slow, quick, quick, slow. As Morgan twisted and moaned with sheer pleasure, Ali responded in kind. As Ali's strong fingers moved inside her, Morgan's mind spun around and around, until she was as close to the edge as she possibly could be.

"You feel incredible," Ali told her, her fingers right where Morgan needed them most.

She wanted to tell Ali she did, too, but she couldn't speak. All Morgan's energy was wrapped up in the physicality of the moment. In replying to Ali in the only way she could. By letting go. One more thrust, one more stroke, and Morgan did just that, coming undone with a delicious moan that started in her throat and landed in her heart.

Morgan flung her head back and coasted through the

crest of the wave, a kaleidoscope of emotions rampaging through her. She wrapped her hand more tightly around Ali's neck as she rode out her orgasm, before finally opening her eyes to check she was still where she'd started. Physically, that was true. But mentally and spiritually, Morgan was somewhere else altogether. From the look in Ali's eyes as she bent to kiss her lips one more time, she'd felt it, too. At least, Morgan hoped she had. And if she hadn't, Morgan wasn't going to let her go tonight until she definitely had.

"That was… I don't even have the words." Morgan had uttered nothing truer in her life. She was depleted, but in the best possible way.

The moment was so raw, so intimate, Morgan almost had to look away. But she didn't, because she was in it too. Just her and Ali. There was nothing else in the world.

Morgan's throat was dry, unlike every other part of her.

Ali stared some more, then looked away. She pulled out of Morgan and rolled away.

It took a few moments for Morgan's body and brain to recalibrate, but eventually, they did. Her heart lurched. Ali didn't look at her. That wasn't the action of someone happy with what had just happened, was it? However, with the sugar rush of sex still glittering inside her, it was hard to bruise the moment.

But she had a sneaking suspicion Ali might try.

Morgan closed her eyes to wallow for a few more gorgeous seconds.

When she opened her eyes, Ali stared at her. She had a look on her face Morgan couldn't compute.

"Why do I feel like you're about to run away?"

Ali winced, then shook her head. She reached over to the coffee table, grabbed a tissue from the box, and wiped her hand. "I can't..." she began. Her gaze searched Morgan's face. Then she dropped it to the floor. Seconds later, Ali rolled over and put her bra and jumper back on.

She jingled once more. The bells weren't welcome.

Morgan held her breath as she waited for Ali to pull the plug.

"My heart says you're perfect. Exquisite." She rolled her gaze up and down Morgan. "And you are." She leaned in and kissed Morgan's shoulders. "But the issue that I'm leaving the country still stands. So maybe we really do finally call this what it is. A festive fling. Then we leave it at that."

Morgan couldn't form a coherent argument right now. It was unfair of Ali to ask.

However, it turned out Ali wasn't going to stick around to chat. In moments, she stood up, ran a hand through her chestnut hair, and stared at herself in the mirror above the fireplace.

Whatever argument she was silently having with herself, she would never win.

Despite her body telling her to stay horizontal, Morgan jumped up, pulled on her pants and jeans, shrugged on her shirt, then faced Ali.

"You've only got one reason this won't work. Because you're moving. I could give you 50 why it just might. Because we know each other. We like each other. We're fucking dynamite together." She stared. Damn, she was beautiful, and also infuriatingly stubborn. "Tell me we're not."

Ali licked her lips, then cast her gaze to the ground. "Being dynamite in bed means nothing when I'm in New York. We don't have enough to keep us tied."

Morgan reached out and held onto the mantelpiece. If Ali kept saying things like that, she was going to need something to keep her upright.

"Why would you say that after you just told me you can't keep your hands off me or stop thinking about me? Why did you kiss me and fuck me like you really meant it?" Morgan shook as she spoke. She was turned on and angry, not a combination she'd ever experienced before. Ali made her feel unique and original things. This one wasn't so welcome. "And don't tell me you didn't mean it, either. I've had bad sex before. I've had disinterested sex. This was not that."

Ali's chest heaved, and she looked away.

At least she wasn't denying that part.

Nobody could.

It was a rock-solid fact.

"I just came to make gingerbread and things got out of hand."

Morgan spluttered, her thoughts flaring red. "That's what you call out of hand?" She couldn't quite believe what Ali was saying.

But then again, she could.

Ali was back in defence mode. Glass half empty. She stuck a hand in her pocket. The same one that had just fucked Morgan. Now it was out of bounds.

"I should go. My family will wonder where I am."

"I wasn't holding you hostage." Morgan did everything she could not to shout, but it wasn't easy. She didn't need her parents getting up to witness this. It was hard enough for her.

Ali stared, then turned.

In the kitchen, there was an awkward pause as Ali eyed the cake box containing the gingerbread pub, along with the tin of home-made biscuits, and tupperware of mince pies. Then she frowned.

"I just realised I didn't drive here. Which means I don't have my car."

Fuck. The last thing Morgan wanted tonight was to drive Ali home. She needed her to disappear, then she could have a breakdown in peace.

"I'll call you a cab, then get you a bag for your baked goods."

Luckily, the taxi said it would arrive in two minutes. When Morgan told Ali, she looked just as relieved as Morgan felt. She went to the drawer where her mum kept her carrier bags, and slid the tin of gingerbread biscuits and the mince pies into a Sainsbury's Bag For Life. Then she held up a finger. "Wait there." She dashed up to her room, battling with herself and questioning her logic with every step, then came down with a wrapped present. She slid it on top of the baked goods.

When she glanced up, Ali shook her head. "Why are you giving me a gift?"

Morgan shrugged. "I told you, our family has a tradition of giving a present on Christmas Eve. I bought you one. It's not exactly the best circumstance to give it to you, but I want you to have it. Take it."

Ali took a deep breath, went to say something, then thought better of it. "Thank you." Her deep brown gaze threatened to swallow Morgan whole.

Morgan ground her teeth together, but luckily, a car horn outside broke the silence. The cab was here.

Ali picked up the bag, then the pub box. "Can you open the front door?"

Morgan nodded, not quite believing this was where tonight ended. But it seemed like it was.

"Happy Christmas, Morgan." Ali turned in the open doorway. "For what it's worth, I'm sorry."

Then, in seconds, she was gone.

# Chapter Twenty-Eight

Ali unlocked the front door, then carefully manoeuvred all her gingerbread products inside. Once they were safely on the hallway table, she pulled the door closed, then unwound her mustard scarf. She buried her head in it, trying to conjure up her real life. Not this fake charade she'd been starring in for the past few days. She had no idea who this person inhabiting her body was. The one who made gingerbread and fucked women at will. Or rather, one specific woman.

She should talk to Tobias. She missed him. So much had happened since she'd left Glasgow. Perhaps she needed a voice of reason to tell her what to do. Her head was resolute and kept instructing her mouth what to say. However, her body was sluggish. It knew something was up. But Ali didn't have the strength to unravel it just yet. Tobias was the king of shagging people and walking away. If anybody would know what to do, it was him.

She glanced at her watch. 11.50pm. Laughter sailed through from the bar, along with a cheer and a chorus of 'Last Christmas'. Ali poked her head into the main space where her mum was cashing up.

"Hey, Mum." She willed her voice to sound more upbeat than she felt. She didn't know how to box up the feelings that coursed through her. How did you rationalise falling for someone, sleeping with them twice, then walking away? Even thinking about it left her dazed, as if she'd just applied a left hook to her own face. Which, in a way, she had.

"There she is! Home for two seconds, then she buggers off. Are you here to stay now?"

Ali blushed. "One hundred per cent. But I am dog-tired. Has Nicole gone?"

Her mum nodded. "Gone to play Santa."

Of course. It was Christmas Eve still, just about. "Is it okay if I slope off to bed, too? I promise I'll be here all week to catch up."

Her mum kissed her cheek. "Get some rest."

Ali gave Brian and the stragglers in the bar a wave, then took the bag Morgan had given her upstairs. She put the baked goods on the counter—had Mum upgraded since the summer?—then sat down at the square wooden table pushed against the wall. She pulled out Morgan's gift and turned it over in her hands. She didn't deserve a gift, she knew that much. The urge to leave and put what happened behind her had been strong when she was there. But now, it seemed callous. She shook her head. She wasn't going to dwell. Otherwise, she'd never forgive herself.

She grabbed her phone from her bag and called Tobias. No answer.

Perhaps it was a sign she should open the gift. It was the least she could do: fulfil Morgan's wishes on this, if nothing else. The wrapping paper had reindeer on it, just like her jumper. She glanced down and flicked a bell. Then immediately silenced it. Ali took a deep breath and tore open the paper.

Inside was a small cardboard box. The price was still in pencil in the corner. £3.49. When she lifted the lid, her heart lurched. She pulled out the toy trumpet and held it with her oversized fingers. It was yellow, red and blue, and supremely plastic. Just as she remembered. More importantly, *Morgan* had remembered, and bought her a gift that meant something.

Damn it all to hell.

She glanced up to the opposite wall, where a photo of her parents in Tenerife was a new installation, too. Her dad grinned at her. Like he was watching her. Telling her to take care and not give away her future for anyone.

Ali's phone lit.

Tobias.

"You called?"

"I did."

"What's up, Buttercup?"

"Everything." Ali slumped in her chair. She didn't have to play it down for Tobias.

"Sounds juicy." He paused. "First up, are you home?"

"Yes, thank god."

"Okay. Second, when I left you last night, you were on the precipice of shagging Morgan, The Love Goddess. Please tell me you did."

Ali didn't even pause. "I did."

"Yes! Finally! And how was it? Did it get your lady juices humming? If it didn't, I don't want to know."

It had done all that and so much more. "Yes, it definitely did." She paused. "But then I drove home with her and told her nothing could happen because I'm going to New York."

Silence on the other end of the line, swiftly followed by laughter.

"Oh Ali, you're so sweet, and *so* fucking lesbian. Way to kill the mood. You're not marrying the woman, you're just having sex with her."

"That's why I'm calling you. I need advice from the king of no-strings sex. How do you do it?"

"Practice," Tobias replied in a low, stern voice. "Also, shutting down all your emotions. It's a skill I learned at the start when men were such shits to me. How the tables have turned."

She knew it was his defence mechanism. They'd discussed it many times before. She also knew he was only half-serious. The other half of him would love to meet someone who mattered.

"How did she take being told nothing could happen?"

Ali frowned. "She wasn't over the moon, but I think we can safely say neither of us is very good at following through, seeing as I just had sex with her again in her parents' lounge."

Tobias spluttered. "What the fuck? Who the hell are you?"

"I have no idea." That was the truth. "It's like she brings out this side to me, this animalistic, primal side that I didn't even know I had."

"I'm not sure what to say to that." He was enjoying this, wasn't he? "And do you like it?"

Ali ran her fingertips over the toy trumpet. Did she? "I think I do."

"I definitely do," he replied. "But telling her it's over and then having sex with her is mixed messages, don't you agree?"

Ali smiled. "I'm aware it could be conceived as such. What do I do now?"

"What do you want to do?"

"I don't fucking know! That's why I'm calling you."

"Tell me one thing—why does you going to New York mean nothing can happen? There's a lot of technology that can help with that. You can have video sex to your heart's content."

Ali grinned. An image of a naked Morgan lying underneath her earlier flashed into her mind.

Not helpful.

"But it won't be the same. I don't want to put pressure on myself when I'm leaving. Plus, I promised my dad I'd give this my all. How can I do that with a new girlfriend to worry about?"

Tobias was silent on the other end for a few seconds. "But what about if, having met Morgan, she's it? What if you end up in New York and all you can think of is her, but she doesn't want to know because you wouldn't consider it in the first place? You've held a torch for this woman for the last 20 years."

"Longer."

"My point exactly! She's shaken you up. What I'm saying is, think long and hard about this decision before you shut it down completely."

# Chapter Twenty-Nine

"Shit the bed, you look ready to drop!" Morgan hugged Annabel after she waddled through the door. She took her coat and hung it on one of the hallway hooks.

"Thanks. I haven't heard that about ten times a day from every person I've met over the past week."

Morgan winced. "Sorry." She greeted Josh as he walked in behind Annabel. He was so tall, he always ducked under normal-sized doorways. He bought his jeans at a special shop that catered for people with legs the length of the M1. "How's my favourite brother-in-law?"

"Looking forward to having dinner with someone other than your grumpy sister." He leaned down and kissed Annabel on the cheek. "She agrees, don't you?"

"Fuck, yes. Pregnancy and me are not friends. The sooner this is out of my body, the better."

Morgan put her arm around her. "Come into the kitchen and have a mince pie. That'll cheer you up."

They followed Morgan into the kitchen, where her mum was already busy making dinner. The turkey was in the oven, the spuds were prepped, as was all the veg. Now it was a case of military precision and timing, of which her mum was a master. Morgan had spent many Christmases watching and learning, but she was still impressed every year.

"What the hell happened to the gingerbread roof?" Annabel stood over it, a grin on her face. "If this is a ploy to get me laughing, you succeeded. This is brilliantly bad."

Morgan ground her teeth together. She'd forgotten about that. It didn't look like her work. It looked like she'd been ambushed.

Annabel looked from her parents to Morgan. "Were you drunk? That's the only way I can explain it."

She shook her head. "It was a joint effort. Me and Ali Bradford."

Her sister frowned. "Ali Bradford, as in little Ali?"

"She's not so little anymore."

Annabel peered closer. "Whatever her day job is, tell her not to give it up for cake decorating."

More looks, which Annabel followed. She frowned. "Is there something I need to know? Something to take my mind off the giant bowling ball currently trying to stop me from breathing?"

"Nothing." Morgan shook her head. "She just wanted to try baking." She walked over to the roof. "For a first time, it's not bad."

"Now I know there must be something you're not telling me. You'd normally be right here with me, laughing too."

Morgan shot her sister a look.

The silence hung in the air.

Annabel tried to take the temperature of the room, then gave up and sat down.

"Josh, I need a cup of tea." She scowled at him.

Josh stood up too quickly, cracking his head on the dining table light fixture. He winced, but ignored any pain, knowing this wasn't his moment. "On it!"

"She was here later than I imagined she might be," Morgan's mum piped up.

"Who?" Morgan asked, dread pooling in her stomach.

"Ali. I heard you in the lounge." Mum paused. "Didn't we, Roger?"

Her dad nodded his head, then stared at his feet.

Morgan wanted to die on the spot. Had they heard the sex, or the arguing?

The sound of Josh filling the kettle pierced the moment, and Morgan had never been so pleased. She wanted to kiss him.

"I'm still not letting this go," Annabel began—quickly followed by a scream.

Morgan swivelled her head to see her sister staring at the floor. When she raised her head, her face was ashen.

"Fuck, fuckety, fuck!" Annabel lifted one foot, then the other. "I think my water just broke. Looks like this baby wants out a little sooner than planned. Damn it, I hope it's not born on Christmas Day. He or she will hate me for the rest of his or her life. I know I would."

"I don't think you get much choice in the matter." Their mum took off her apron and handed it to Morgan. "Roger, get the car keys."

Annabel shook her head. "It could be ages yet, Mum, and I haven't even had a contraction." Right at that moment, she doubled over. "Okay, first contraction!" she shouted.

Alarm spread over Josh's and Mum's faces.

Her dad stepped in. "You and Josh are her birthing team,

so we all need to go, just in case. I'll drive us to the hospital. Are you okay finishing up the dinner and driving your mum's car over later?"

Morgan nodded. "Of course."

Moments later, coats were back on, and Annabel was escorted to the car.

"If you have it quickly, you could be back in time for the turkey!" Morgan shouted.

She got a middle finger from the pregnant woman in return.

\* \* \*

Even though her mum was in her sister's birthing party, she still found time to message Morgan with precise instructions for finishing the Christmas dinner.

'The potatoes need longer than you think. The parsnips need honey and garlic powder. Make sure you whisk the gravy with the meat juices once it's rested. The turkey comes out at midday!' It made Morgan smile. There was no way she was doing that with the gravy either. Seemed a bit much. She'd add the meat juices to a jug of Bisto and hope her mum was too wowed by her new grandchild to notice.

Keeping busy also meant she was distracted, and so less likely to think about the last few days. About last night. About baking gingerbread in this very kitchen with Ali. Getting fucked on the lounge floor by Ali. Morgan's insides pulsed and her cheeks flushed with warmth at the memory. Even if they would be the shortest-lived couple of the century—did they even count as a couple?—she'd look back on the last few days with a certain fondness. She was still getting over how good she and Ali Bradford were together. Also, how stubborn Ali was once she'd made up her mind. Even when she was clearly breaking both their hearts. Definitely Morgan's. She could only hope Ali felt the same deep down.

Maybe she should talk to Nicole, ask her to make Ali see sense. Only, that would mean Nicole would have to know, and Ali didn't want that. She wanted to sweep what had happened this week under the carpet, write it off as a festive fling. Maybe, in time, Morgan could do the same.

She slid her hands into her mum's padded red oven gloves and opened the oven door. Heat licked her face, but the smell of roasted meat made her mouth water. She pulled out the turkey—enough to feed an army by the size of it—and moved it to the end of the island. Then she got two clean tea towels from the second drawer down and tucked them around the bird. That could rest while she got on with the rest of the dinner.

Two hours later, Morgan sat at the island with a well-earned cup of coffee, phone in hand, willing more updates from anyone. Her sister. Her mum. Ali. It was all quiet. She'd come home to spend time with her family. This was not how she'd envisioned Christmas Day.

She keyed Ali's name into Instagram and scrolled until she found her. Her profile was private. She couldn't stalk her there. What was Ali doing? Was she thinking about her, about last night, or was it all boxed up and done? Morgan would love to know.

She sipped the last of her coffee, then jumped off the stool and put her blue mug in the dishwasher. The dinner was in containers on the side. She put the lids on, wriggled most of it into the fridge, then got her phone, house keys, car keys and put them all in her bag. Her phone vibrated, and she dug it out.

'Come quickly, she's had the baby. It's a girl!' That was from her dad.

Morgan blinked, delight blooming in her chest. She was an aunty. How about that?

Her finger hovered over WhatsApp. The person she most wanted to share the news with was Ali. But she couldn't. It was Christmas Day, and they'd agreed that today was off-limits. Instead, she walked through to the hallway and slipped on her coat and scarf, along with her Christmas pudding hat. Then she pulled the front door closed, and got into her mum's bright yellow Polo, adjusting the mirrors as she gunned the engine.

She was off to meet her baby niece.

She was going to focus on that.

Not on Ali Bradford one tiny bit.

\* \* \*

The good thing about driving on Christmas Day was that the mid-afternoon traffic was almost non-existent. Morgan had to drive by The Rising Sun to get on the main road to the hospital, but she tried to put that out of her mind. She stabbed the radio until it spewed out a festive hit and settled back. She missed driving, but she didn't have a car in Glasgow. Maybe she should get one. At least then, she'd never have a trip home like the one she'd just endured. Although if that hadn't happened, she'd never have reconnected with Ali. She'd never have had some of the best orgasms of her life.

Maybe if she got a car, she could go on trips with Ali.

Only Ali was going to New York. She'd made that very clear indeed.

Morgan flicked on her indicator to turn right onto the road that housed The Rising Sun. She wasn't going to look as she drove past. There wasn't another car in sight.

"And now, it's time for that well-known Christmas classic, 'Stay Another Day' by East 17," said the radio announcer.

Morgan rolled her eyes. "It's not a Christmas classic, it was just released in December and has bells in it!" she vented, then glanced down to locate the tuner button. Was it left or right? Was this the volume or the tuner button? She squinted at the radio, then stabbed one button. Nothing happened. She stabbed the one next to it. The car filled with static noise.

"Goddammit," she muttered. Irritation scratched her skin.

When she looked up, a grey car headed straight for her.

Morgan clutched the steering wheel as fear pierced her everywhere. Where the hell had the car come from and why wasn't the driver even looking up? Was he trying to tune his radio, too?

Everything went into slow-motion as Morgan dragged the steering wheel left to avoid the full-on collision. But the other car wasn't moving, and it was almost upon her.

She'd spied it too late. The air in the car flickered and buzzed. Inevitability slapped her in the face.

"Fuck!" she screamed as she closed her eyes and waited for the brutal impact.

# Chapter Thirty

Her nephew Harrison hurtled into the lounge in his brand-new Superman costume, one arm raised up high. He climbed onto the cream sofa with his too-short, four-year-old legs, then flung himself off, shouting "I'm Superman!" When he landed in a heap on the lounge carpet, he seemed momentarily stunned. But then, as only kids do, he righted himself, narrowed his gaze, and ran through the entire process again.

On the third failed attempt to fly, Nicole reached over and grabbed him, giving him a hug to stop another flight. It distracted him for a moment. Next to her, her husband, Stuart, was studiously ignoring the noise, engrossed in his phone.

To Ali's right, her mum hovered over the gingerbread pub, a gingerbread star in her hand.

"This pub is just the perfect gift. It almost seems a crime that we might have to eat it." She paused. "I still can't believe you mended the table and baked gingerbread stars with Morgan last night. A baker in this family. I barely recognise you."

Ali puffed out her chest, as if Paul Hollywood had just given her a handshake. None of it would have been possible without Morgan. She bought the pub, broke the pub, then fixed the pub. She was the communications and solutions expert.

The absolute best way she communicated with Ali was with her lips pressed against hers, and her fingers deep inside Ali. She blinked, then shook herself. Thoughts like that were not safe for Christmas Day.

What was Morgan doing right now?

Ali glanced up at the fireplace, a framed photo of her parents smiling back at her, so happy together on their wedding day. They had many more years of happiness, as her mum kept telling her. She always said she wasn't going to dwell on the past, but look to the future. That's exactly what Ali was doing in prioritising New York.

Although she knew what Tobias had said was also true.

Had she made the wrong decision? Was Morgan someone she should give more thought to? She hadn't slept last night thinking about it.

What if she was turning down the love of her life?

That thought made her jump up from the sofa. Christmas dinner sat heavy in her stomach. It had been delicious, but she'd overdone it on the roasties.

"Anyone want a wine top-up?"

Her mum nodded. "I might have my first glass with dessert. I'll get the crumble and custard ready soon."

They'd all agreed on a rest after their lunch. The queen's speech, followed by a spot of present opening. Her mum had bought her an NYC baseball cap, along with a New York guidebook, as if the internet didn't exist. The whole family had been thrilled with their double lot of gifts—the originals, and the ones Ali had bought in Lower Greeton. The village where everything changed.

Ali grabbed the chardonnay from the fridge and unscrewed

the cap. She refilled her glass, then poured a new one for her mum, who'd followed her in and now leaned against the counter.

"Dinner was delicious."

Mum nodded. The bags under her eyes were far more pronounced since the summer. That's what came of grief, and having to run a business solo.

Ali walked over and gave her a hug. It was spontaneous, and her mum seemed surprised. Eventually, she gave in and hugged her back. When Ali let go, her mum looked at her with suspicion.

"What was that for?"

She shook her head. "No reason. It's just been a while since I've been in this kitchen with you. I'm allowed to hug my mum, right?"

"Always."

Her mum took a seat at the table. Outside, the white clouds persisted. Snow was forecast, but it hadn't arrived yet. Ali sat at right angles to her mum and they clinked glasses.

"Merry Christmas!"

Her mum smiled. "It's good to have you home. Did I say that already?"

"Once or twice. I'm glad to be here spending it with you."

"I love your shirt, too." Her mum stroked her arm. "Are they foxes or dogs?"

Ali smiled. "They're reindeer."

Her mum peered over her glasses. "Are they really? Very stylish and festive."

They heard a wail from the other room, followed by the sound of crying.

"You think Harrison has finally learned the costume doesn't give him special powers?" Her mum laughed, then peered over the top of her glasses. "Can I ask you a question? No getting mad at me."

Ali stilled. "Sure."

Her mum held her gaze. "Morgan. Is anything going on? I know I mentioned it on the phone, but you told me in no uncertain terms that nothing was going on, so I believed you. But now your sister reckons there is, but I don't want to assume. Then, you did bake gingerbread, and that's very out of character."

Ali pressed her teeth together. Did she know the answer to that question?

"We hit it off while we were travelling. Something happened, but it can't go anywhere with me going to New York, so I've nipped it in the bud." Her heart pulled the duvet over its head. She tried to stop the sides of her mouth turning downwards, but she wasn't sure she was successful.

"You look and sound thrilled about that decision." Her mum paused. "Why couldn't it work? There are things called planes."

"It's a long way, Mum. Expensive, too. Besides, you know what Dad said. To travel, follow my dreams, and not let anything or anyone tie me down or stand in my way. I'm trying to honour his wishes."

Mum sipped her wine, then sat back. "Your father said a lot of things, but they were mainly about him. He wanted to travel with no ties, but then we met and had Nicole, then you, and he never regretted that. Not for a second. Plus, we still got to travel, just with you kids in tow. He wanted you to live the life he didn't, but he wouldn't have traded the life he had for anything."

She exhaled. "He wanted you to have adventures, but also

to find love, too. I want that for you as well. It's what any parent wants for their child. Love and happiness. You've got the adventure lined up with your new job, but maybe Morgan's an adventure you hadn't bargained for. An exciting, unexpected one. If she is, and you like her, be open to it. If you want to make it work, you will. You can have a new job *and* a new girlfriend. If it's on offer, why not have it all?"

A loud, clattering crunch of metal made them both jump. Ali's blood froze.

Her mum dashed into the lounge. "You okay?" Her voice was frantic. Neither of them could bear anything else happening to someone they loved this year.

"It's outside," Nicole shouted.

Ali dashed to the window. Two cars had smashed into each other almost outside the pub. On Christmas Day of all days. Smoke spewed from the yellow car's bonnet.

"Is someone dialling an ambulance?" Ali shouted. She ran through to the lounge, where Nicole nodded, talking into her phone.

"Let's go down and see if we can help, shall we?"

Ali nodded at her mum. They grabbed their coats and keys, went through the pub, which Ali always found eerie when it was empty, then unlocked the door to the street.

It was only when Ali got up close that her heart jumped into her throat and her bones turned to jelly.

She stopped, then stared. Her pulse sprinted, then screamed. All the air left her body. She couldn't quite process what she saw.

Because Morgan sat in the driving seat of the sunshine-yellow car.

Walt, the old guy from their plane, was in the other.

They'd had a head-on collision. Both airbags were fully inflated, and blood oozed from Morgan's forehead.

Ali immediately ran around to Morgan's door and tried to open it, but it was crinkled from impact and jammed shut.

She rattled the handle and banged on the window. "Morgan!"

*Please let her be okay!* Ali put a hand to her hair and pulled. Why had she said all those things when she didn't mean them? Why had she let Morgan think she was willing to let her go? She wasn't. She wanted her in her life. But now it might be too late to tell her.

"Morgan!"

They'd only just found each other. She couldn't lose her now. All the potential futures she'd imagined overnight exploded into a million fragile pieces. Ali's heart sank to its knees, trying to piece her future back together. Blood roared in her ears.

"Morgan! Stay awake, you hear me? Stay awake!"

She didn't open her eyes.

\* \* \*

Ali paced the waiting room in the A&E, flashes of doing exactly the same thing this summer with her dad far too fresh in her mind. She still remembered the nicotine-coloured walls, the posters with curling edges. This room only had a tiny window, which meant a severe lack of light and hope while you waited for any news. Ali's mum sat on the edge of her blue plastic seat, ready to spring at any moment. Being back here wasn't easy for either of them.

Her mum checked her watch, then stood up. "Shall we go outside for a bit of air? I always find hospitals so stifling."

Ali bit her top lip. "I don't want to miss any news."

"They've only just taken her in, and she was stable in the ambulance. We won't hear anything for a while yet."

Her mum was probably right. Ali followed her out into the cold, biting air. She pulled her scarf close. "You sure we won't miss anything?"

"Positive," her mum replied. "I have more experience in hospitals than you, remember? Plus, anything's better than sitting and thinking about the last time we were here."

Ali stepped forward and pulled her mum into her second hug of the day. She squeezed her tight.

Her mum shivered in her embrace.

"Thanks for coming with me."

"Good job I hadn't had a drink so I could drive, isn't it?" She held Ali at arm's length. "She's going to be okay, sweetheart. They're just checking her out as a precaution. But she was talking when she got out of the ambulance they said, so that's a good sign."

Ali knew all of that on the surface, but until she saw and spoke to Morgan herself, she wasn't going to be calmed.

Her mum steered her to a nearby bench, and they sat down. Ali leaned her head on her mum's shoulder and took a deep breath.

"We slept together. Twice. But I told her nothing could happen because I was going to America. Bad timing."

Her mum's arm snaked around her. They sat like that for at least a minute without talking.

"But this has made you see that maybe you might have

feelings for her?" She paused. "I have to say, the whole gingerbread thing was a big sign."

Ali swallowed down, then nodded. "It doesn't make any sense. We only slept together for the first time two days ago."

Laughter from her mum. "I told you about when your dad and I met? In that bar in Tenerife? How I knew he was going to be important to me by the end of our first drink, even though he didn't know, the dozy berk." Her face creaked as she smiled. "Plus, this is not out of the blue, is it? You've always liked Morgan. It's not just a few days. She's been in your life for decades."

Did everyone know about her crush on Morgan? She guessed when you were little, it was hard to hide things. Even when you were an adult. Apparently, baking gingerbread on Christmas Eve is a dead giveaway.

Ali wriggled out of her mum's embrace and sat back, lifting her head to the sky. Right at the moment, it started to snow.

Her mum mirrored her stance, and they both opened their mouths, letting the snow fall in.

"I asked your dad for some snow and he delivered." Her mum raised a thumb in the air. "Cheers, love!"

A tear stained Ali's cheek, but she smiled all the same. "Happy Christmas, Dad!"

They sat side by side, laughing through the tears, mother and daughter getting their thoughts in order before they spoke.

"Have you spoken to Morgan about going, about how you're feeling?"

Ali shook her head. "I didn't truly know until I saw her in that car. I wanted to dive in and rescue her. She can't be hurt." Ali would never forgive herself.

"She won't be." Her mum's fingers wrapped around Ali's. "You haven't spoken at all?"

"We have. She wants to see where it goes. Even if I go to New York. She said she'll wait for me, and come to visit."

"I don't see a problem, then."

"Maybe I shouldn't go to New York at all. Maybe I should move closer to home to see you more. I've been a bad daughter this year, I know." Ali slumped forward as she spoke.

"Don't talk nonsense. Your dad got one thing right—this is a great opportunity, and you're not passing it up for me. You're going, no question. Coming home when you don't want to *would* make you a bad daughter." She squeezed again. "Look at me, Ali."

Ali sighed, then straightened up. She turned to her mum, her eyes still glassy. But no matter what, her mum always had her best interests at heart. Even when her heart was clearly breaking being back here.

"If you think Morgan is someone who could be important to you, what's the harm in trying? If it doesn't work out, at least you tried. New York isn't the moon, you can come back, she can visit. Just not when I'm there, because I want my little girl all to myself." She leaned in and kissed Ali's cheek. "Don't put your life on hold in any area. It's short. Grab happiness where you can, while you can."

"You sound like one of those cheesy posters."

"I like those cheesy posters." Her mum gave her a wink, then shivered. "While this snow is lovely, it's also freezing. Shall we go in and see if Morgan's family has found her yet? They might appreciate a friendly face."

Ali got up and held out her hand. Her mum took it.

"I know you're worried, but try to smile. Morgan will appreciate it when you see her."

\* \* \*

An hour later, Ali's black Docs squeaked on the shiny corridor floors as she carefully carried two coffees back to the waiting area. When she arrived, Mrs Scott stood there, red eyes, mascara streaked down her face. Ali almost dropped the coffees, but held on. When she put them down, Mrs Scott wasted no time in pulling her into a bear hug.

"I can't tell you how grateful I am to you both!" she said when she let Ali go. "You calling the ambulance right away, being there on the scene, then calling us, too. You really saved the day. Luckily, we were already here, so we didn't have far to go."

"Have you seen Morgan?" Ali needed to know.

Mrs Scott nodded, her wiry bob static. "I have. She's fine. I mean, shook up, but more concerned about the other driver. Who is also fine. You two know him, I believe?"

Ali nodded. "He was on our flight back. The one we never took. His daughter lives in Dartmouth."

"Apparently he was on his way to get cranberry sauce from the corner shop, and he was checking his sat nav and not looking where he was going. He was very apologetic, and luckily, they're both walking away with cuts and bruises, but nothing else."

Relief soaked Ali to her very core. Ever since she walked out the door of Morgan's family home last night, she'd had a sense of foreboding she'd done the wrong thing. Even when Tobias and her mum pointed it out, she was still on the fence. But this accident had shown her what was important to her.

That was Morgan.

It had always been Morgan.

Her whole body filled with warmth at that thought. She needed to see her, to tell her what she felt. To tell her she'd changed her mind. She really hoped it wasn't too late. What if Morgan had banged her head and realised the past few days were something to be chalked off? There was only one way to find out.

"You must be so relieved, Diane," her mum said. "I know if that was Nicole or Ali, I'd be frantic."

Diane threw up her hands. "I know! Both daughters in hospital on Christmas Day doesn't sound promising, does it? But luckily, they're both fine. One of them, in fact, has just given birth." Her face lit up as she spoke.

"That's wonderful news!" Her mum hugged Diane.

They'd known each other all their lives, too. Standing at the school gates. Toasting their daughters' successes. Lifting them back up after they fell down in whatever way. Ali was suddenly immensely grateful to them both. These wise, wonderful women. She hoped she became half the woman they both were.

"What did she have?" Ali asked.

Diane's smile, if it were possible, got even wider. "A girl. They've called her Camille, after my mother. Born on Christmas Day and named after the woman who simply adored Christmas. It really couldn't be more fitting." She leaned over. "I'm going back to see the new arrival and her parents. Roger's in with Morgan right now, but poke your head in.

She's been asking for you. She knows you were there. Kick him out, have a little time for yourselves. Just the two of you." Diane wrapped her fingers around Ali's hand, held her gaze, and squeezed. "I think she'd really like that."

# Chapter Thirty-One

If cooking dinner solo hadn't been how Morgan anticipated spending her Christmas Day, a car crash and a hospital stay trumped that by a country mile. If she'd seen a script of her life over the past week, she'd have sent it back to the writer's room, telling them it was too far-fetched. But it was real. Morgan had the bruises to prove it.

She stared out the window. It was snowing. Where was Ali right now? Was she still here, or was she back at the pub, staring out at the snow? She still wasn't sure it was romantic, but she'd always remember the last few days as just that. Whatever happened next.

When she'd opened her eyes and seen Ali's scared face in front of her own, Morgan had panicked. Did she look that bad? Was her leg about to fall off? She was in shock. Maybe the pain would come later. But none of it had. Instead, she'd been whisked away in an ambulance, and she was still very much alive.

Someone clearing their throat made Morgan look up. When she saw who it was, the sun came out in her heart.

"You came." She sounded croakier than she'd imagined.

Ali gave her a shy smile. "I did. I was hardly going back to my Christmas Day after seeing you in a crash, was I?"

"I hoped not." But Morgan hadn't dared to dream. "Are you coming in?" She patted the edge of the bed beside her. "Sit, please. But don't judge me. I might not look my best."

Ali shook her head and followed Morgan's instructions.

When Morgan saw what was in her hand, a grin spread across her features. "Are those for me?"

"I couldn't turn up empty-handed, could I? Especially not for the chocolate-giving queen." Ali put the box of Celebrations on Morgan's bedside table. "It's about time someone brought you a box of these, isn't it?"

Morgan nodded as hope bloomed inside. "Nobody ever brings me chocolates."

"Maybe that's about to change."

Morgan gulped, but didn't allow her brain to wander. She was still alive, and simply having Ali this close made her limbs relax. She sensed something had changed since last night, but she wasn't sure what. However, after the day she'd had, she wasn't leaving anything to chance. She reached out her fingers and brushed them along Ali's forearm.

Ali stilled, caught her gaze, then grasped Morgan's fingers in her own and squeezed.

Morgan's eyelids fluttered shut briefly. Her chest ached with anticipation.

"I saw your mum. She said you were okay. Is that true? No internal issues?" Ali's voice cracked with concern.

"I'm lucky. Walt wasn't going too fast, neither was I, so we should both be fine. He popped his head in when he was being wheeled on the trolley to apologise." Morgan shook her head. "It wasn't all his fault, though. I was trying to change the radio station because 'Stay Another Day' came on and you know what I think about that. It's not a Christmas song."

Ali put a hand to her forehead. "Will you let that go? The irony is, I want *you* to stay another day. We all do. Please, from now on, accept East 17 for what it is."

Morgan gave her a weak smile. "I'll try." She peered closer. "I like your shirt. Are they dogs or foxes?"

"They're bloody reindeer!" Ali pulled the material out. Now she looked closer, they did look a little like foxes. With small antlers.

Anyway.

She eyed Morgan and shook her head. "I was so worried when I saw you. I feared the worst." She paused, her eyes searching Morgan's face. "But it made me realise what's important. What I want. What you mean to me."

Morgan tried to sit up, then winced. Somehow, she didn't want to be slumped for this announcement. She wanted to be upright and fully present.

"Do you need help?" Ali got up, plumped up a couple of pillows, and helped Morgan sit up. She stopped midway as she drew back, their gazes connecting.

Morgan put a hand on her arm.

Ali glanced down at it, then back up to Morgan.

"Are you saying what I think you're saying?" Morgan couldn't be sure until Ali said the words. "You know what I want to happen, but I have to hear it from you, too."

Ali gave her the faintest of nods. "I'm saying, seeing you in a crash made me realise I don't want to be without you. The thought of something happening to you was too real and if anything had, I would have spent the rest of my life regretting it. And yes, my original point still stands. It's terrible timing. I'm just about to live in New York."

Morgan's grin ripened to the point of splitting. "I've always loved New York."

Ali laughed. "I'm glad, because you might visit more than you'd bargained for." She paused. "Morgan Scott, if you're prepared to deal with our time and distance differences and see where this goes, then I am, too." She leaned in closer, so their lips were now inches apart.

Morgan's heart thumped in her chest. She wasn't sure this amount of adrenaline was great for somebody who was just getting over a car crash, but honestly, she didn't care. If she was going to die, there were worse ways to go than having Ali Bradford telling her she wanted to make a go of things and laying a kiss on her lips.

"Turns out," Ali continued, "I'm not quite over my childhood crush."

Then she moved her lips forward and pressed them to Morgan's, making Morgan's heart dance like nobody was watching.

Last night, as she'd slept fitfully, Morgan hadn't thought this would ever happen again. If that had come true, it would have been a crime. Now, even though Ali's kiss was light, tentative—Morgan was lying in a hospital bed—it still lit up Morgan's body. Ali's lips painted visions of a future in Morgan's mind. A future filled with kisses, with laughter, with love.

When Ali pulled away, Morgan blinked. Love? She wouldn't say that just yet. She didn't want to scare Ali away when she'd only just come back onboard.

But what a Christmas Day this was turning out to be. One for the ages.

Ali's gaze roamed Morgan's face, concern flickering in her eyes. "That didn't hurt, did it?"

Morgan laughed, then wished she hadn't. With her bruises, laughter was not the best medicine.

"Your kiss did the opposite of hurt. It gave me hope." Then she closed her eyes, embarrassed.

But Ali squeezed her hand. "I couldn't sleep last night, questioning everything. All throughout today, I was thinking about you, wondering what you were doing. Something wasn't right. I hope I would have worked out that I liked you too much to lose you. Enough to give us a go. But someone once told me I am notoriously glass half empty, and they might have a point." Ali screwed up her face and gave Morgan a rueful smile. "I'm really sorry for everything I said and did, for all the ridiculousness that blurted out of my mouth. My only defence is that I'm completely stubborn and stupid."

Morgan smiled. "You're only a bit stupid. But a lot stubborn. Good job you're also gorgeous and finally come to your senses, isn't it?" She paused. "Are you finally admitting this might not be a festive fling? That you might just have feelings for me?"

Ali laid the lightest of kisses on her lips, then nodded. "Of course I have feelings for you. How could I not? You're Morgan Scott. The woman of my dreams. Now a reality who's not as perfect as I always thought. Which is a good thing." Ali paused. "But to be clear, you *are* perfect in a lot of ways, though."

Morgan's grin reattached itself to her face. "What ways are those?"

Ali cocked an eyebrow. "You're pretty darn kissable, for

one. You've got great tits." Another kiss. "And I almost cried when I opened your present last night. That was perfect."

"I'm glad you liked it. I'll look forward to you playing me something later. Plus, I thought it was about time I made up for my crimes of 30 years ago." Morgan gazed into Ali's eyes. "But I'm curious. How am I not perfect?"

Ali flicked her head to the window. "You don't think snow's romantic, and you think romance is for summer. Have I changed your mind on that one?"

"I think you're living proof that romance and snow are the perfect couple."

They both stared out the window as the snow fell in droves.

Ali sat on the bed, her bodyweight warming Morgan deliciously. "A little like us?"

"I hope so." Morgan had never meant three little words as much in her entire life.

"Plus, if you're coming to New York in winter, they have bucket loads of snow, so you might have to get used to it. I bought you a present that'll help, too."

"I'm intrigued. Just don't make me ride a tandem bike in a snowstorm again, okay? Once is enough to last a lifetime."

Ali let out a howl of laughter at that. "Pinky promise."

They were both silent for a few moments. The weight of their words and decisions settled on them like a cashmere blanket.

"I'm really glad you've changed your mind."

"Me, too." Ali moved her mouth from side to side. "You sure you're up for it? I might be there over six months. It could be a year. Maybe two."

Morgan shrugged. "We'll cope. I can visit and work from

there. Plus, there's Zoom, WhatsApp, phone sex." She laughed, then winced with the pain. Ali fussed over her, but Morgan shook her head. "I just need to stop laughing. Say something serious, please."

Ali stroked her chin with her thumb and forefinger, then held Morgan in place with her gaze. "Serious, huh? Okay, how about this." She hopped off the bed, then got down on one knee.

Every organ Morgan possessed froze. Her heart, her lungs, her brain. What the actual fuck?

"Morgan Scott," Ali said.

Morgan ground her teeth together as her psyche screamed.

"Will you be my girlfriend?"

*Oh thank the fucking stars!*

Ali jumped to her feet, shaking with laughter. "You should have seen your face."

"I said serious, not heart-stopping!"

Honest-to-fucking-god.

"I'm sorry." Ali leaned in and kissed her cheek. "I just couldn't resist." She paused. "You haven't given me an answer, by the way."

Morgan rolled her eyes. "It's a yes, although it should be a no after that stunt." She pressed her head back into pillows, glanced out the window, then back to Ali. "What a fucking Christmas Day. It's snowing, I've got a ridiculously hot girlfriend, and a new niece." She stared at Ali. "Life is good. A wise woman once told me I might meet the love of my life on New Year's Eve. Now, are you going to spend New Year with me this year in Glasgow, girlfriend?"

Ali leaned forward again and kissed Morgan's lips. "I thought you'd never ask."

# Epilogue

## One Year Later

"Camille!" Annabel sighed. "Josh, will you grab her before she crawls right across the bar and pulls over the massive tree?" Josh was already on it, squatting down to scoop up his toddler daughter. He then stuck his face into her stomach and blew a raspberry, which drew giggles from the little girl.

To Ali's right, her mum and Diane sat at the end of the table, laughing about something and drinking a glass of Chablis. Her mum's fake tan was far more bronzed this year. She'd told the whole family to destroy any evidence of last year's dodgy orange hue.

They were also all under strict instructions to not get in a car this year, either. "No hospital visits this Christmas. Everybody understand?" Diane had told them the night before. There had been nods all round.

What a difference a year made.

At the table set for 12, Morgan's dad reached over and popped another pig-in-a-blanket into his mouth. Then he sat back, patting his stomach. "I need to stop eating those, don't I? The trouble is, they're so moreish!"

"You're not wrong, Roger." Nicole leaned over and got one for herself and Stuart, then one for Harrison, who was thankfully non-flying this Christmas. This year, he'd come dressed as a dinosaur, which meant he just had to roam around and roar. Everyone preferred the dinosaur to Superman.

Over the past year, with Morgan flying back and forth to see her and vice versa, their families had become more friendly. So much so that when Elaine had invited the Scotts over to spend Christmas Day at the pub—"with no one else, not open, just us!"—they had readily agreed. Diane and Roger had brought an array of elaborate desserts and a cheeseboard for afters, while Ali and Morgan had taken charge of the dinner. As Morgan had told anyone who would listen all day long, "I did it all last year and nobody appreciated it. This year, it would be nice if someone did." Morgan had done most of the cooking, but under her watchful eye, Ali had become a useful sous chef. She could cook far more than a tortilla these days.

"That was a gorgeous dinner, even if I say so myself." Ali rubbed a hand up and down Morgan's thigh as she spoke.

Morgan slipped her a sultry grin. "Not that I want to do it every year." She turned to her dad. "You and Mum can take over again any time you like."

But Roger shook his head. "No, it's over to you now. Plus, we hardly ever get to enjoy your cooking these days. You're in Glasgow or New York, so it's a treat when it happens."

Ali felt a little guilty about stealing more of Morgan's time away from her family, but they'd survive. She'd flown back into Glasgow on December 20th, and together, she and Morgan had hopped into Morgan's snazzy new purple Mini (replete with furry festive dice), and driven the length of the country to come home for the holidays. After last year's calamitous trip, they'd both agreed they were taking no chances. They'd managed the drive in just over eight hours, with not a single hiccup. Their luck was changing. That was definitely true, as proven by the past year.

Roger leaned over and refilled their glasses with the Shiraz he'd bought.

"I like your shirt, by the way. Very jaunty," he told Ali.

She glanced down. "Thank you. I thought I'd be clear this year and go for something obvious after last year's fox/dog/reindeer headache."

Morgan smirked. "I love your foxy reindeer shirt. But this one's good, too. Christmas trees are always a winner. We should send one to Dave, the Christmas tree man."

"He would love it!" Ali had already made sure everyone in Glasgow shopped with Dave for their tree, Morgan and Tobias included.

Nicole, dressed in an eye-popping bubble gum-pink dress, turned to Morgan. "How are you feeling about relocating for good? I can't believe you're going, by the way. You hook up with my sister, almost become my sister for reals, and then you bugger off to New York." She gave an exaggerated eye roll, then winked at Morgan.

Ali loved that as well as landing the most gorgeous girlfriend in the world, Morgan and Nicole had got closer in the past 12 months, too.

Morgan took a sip of her wine before she replied. "It's not forever, but I'm looking forward to living in the Big Apple.

Who wouldn't be? I can live out my American dreams in the city that never sleeps."

"I'm sure you'll have a ball. I'm just jealous."

Morgan poked Nicole's shoulder. "You know the solution? Come and see us. We've got a lovely apartment with a very comfy sofabed."

Ali nodded. "I've told everyone the same. That includes you and Diane, Roger." She'd said the same to her mum, and eventually got her to visit in September for a week. Getting her away from the pub for that long had been a feat. Ali hoped they'd be able to perform the same magic next year, too.

Ali's job had gone very well. So well, she was now an integral part of the team, and was likely to stay in New York for at least another year, maybe more. All of which meant that after careful consultation with her employers and potential clients in the US, Morgan had taken the leap and was about to move to be with Ali. Long distance had proved a challenge they were up to, but Ali couldn't wait for the moment they were both on the same continent and in the same time zone every day. She couldn't wait until they were sharing the same bed every night.

Morgan had visited almost every month when Ali hadn't flown back herself, and they'd already had some magical times in their new home city. If Ali had thought their first kisses and sex were good, they'd built over the year to spectacular levels. But it wasn't just about sex. It was about love. She'd told Morgan she loved her at the top of the Empire State Building. Morgan had said it right back, and they'd kissed, long and hard. After being so worried and fearful that long distance simply wouldn't work, Morgan had showed her it could. That if you really wanted something, you could make it happen.

Ali really wanted Morgan, and the feeling was mutual. One year on from their spectacularly eventful Christmas, their lives were just about to get more settled than ever. Mundane. But if it was mundane with Morgan Scott, Ali would take it any day.

She leaned over and laid a kiss on Morgan's lips, then gave her girlfriend a beaming smile. She was certain they were going to stay the distance. That Morgan Scott would one day be her wife. If she had any say in it at all, Ali was going to make it happen.

"What was that for?" Morgan kissed her back.

"Just because you're you."

They stared, then laughed. They did that a lot. Whenever they were in Glasgow, Tobias told them they were nauseating. Ali could live with it.

"Hey, lovebirds." Ali looked up, and was nearly struck in the head by one of Camille's flailing legs. "Can you take her for a minute so she doesn't swallow the pub? We need to get madam's birthday cake sorted before we do dessert."

Ali took the chunk that was Camille and kissed her cheek. She wriggled in her arms. She smelled of sugar and spice, probably because she'd just smudged some of Diane's delicious mince pies into her chubby cheeks. Camille pressed her sticky fingers to Ali's nose, and Morgan smiled her way.

"You look good with a baby," she told her.

Ali grabbed Camille's hands in hers and gave Morgan a look. "Don't be getting ideas." Camille danced on Ali's lap, rocking her tiny bum back and forth. "Although you are cute, aren't you? Happy birthday, Camille. What a year it's been. I hope your first year of life has been as good as my most recent."

Morgan leaned over and kissed Ali's cheek. "Couldn't possibly be," she told her.

\* \* \*

They walked back to Morgan's family home, even though it was a 45-minute trek. Morgan had favoured getting in the cab with her parents, but Ali had insisted on the walk to get some air. Plus, it was still snowing lightly, and she wanted to make the most of it.

"You love snow, now, admit it." Ali snaked an arm through Morgan's.

"It's the most romantic thing ever," Morgan replied, one eyebrow raised. "Did you have a good Christmas Day? The first one with our blended families?"

"It was the best. Fab to bring everyone together, and I think it's really helped Mum to have your family around this year. We all still miss Dad, but with so much love and laughter in the air, you don't get as much time to mope, do you?"

That was the plain truth. This year had been hard, but they'd got through all the milestones once now: Dad's birthday, Christmas, her parents' anniversary, Father's Day. She knew grief appeared at odd times, but she also knew that with Morgan by her side, and her family strong and happy back home, she could cope. Life had a funny way of working itself out sometimes. This was one of those times when all her stars had aligned. Especially now Morgan was moving to New York to be with her.

Sometimes, Ali felt like she was living in the pages of a romance novel, but it was actually her life. She woke up grateful they'd reconnected every single day.

"We're driving back the day after Boxing Day?"

Up above, the stars twinkled at them, just as they had the year before. To Ali's right, a neon bar sign flashed on and off in the front window of a house, proclaiming to the world they had 'Cocktails!' Had anybody ever knocked and asked for one?

"Yep," Morgan replied, blowing out a breath of smoky air. "I've got a bit of work to do, and then it's a Hogmanay party for the ages at yours, right?"

"At Tobias's flat, not mine. He's fully paying the rent now he's officially moved in and not just house-sitting. Means we're not responsible for clear-up, which suits me fine."

"I'll second that." Morgan pulled Ali close. "I heard from Imogen and Sam. They're coming to the party, bringing a couple of their friends, too." They'd met up with Imogen and Sam when they were back in Glasgow in the summer, and got on great. Imogen never tired of telling the story of how they met, and how she knew Ali and Morgan should be together before they did. Ali knew it would come up again at New Year.

"The party will be heaving, but that's just the way Tobias would want it. He'd be so ashamed if nobody came."

"He doesn't have to worry," Morgan replied. "Did I tell you he knitted me a scarf after I told him I liked yours?"

Ali nodded. She was thrilled that Morgan and Tobias got on so well. They met up when she wasn't there, and Morgan's new scarf was a warm grey colour with blue hues. It really brought out the flecks of teal in her gorgeous eyes. Tobias had also adopted Snowy the cat, but Ali and Morgan were both frequent visitors.

"The morning after, can we go to Francesco's for a dirty hangover sandwich?"

"Of course, I would expect nothing else." Morgan stopped Ali under a streetlight, then before she could say a word, she leaned down and kissed her.

All Ali's thoughts flew from her head, and her feet lifted off the ground. Or at least, that's how it felt. Morgan's kisses had that effect on her. She only wished she'd started having them earlier in her life. But now she had them, she would never let them go.

She stared up into her rich gaze, "Today has been ideal. Just like you. I love you, Morgan Scott." She never tired of saying it.

The skin around Morgan's eyes crinkled as she smiled. "I love you, too, Alison Bradford. My original glass-half-empty girl, now transformed into a glass half full."

Ali frowned. "I reserve the right to be glass half empty when I want to be."

"Of course you do." Morgan laughed, then kissed her again. "You think we'll be in New York for Christmas next year? They have a Ferris wheel on Coney Island. I looked it up. Perhaps we could go when I move."

Ali gave her a doubting look. "No fucking way you're getting me back on one of those again."

"Not even if I promise to kiss you again?"

"I can kiss you any time now. I don't need to be 100ft off the ground to do it."

"Although my kisses sweep you off your feet, right? Just so we're clear?"

Ali rolled her eyes. She was incorrigible. "You're a fucking magician," she told her. "Happy?"

Morgan grinned. "I really am. More than I ever thought possible."

THE END

*Want more from me? Sign up to join my VIP Readers'*
*Group and get a FREE lesbian romance,*
**It Had To Be You!** *Claim your free book here:*
*www.clarelydon.co.uk/it-had-to-be-you*

# Did You Enjoy This Book?

If the answer's yes, I wonder if you'd consider leaving me a review wherever you bought it. Just a line or two is fine, and could really make the difference for someone else when they're wondering whether or not to take a chance on me and my writing. If you enjoyed the book and tell them why, it's possible your words will make them click the buy button, too! Just hop on over to wherever you bought this book — Amazon, Apple Books, Kobo, Bella Books, Barnes & Noble or any of the other digital outlets — and say what's in your heart. I always appreciate honest reviews.

Thank you, you're the best.

Love,
Clare x

# Also by Clare Lydon

## Other Novels
A Taste Of Love
Before You Say I Do
Change Of Heart
Christmas In Mistletoe
It Started With A Kiss
Nothing To Lose: A Lesbian Romance
Once Upon A Princess
One Golden Summer
The Long Weekend
Twice In A Lifetime
You're My Kind

## London Romance Series
London Calling (Book One)
This London Love (Book Two)
A Girl Called London (Book Three)
The London Of Us (Book Four)
London, Actually (Book Five)
Made In London (Book Six)
Hot London Nights (Book Seven)
Big London Dreams (Book Eight)

## All I Want Series
Two novels and four novellas chart the course
of one relationship over two years.

## Boxsets
Available for both the London Romance series and
the All I Want series for ultimate value. Check out
my website for more: www.clarelydon.co.uk

Printed in Great Britain
by Amazon